Before I Die

Before I Die

jenny downham

David Fickling Books

OXFORD · NEW YORK

A DAVID FICKLING BOOK

David Fickling Books and the colophon are trademarks of David Fickling.

Visit us on the Web! www.randomhouse.com/teens

Educators and librarians, for a variety of teaching tools, visit us at
www.randomhouse.com/teachers

The Library of Congress has cataloged the hardcover edition of this work as follows:
Downham, Jenny.
Before I die / Jenny Downham.
p. cm.
Summary: A terminally ill teenaged girl makes and carries out a list
of things to do before she dies.
ISBN 978-0-385-75155-1 (trade) — ISBN 978-0-385-75158-2 (lib. bdg.)
[1. Terminally ill—Fiction. 2. England—Fiction.] I. Title.
PZ7.D75918Be 2007
[Fic]—dc22   2007020284

ISBN 978-0-385-75183-4 (tr. pbk.)

Printed in the United States of America
May 2009

10 9 8 7 6 5

First Trade Paperback Edition

For Louis and Archie, with love

One

I wish I had a boyfriend. I wish he lived in the wardrobe on a coat hanger. Whenever I wanted, I could get him out and he'd look at me the way boys do in films, as if I'm beautiful. He wouldn't speak much, but he'd be breathing hard as he took off his leather jacket and unbuckled his jeans. He'd wear white pants and he'd be so gorgeous I'd almost faint. He'd take my clothes off too. He'd whisper, 'Tessa, I love you. I really bloody love you. You're beautiful' – exactly those words – as he undressed me.

I sit up and switch on the bedside light. There's a pen, but no paper, so on the wall behind me I write, *I want to feel the weight of a boy on top of me*. Then I lie back down and look out at the sky. It's gone a funny colour – red and charcoal all at once, like the day is bleeding out.

I can smell sausages. Saturday night is always sausages. There'll be mash and cabbage and onion gravy too. Dad'll have the lottery ticket and Cal will have chosen the numbers and they'll sit in front of the TV and eat dinner from trays on their laps. They'll watch *The X Factor*, then they'll watch *Who Wants to Be a Millionaire?* After that, Cal will have a bath and go to bed and Dad'll drink beer and smoke until it's late enough for him to sleep.

He came up to see me earlier. He walked over to the window and opened the curtains. 'Look at that!' he said as light flooded the room. There was the afternoon, the tops of the trees, the sky. He stood silhouetted against the window, his hands on his hips. He looked like a Power Ranger.

'If you won't talk about it, how can I help you?' he said, and he came over and sat on the edge of my bed. I held my breath. If you do it for long enough, white lights dance in front of your eyes. He reached over and stroked my head, his fingers gently massaging my scalp.

'Breathe, Tessa,' he whispered.

Instead, I grabbed my hat from the bedside table and yanked it on right over my eyes. He went away then.

Now he's downstairs frying sausages. I can hear the fat spitting, the slosh of gravy in the pan. I'm not sure I should be able to hear that from all the way upstairs, but nothing surprises me any more. I can hear Cal unzipping his coat now, back from buying mustard. Ten minutes ago he was given a pound and told, 'Don't talk to anyone weird.' While he was gone, Dad stood on the back step and smoked a fag. I could hear the whisper of leaves hitting the grass at his feet. Autumn invading.

'Hang your coat up and go and see if Tess wants anything,' Dad says. 'There's plenty of blackberries. Make them sound interesting.'

Cal has his trainers on; the air in the soles sighs as he leaps up the stairs and through my bedroom door. I pretend to be asleep, which doesn't stop him. He leans right over and whispers, 'I don't care even if you never speak to me again.' I open one eye and find two blue ones. 'Knew you were faking,' he says, and he grins wide and lovely. 'Dad says, do you want blackberries?'

'No.'

'What shall I tell him?'

'Tell him I want a baby elephant.'

He laughs. 'I'm gonna miss you,' he says, and he leaves me with an open door and the draught from the stairs.

Two

Zoey doesn't even knock, just comes in and plonks herself down on the end of the bed. She looks at me strangely, as if she hadn't expected to find me here.

'What're you doing?' she says.

'Why?'

'Don't you go downstairs any more?'

'Did my dad phone you up?'

'Are you in pain?'

'No.'

She gives me a suspicious look, then stands up and takes off her coat. She's wearing a very short red dress. It matches the hand-bag she's dumped on my floor.

'Are you going out?' I ask her. 'Have you got a date?'

She shrugs, goes over to the window and looks down at the garden. She circles a finger on the glass, then she says, 'Maybe you should try and believe in God.'

'Should I?'

'Yeah, maybe we all should. The whole human race.'

4

'I don't think so. I think he might be dead.'

She turns round to look at me. Her face is pale, like winter. Behind her shoulder, an aeroplane winks its way across the sky.

She says, 'What's that you've written on the wall?'

I don't know why I let her read it. I guess I want something to happen. It's in black ink. With Zoey looking, all the words writhe like spiders. She reads it over and over. I hate it how sorry she can be for me.

She speaks very softly. 'It's not exactly Disneyland, is it?'

'Did I say it was?'

'I thought that was the idea.'

'Not mine.'

'I think your dad's expecting you to ask for a pony, not a boyfriend.'

It's amazing, the sound of us laughing. Even though it hurts, I love it. Laughing with Zoey is absolutely one of my favourite things, because I know we've both got the same stupid pictures in our heads. She only has to say, 'Maybe a stud farm might be the answer,' and we're both in hysterics.

Zoey says, 'Are you crying?'

I'm not sure. I think I am. I sound like those women on the telly when their entire family gets wiped out. I sound like an animal gnawing its own foot off. Everything just floods in all at once – like how my fingers are just bones and my skin is practically see-through. Inside my left lung I can feel cells multiplying, stacking up, like ash slowly filling a vase. Soon I won't be able to breathe.

'It's OK if you're afraid,' Zoey says.

5

'It's not.'

'Of course it is. Whatever you feel is fine.'

'Imagine it, Zoey – being terrified all the time.'

'I can.'

But she can't. How can she possibly, when she has her whole life left? I hide under my hat again, just for a bit, because I'm going to miss breathing. And talking. And windows. I'm going to miss cake. And fish. I like fish. I like their little mouths going, open, shut, open.

And where I'm going, you can't take anything with you.

Zoey watches me wipe my eyes with the corner of the duvet.

'Do it with me,' I say.

She looks startled. 'Do what?'

'It's on bits of paper everywhere. I'll write it out properly and you can make me do it.'

'Make you do what? The thing you wrote on the wall?'

'Other stuff too, but the boy thing first. You've had sex loads of times, Zoey, and I've never even been kissed.'

I watch my words fall into her. They land somewhere very deep.

'Not loads of times,' she says eventually.

'Please, Zoey. Even if I beg you not to, even if I'm horrible to you, you must make me do it. I've got a whole long list of things I want to do.'

When she says, 'OK,' she makes it sound easy, as if I only asked her to visit me more often.

'You mean it?'

'I said so, didn't I?'

I wonder if she knows what she's letting herself in for.

I sit up in bed and watch her fiddle about in the back of my wardrobe. I think she's got a plan. That's what's good about Zoey. She'd better hurry up though, because I'm starting to think of things like carrots. And air. And ducks. And pear trees. Velvet and silk. Lakes. I'm going to miss ice. And the sofa. And the lounge. And the way Cal loves magic tricks. And white things – milk, snow, swans.

From the back of the wardrobe, Zoey pulls out the wrap-dress Dad bought me last month. It's still got the price on.

'I'll wear this,' she says. 'You can wear mine.' She starts to unbutton her dress.

'Are you taking me out?'

'It's Saturday night, Tess. Ever heard of it?'

Of course. Of course I have.

I haven't been vertical for hours. It makes me feel a bit strange, sort of empty and ethereal. Zoey stands in her underwear and helps me put on the red dress. It smells of her. The material is soft and clings to me.

'Why do you want me to wear this?'

'It's good to feel like you're somebody else sometimes.'

'Someone like you?'

She considers this. 'Maybe,' she says. 'Maybe someone like me.'

When I look at myself in the mirror, it's great how different I look – big-eyed and dangerous. It's exciting, as if anything is possible. Even my hair looks good, dramatically shaved rather than only just growing. We look at ourselves, side by side, then she steers me away from the mirror and makes me sit down on the bed. She brings my make-up basket from the dressing table and sits next to me. I concentrate on her face as she smears foundation onto her finger and dabs at my cheeks. She's very pale and very blonde and her acne makes her look kind of savage. I've never had a spot in my life. It's the luck of the draw.

She lines my lips and fills in the space with lipstick. She finds some mascara and tells me to look right at her. I try to imagine what it might be like to be her. I often do this, but I can never really get my head round it. When she makes me stand up in front of the mirror again, I glitter. A little like her.

'Where do you want to go?' she says.

There are loads of places. The pub. A club. A party. I want a big dark room you can barely move in, with bodies grinding close together. I want to hear a thousand songs played incredibly loud. I want to dance so fast that my hair grows long enough to trample on. I want my voice to be thunderous above the throb of bass. I want to get so hot that I have to crunch ice in my mouth.

'Let's go dancing,' I say. 'Let's go and find some boys to have sex with.'

'All right.' Zoey picks up her handbag and leads me from the bedroom.

Dad comes out of the lounge and halfway up the stairs. He pretends he was going to the loo, and acts all surprised to see us.

'You're up!' he says. 'It's a miracle!' And he nods grudging respect at Zoey. 'How did you manage it?'

8

Zoey smiles at the floor. 'She just needed a little incentive.'

'Which is?'

I lean on one hip and look him right in the eye. 'Zoey's taking me pole dancing.'

'Funny,' he says.

'No, really.'

He shakes his head, runs a hand in circles over his belly. I feel sorry for him, because he doesn't know what to do.

'OK,' I say. 'We're going clubbing.'

He looks at his watch as if that'll tell him something new.

'I'll look after her,' Zoey says. She sounds so sweet and wholesome I almost believe her.

'No,' he says. 'She needs to rest. A club will be smoky and loud.'

'If she needs to rest, why did you phone me?'

'I wanted you to talk to her, not take her away!'

'Don't worry,' she laughs. 'I'll bring her back.'

I can feel all the happiness sliding out of me because I know Dad's right. I'd have to sleep for a week if I went clubbing. If I use up too much energy, I always pay for it later.

'It's OK,' I say. 'It doesn't matter.'

Zoey grabs my arm and pulls me behind her down the stairs. 'I've got my mum's car,' she says. 'I'll bring her home by three.'

My dad tells her no, it's too late; he tells her to bring me back by midnight. He says it several times as Zoey gets my coat from the closet in the hall. As we go through the front door, I call goodbye, but he doesn't answer. Zoey shuts the door behind us.

'Midnight's OK,' I tell her.

She turns to me on the step. 'Listen, girl, if you're going to do this properly, you're going to have to learn to break the rules.'

'I don't mind being back by midnight. He'll only worry.'

'Let him — it doesn't matter. There are no consequences for someone like you!'

I've never thought about it like that before.

Three

Of course we get into the club. There are never enough girls to go round on a Saturday night and Zoey's got a great body. The bouncers drool over her as they wave us to the front of the queue. She does a little shimmy for them as we go through the door and their eyes follow us across the lobby to the cloakroom. 'Have a lovely evening, ladies!' they call. We don't have to pay. We're absolutely in charge.

After checking in our coats, we go to the bar and get two Cokes. Zoey adds rum to hers from the hip flask she keeps in her bag. All the students at her college do this, she says, because it makes going out cheaper. Not drinking is one prohibition I'm going to stick to, because it reminds me of radiotherapy. I once got wasted between treatments on a mixture of stuff from Dad's drinks cabinet, and now the two are stuck together in my head. Alcohol and the taste of total body irradiation.

We lean on the bar to survey the place. It's packed already, the dance floor hot with bodies. Lights chase across breasts, arses, the ceiling.

Zoey says, 'I've got condoms, by the way. They're in my bag when you need them.' She touches my hand. 'You all right?'

'Yeah.'

'Not freaking out?'

'No.'

A whole room dizzy with Saturday night is exactly what I wanted. I've begun my list and Zoey's doing it with me. Tonight I'm going to cross off number one – sex. And I'm not going to die until all ten are done.

'Look,' Zoey says. 'What about him?' She's pointing to a boy. He's a good dancer, moving with his eyes shut, as if he's the only one here, as if he doesn't need anything other than the music. 'He comes every week. Don't know how he gets away with smoking dope in here. Cute, isn't he?'

'I don't want a druggie.'

Zoey frowns at me. 'What the hell are you talking about?'

'If he's out of his head, he won't remember me. I don't want anyone pissed either.'

Zoey slaps her drink down on the bar. 'I hope you're not expecting to fall in love. Don't tell me that's on your list.'

'Not really.'

'Good, because I hate to remind you, but time isn't on your side. Now let's get on with it!'

She pulls me with her towards the dance floor. We get close enough for Stoner Boy to notice us, and then we dance.

And it's all right. It's like being in a tribe, all of us moving and breathing at the same pace. People are looking, checking each other out. No one can take it away. To be here dancing on this Saturday night, dragging the eyes of a boy towards me in Zoey's red dress. Some girls never have this. Not even this much.

I know what'll happen next because I've had plenty of time for reading and I know all the plots. Stoner Boy will come closer to check us out. Zoey won't look at him, but I will. I'll gaze for a second too long and he'll lean towards me and ask me my name. 'Tessa,' I'll say, and he'll repeat it – the hard 'T', the sibilance of that double 's', the hopeful 'a'. I'll nod to let him know he got it right, that I'm pleased with how sweet and new it sounds on his tongue. Then he'll hold out both arms, palms up, as if saying, *I give in, what can I do with all that beauty?* I'll smile coyly and look at the floor. This tells him he can make a move, that I won't bite, that I know the game. He'll wrap me in his arms then and we'll dance together, my head against his chest, listening to his heart – a stranger's heart.

But that's not what happens. I forgot three things. I forgot that books aren't real. I also forgot that I don't have time for flirting. Zoey remembers. She's the third thing I forgot. And she's moving in.

'This is my friend,' she shouts to Stoner Boy above the music. 'Her name's Tessa. I'm sure she'd like a drag on that joint of yours.'

He smiles, passes it over, takes us both in, his gaze lingering on the length of Zoey's hair.

'It's pure grass,' Zoey whispers. Whatever it is, it's thick and pungent at the back of my throat. It makes me cough, makes me dizzy. I pass it to Zoey, who inhales deeply, then passes it back to him.

The three of us are joined now, moving together as the bass pounds up through our feet and into our blood. Kaleidoscopic images flicker from the video screens on the walls. The joint goes round again.

I don't know how much time goes by. Hours maybe. Minutes. I know I mustn't stop and that's all I know. If I keep dancing, the dark corners of the room won't creep any nearer, and the silence between tracks won't get any louder. If I keep dancing, I'll see ships on the sea again, taste cockles and whelks and hear the creak snow makes when you're the first one to stand on it.

At some point Zoey passes over a fresh joint. 'Glad you came?' she mouths.

I pause to inhale, stupidly stand still a second too long, forgetting to move. And now the spell is broken. I try to claw back some enthusiasm, but I feel as if a vulture is perched on my chest. Zoey, Stoner and all the other dancers are far away and unreal, like a TV programme. I don't expect to be included any more.

'Back in a minute,' I tell Zoey.

In the quiet of the toilet, I sit on the bowl and contemplate my knees. If I gather up this little red dress just a bit further, I can see my stomach. I still have red patches on my stomach. And on my thighs. My skin is as dry as a lizard's, however much cream I smooth in. On the inside of my arms are the ghosts of needle marks.

I finish peeing, wipe myself and pull the dress back down.

When I leave the cubicle, Zoey's waiting by the hand dryer. I didn't hear her come in. Her eyes are darker than before. I wash my hands very slowly. I know she's watching me.

'He's got a friend,' she says. 'His friend's cuter, but you can have him, since it's your special night. They're called Scott and Jake and we're going back to their place.'

I hold onto the edge of the sink and look at my face in the mirror. My eyes seem unfamiliar.

'One of the Tweenies is called Jake,' I say.

'Look,' Zoey says, pissed off now, 'do you want to have sex or not?'

A girl at the sink next to mine shoots me a glance. I want to tell her that I'm not what she thinks. I'm very nice really, she'd probably like me. But there's not time.

Zoey drags me out of the toilet and back towards the bar. 'There they are. That one's yours.'

The boy she points to has his hands flat against his groin, his thumbs looped through his belt. He looks like a cowboy with far-away eyes. He doesn't see us coming, so I dig my heels in.

'I can't do it!'

'You can! Live fast, die young, have a good-looking corpse!'

'No, Zoey!'

My face feels hot. I wonder if there's a way of getting air in here. Where's the door we came in from?

She scowls at me. 'You asked me to make you do this! What am I supposed to do now?'

'Nothing. You don't have to do anything.'

'You're pathetic!' She shakes her head at me, stalks off across the dance floor and out to the foyer. I scurry after her and watch her hand in the ticket for my coat.

'What are you doing?'

'Getting your coat. I'll find you a cab, so you can piss off home.'

'You can't go back to their house on your own, Zoey!'

'Watch me.'

She pushes open the door and surveys the street. It's quiet out here now the queue has gone, and there aren't any cabs. Along the pavement some pigeons peck at a takeaway chicken box.

'Please, Zoey, I'm tired. Can't you drive me home?'

She shrugs. 'You're always tired.'

'Stop being so horrible!'

'Stop being so boring!'

'I don't want to go back to some strange boys' house. Anything could happen.'

'Good. I hope it does, because precisely zero is going to happen otherwise.'

I stand awkwardly, suddenly afraid. 'I want it to be perfect, Zoey. If I have sex with a boy I don't even know, what does that make me? A slag?'

She turns on me, her eyes glittering. 'No, it makes you alive. If you get in a cab and go home to Daddy, what does that make you?'

I imagine climbing into bed, breathing the dead air of my room all night, waking up to the morning and nothing being any different.

16

Her smile is back. 'Come on,' she says. 'You can tick the first thing off that bloody list of yours. I know you want to.' Her smile's contagious. 'Say yes, Tessa. Come on, say yes!'

'Yes.'

'Hurrah!' She grabs my hand, steers me back to the door of the club. 'Now text your dad and say you're staying at mine, and let's get a move on.'

Four

'Don't you like beer?' Jake says.

He's leaning against the sink in his kitchen and I'm standing too close to him. I'm doing it on purpose.

'I just fancied some tea.'

He shrugs, chinks his beer bottle against my cup, and tips his head back to swig. I watch his throat as he swallows, notice a small pale scar under his chin, a thin ribbon from some long ago accident. He wipes his mouth with his sleeve, sees me staring.

'You OK?' he asks.

'Yeah. You?'

'Yeah.'

'Good.'

He smiles at me. He has a nice smile. I'm glad. It would be so much harder if he was ugly.

Half an hour ago Jake and his mate Stoner Boy grinned at each other as they led me and Zoey into their house. Those grins said they'd scored. Zoey told them not to make any assumptions, but still we walked into their lounge and she let Stoner take her coat.

She laughed at his jokes, accepted the joints he made for her and got steadily wrecked.

I can see her through the door. They've put music on, some mellow jazz number. They've turned off the lights to dance, moving together in slow, stoned circles on the carpet. Zoey has one hand in the air holding a joint, the other tucked into Stoner's belt at the back of his trousers. He has both arms wrapped around her so that they appear to be holding each other up.

I feel suddenly sensible, drinking tea in the kitchen, and realize I need to get on with my plan. This is about me, after all.

I gulp my tea down, put the cup on the draining board and move even closer to Jake. The tips of our shoes touch.

'Kiss me,' I say, which sounds ridiculous as soon as I say it, but Jake doesn't seem to mind. He puts down his beer and leans towards me.

We kiss quite gently, our lips just brushing, only a hint of breath from him to me. I've always known I'd be good at kissing. I've read all the magazines, the ones that tell you about nose bumping and excess saliva and where to put your hands. I didn't know it would feel like this though, the soft scour of his chin on mine, his hands gently searching my back, his tongue running along my lips and into my mouth.

We kiss for minutes, pressing our bodies closer, leaning in to each other. It's such a relief to be with someone who doesn't know me at all. My hands are brave, dipping into the curve where his spine ends and stroking him there. How healthy he feels, how solid.

I open my eyes to see if he's enjoying it, but I'm drawn instead to the window behind him, to the trees surrounded by night out there. Little black twigs tap at the glass like fingers. I snap my eyes shut and grind myself closer to him. I can feel just how hard he wants me through my little red dress. He makes a small moaning noise at the back of his throat.

'Let's go upstairs,' he says.

He tries to move me towards the door, but I put my hand flat against his chest to keep him at bay while I think.

'Come on,' he says. 'You want to, don't you?'

I can feel his heart pulsing through my fingers. He smiles down at me, and I do want to, don't I? Isn't this why I'm here?

'OK.'

His hand is hot as he laces our fingers together and leads me through the lounge to the stairs. Zoey's kissing Stoner Boy. She has his back against the wall and her leg between his. When we walk past, they hear us and they both turn round. They look dishevelled and hot. Zoey wiggles her tongue at me. It glistens like a fish in a cave.

I let go of Jake to get Zoey's bag from the sofa. I rummage around in it, aware of everyone's eyes on me, the slow grin on Stoner's face. Jake's leaning against the doorframe, waiting. Is he giving the thumbs-up? I can't look. I can't find the condoms either, don't even know if it's a box or a packet, or really what they look like. In my embarrassment, I decide to take the entire bag upstairs. If Zoey needs a condom, she'll just have to come and get it.

'Let's go,' I say.

I follow Jake up the stairs, concentrate on the sway of his hips to keep myself cheerful. I feel a bit strange, dizzy and slightly nauseous. I didn't think that walking up the stairs behind a guy would remind me of hospital corridors. Maybe I'm just tired. I try to remember the rules about feeling sick – whenever possible get lots of fresh air, open a window or go outside if you can. Get good at distraction therapy – do something, anything, to keep your mind off it.

'In here,' he says.

His bedroom's nothing special – a small room with a desk, a computer, scattered books on the floor, a chair and a single bed. On the walls are a few black and white posters – jazz musicians mostly.

He looks at me looking at his room. 'You can put your bag down,' he says.

He picks up dirty laundry from the bed and chucks it on the floor, straightens the duvet, sits down and pats the space next to him.

I don't move. Because if I sit down on that bed, then I need the lights off.

'Could you light that candle?' I say.

He opens a drawer, pulls out matches and gets up to light the candle on the desk. He turns off the main light and sits back down.

Here is a real breathing boy, looking up at me, waiting for me. This is my moment, but I can feel my chest ticking. Maybe the only way to get through this without him thinking I'm a complete idiot

21

is to pretend to be someone else. I decide to be Zoey, and begin to undo the buttons on her dress.

He watches me do it, one button, two buttons. He runs his tongue across his lips. Three buttons.

He stands up. 'Let me do that.'

His fingers are quick. He's done this before. Another girl, a different night. I wonder where she is now. Four buttons, five, and the little red dress slides from shoulder to hip, falls to the floor and lands at my feet like a kiss. I step out·of it and stand before him in just my bra and knickers.

'What's that?' He frowns at the puckered skin on my chest.

'I was ill.'

'What was wrong with you?'

I shut him up with kisses.

I smell different now I'm practically naked – musky and hot. He tastes different – of smoke and something sweet. Life maybe.

'Aren't you taking your clothes off?' I ask in my best Zoey voice.

He pulls up his T-shirt, over his face, his arms raised. For a second he can't see me, but he's exposed – his narrow chest, freckled and young, the dark shine of hair under his armpits. He chucks his T-shirt on the floor and kisses me again. He tries to unbuckle his belt without looking, with only one hand, but can't do it. He pulls away, looking at me all the while as he fumbles at button and zip. He steps out of his trousers and stands before me in his underwear. There's a moment when maybe he's uncertain, and he hesitates, seems shy. I notice his feet, innocent as daisies in their white socks, and I want to give him something.

'I've never done this before,' I say. 'Not all the way with a guy.' The candle gutters.

He doesn't say anything for a second, then shakes his head like he just can't believe it. 'Wow, that's amazing.'

I nod.

'Come here.'

I bury myself in his shoulder. It's comforting, as if things may be all right. He wraps one arm around me, the other creeping up my back to stroke my neck. His hand is warm. Two hours ago I didn't even know his name.

Maybe we don't have to have sex. Maybe we could just lie down and snuggle up, find sleep in each other's arms under the duvet. Maybe we'll fall in love. He'll hunt for a cure and I'll live for ever.

But no. 'Have you got condoms?' he whispers. 'I've run out.'

I reach for Zoey's bag and tip it upside down on the floor at our feet and he helps himself, puts the condom on the bedside table ready and starts to pull off his socks.

I take off my bra slowly. I've never been naked in front of a guy before. He looks at me as if he wants to eat me and is wondering where to start. I can hear my heart thumping. He has trouble with his pants, easing them over his hard-on. I pull off my knickers, find myself shivering. We're both naked. I think of Adam and Eve.

'It'll be OK,' he says, and he takes me by the hand and leads me to the bed, pulls down the duvet and we climb in. It's a boat. It's a den. It's somewhere to hide.

23

'You're gonna love it,' he says.

We start to kiss, slowly at first, his fingers lazily tracing the lines of my bones. I like it – how gentle we are with each other, our slowness under the candle's glow. But it doesn't last long. His kisses become deeper, his tongue thrusting quickly, like he can't get close enough. His hands are busy too now, squeezing and rubbing. Is he looking for something in particular? He keeps saying, 'Oh yeah, oh yeah,' but I don't think he's saying it to me. His eyes are closed, his mouth is full of my breast.

'Look at me,' I tell him. 'I need you to look at me.'

He leans up on one elbow. 'What?'

'I don't know what to do.'

'You're fine.' His eyes are so dark I don't recognize him. It's as if he's changed into someone else, is not even the half-stranger he was a few minutes ago. 'Everything's fine.'

And he goes back to kissing my neck, my breasts, my stomach until his face disappears from me again.

His hand works its way down too, and I don't know how to tell him not to. I move my hips away from him, but he doesn't stop. His fingers flicker between my legs, and I gasp with shock, because no one has ever done that to me before.

What's wrong with me that I don't know how to do this? I thought I'd know what to do, what would happen. But this is spiralling away from me, as if Jake's making me do it, when I'm supposed to be in charge.

I cling to him, wrap my hands round his back and pat him there, like he's a dog that I don't understand.

24

He eases himself up the bed and sits up.

'All right?'

I nod.

He reaches over to the table where he left the condom. I watch him put it on. He does it quickly. He's a condom expert.

'Ready?'

I nod again. It seems rude not to.

He lies down, moves my legs apart with his, presses himself closer, his weight on top of me. Soon I'll feel him inside me and I'll know what all the fuss is about. This was my idea.

I notice lots of things while the red neon numbers on his radio alarm move from 3:15 to 3:19. I notice that his shoes are on their side by the door. The door isn't shut properly. There's a strange shadow on the ceiling in the far corner that looks like a face. I think of a fat man I once saw sweating as he jogged down our street. I think of an apple. I think that a safe place to be would be under the bed, or with my head on my mother's lap.

He supports himself with his arms, moving slowly above me, his face turned to one side, his eyes tight shut. This is it. It's really happening. I'm living it now. Sex.

When it's finished, I lie under him feeling mostly silent and small. We stay like this for a bit, then he rolls off and peers at me through the dark.

'What is it?' he says. 'What's wrong?'

I can't look at him, so I move closer, bury myself deeper, hide in his arms. I know I'm making a complete fool of myself. I'm snuffling all over him like a baby, and I can't stop, it's horrible.

He sweeps his hand in circles on my back, whispers 'Shush' into my ear, eventually eases me away so he can see me.

'What is it? You're not going to say you didn't want to, are you?'

I wipe my eyes with the duvet. I sit up, my feet dangling over the edge of the bed onto the carpet. I sit with my back to him, blinking at my clothes. They're unfamiliar shadows scattered on the floor.

When I was a kid, I used to ride on my dad's shoulders. I was so small he had to hold my back with both hands to stop me tipping, and yet I was so high I could splash my hands through leaves. I could never tell Jake this. It wouldn't make any difference to him. I don't think words reach people. Maybe nothing does.

I scramble into my clothes. The red dress seems smaller than ever; I pull it down, trying to cover my knees. Did I really go to a club looking like this?

I slip on my shoes, gather the things back into Zoey's bag.

Jake says, 'You don't have to go.' He's leaning up on one elbow. His chest seems pale as the candle flickers.

'I want to.'

He flings himself back onto the pillow. One arm hangs over the side of the bed; his fingers curl where they touch the floor. He shakes his head really slowly.

Zoey's downstairs on the sofa, asleep. So is Stoner Boy. They lie together, their arms entwined, their faces next to each other. I hate it that it's OK for her. She's even wearing his shirt. Its sweet buttons in little rows make me think of that sugar house in the children's story. I kneel beside them and stroke Zoey's arm very lightly. Her arm is warm. I stroke her until she opens her eyes. She blinks at me. 'Hey!' she whispers. 'Finished already?'

I nod, can't help grinning, which is weird. She untangles herself from Stoner's arms, sits up and surveys the floor.

'Is there any gear about?'

I find the tin with the dope in it and hand it to her, then I go to the kitchen and get a glass of water. I think she'll follow me, but she doesn't. How can we talk with Stoner there? I drink the water, put the glass on the draining board and go back to the lounge. I sit on the floor at Zoey's feet as she licks a Rizla and sticks it to another, licks a second, straps that down too, tears off the edges.

'Well?' she says. 'How did it go?'

'OK.'

A pulse of light through the curtain blinds me. I can only see the shine of her teeth.

'Was he any good?'

I think of Jake upstairs, his hand trailing the floor. 'I don't know.'

Zoey inhales, regards me curiously, exhales. 'You have to get used to it. My mum once said that sex was only three minutes of pleasure. I thought, Is that all? It's going to be more than that for me! And it is. If you let them think they're great at it, somehow it turns out all right.'

I stand up, walk to the curtains and open them wider. The streetlights are still on. It's nowhere near morning.

Zoey says, 'Have you just left him up there?'

27

'I guess so.'

'That's a bit rude. You should go back and have another go.'

'I don't want to.'

'Well, we can't go home yet. I'm wrecked.'

She stubs the joint out in the ashtray, settles herself back down next to Scott and shuts her eyes. I watch her for ages, the rise and fall of her breathing. A string of lights along the wall casts a gentle glow across the carpet. There's a rug too, a little oval with splashes of blue and grey, like the sea.

I go back to the kitchen and put the kettle on. There's a piece of paper on the counter. On it someone's written, *Cheese, butter, beans, bread*. I sit on a stool at the kitchen table and I add, *Butterscotch chocolate, six-pack of Creme Eggs*. I especially want the Creme Eggs, because I love having those at Easter. It's two hundred and seventeen days until Easter.

Perhaps I should be a little more realistic. I cross out the Creme Eggs and write, *Chocolate Father Xmas, red and gold foil with a bell round its neck*. I might just get that. It's one hundred and thirteen days until Christmas.

I turn the little piece of paper over and write, *Tessa Scott*. A good name of three syllables, my dad always says. If I can fit my name on this piece of paper over fifty times, everything will be all right. I write in very small letters, like a tooth fairy might write to answer a child's letter. My wrist aches. The kettle whistles. The kitchen fills with steam.

Five

Sometimes on a Sunday Dad drives me and Cal to visit Mum. We get the lift up to the eighth floor, and usually there's a moment when she opens the door and says, 'Hey, you!' and includes all three of us in her gaze. Dad usually loiters for a while on the step and they talk.

But today when she opens the door, Dad's so desperate to get away from me that he's already moving back across the hallway towards the lift.

'Watch her,' he says, jabbing a finger in my direction. 'She's not to be trusted.'

Mum laughs. 'Why, what did she do?'

Cal can hardly contain his excitement. 'Dad told her not to go clubbing.'

'Ah,' Mum says. 'That sounds like your father.'

'But she went anyway. She only got home just now. She was out all night.'

Mum smiles at me fondly. 'Did you meet a boy?'

'No.'

'I bet you did. What's his name?'

'I didn't!'

Dad looks furious. 'Typical,' he says. 'Bloody typical. I might've known I wouldn't get any support from you.'

'Oh, shush,' Mum says. 'It hasn't done her any harm, has it?'

'Look at her. She's completely exhausted.'

All three of them take a moment to look at me. I hate it. I feel dismal and cold and my stomach aches. It's been hurting since having sex with Jake. No one told me that would happen.

'I'll be back at four,' Dad says as he steps into the lift. 'She's refused to have her blood count checked for nearly two weeks, so phone me if anything changes. Can you manage that?'

'Yes, yes, don't worry.' She leans over and kisses my forehead. 'I'll look after her.'

Cal and me sit at the kitchen table, and Mum puts the kettle on, finds three cups amongst the dirty ones in the sink and swills them under the tap. She reaches into a cupboard for tea bags, gets milk from the fridge and sniffs it, scatters biscuits on a plate.

I put a whole Bourbon in my mouth at once. It tastes delicious. Cheap chocolate and the rush of sugar to my brain.

'Did I ever tell you about my first boyfriend?' Mum says as she plonks the tea on the table. 'His name was Kevin and he worked in a clock shop. I used to love the way he concentrated with that little eye-piece nudged into his face.'

Cal helps himself to another biscuit. 'How many boyfriends have you actually had, Mum?'

She laughs, pushes her long hair back over one shoulder. 'Is that an appropriate question?'

'Was Dad the best?'

'Ah, your father!' she cries, and clutches her heart melodramatically, which makes Cal roar with laughter.

I once asked Mum what was wrong with Dad. She said, 'He's the most sensible man I've ever met.'

I was twelve when she left him. She sent postcards for a while from places I'd never heard of – Skegness, Grimsby, Hull. One of them had a picture of a hotel on the front. *This is where I work now*, she wrote. *I'm learning how to be a pastry chef and I'm getting very fat!*

'Good!' Dad said. 'I hope she bloody bursts!'

I put her postcards on my bedroom wall – Carlisle, Melrose, Dornoch.

We're living in a croft like shepherds, she wrote. *Did you know that they use the windpipe, lungs, heart and liver of a sheep to make haggis?*

I didn't, and I didn't know who she meant by 'we', but I liked looking at the picture of John o'Groats with its vast sky stretching across the Firth.

Then winter came and I got my diagnosis. I'm not sure she believed it at first, because it took her a while to turn round and make her way back. I was thirteen when she finally knocked on our door.

'You look lovely!' she told me when I answered it. 'Why does your father always make everything sound so much worse than it is?'

'Are you coming back to live with us?' I asked.

'Not quite.'

And that's when she moved into her flat.

It's always the same. Maybe it's lack of money, or perhaps she wants to make sure I don't over-exert myself, but we always end up watching videos or playing board games. Today, Cal chooses the Game of Life. It's rubbish, and I'm crap at it. I end up with a husband, two children and a job in a travel agent's. I forget to buy house insurance, and when a storm comes, I lose all my money. Cal, however, gets to be a pop star with a cottage by the sea, and Mum's an artist with a huge income and a stately home to live in. When I retire, which happens early because I keep spinning tens, I don't even bother counting what's left of my cash.

Cal wants to show Mum his new magic trick next. He goes to get a coin from her purse, and while we're waiting, I drag the blanket off the back of the sofa and Mum helps me pull it over my knees.

'I've got the hospital next week,' I tell her. 'Will you come?'

'Isn't Dad going?'

'You could both come.'

She looks awkward for a moment. 'What's it for?'

'I've been getting headaches again. They want to do a lumbar puncture.'

She leans over and kisses me, her breath warm on my face. 'You'll be fine, don't worry. I know you'll be fine.'

Cal comes back in with a pound coin. 'Watch very carefully, ladies,' he says.

But I don't want to. I'm bored of watching things disappear.

In Mum's bedroom, I hitch my T-shirt up in front of the wardrobe mirror. I used to look like an ugly dwarf. My skin was grey and if I poked my tummy it felt like an over-risen lump of bread dough and my finger disappeared into its softness. Steroids did that. High-dosage prednisolone and dexamethasone. They're both poisons and they make you fat, ugly and bad-tempered.

Since I stopped taking them I've started to shrink. Today, my hips are sharp and my ribs shine through my skin. I'm retreating, ghost-like, away from myself.

I sit on Mum's bed and phone Zoey.

'Sex,' I ask her. 'What does it mean?'

'Poor you,' she says. 'You really did get a crap shag, didn't you?'

'I just don't understand why I feel so strange.'

'Strange how?'

'Lonely, and my stomach hurts.'

'Oh, yeah!' she says. 'I remember that. Like you've been opened up inside?'

'A bit.'

'That'll go away.'

'Why do I feel as if I'm about to cry all the time?'

'You're taking it too seriously, Tess. Sex is a way of being with someone, that's all. It's just a way of keeping warm and feeling attractive.'

She sounds odd, as if she's smiling.

'Are you stoned again, Zoey?'

'No!'

'Where are you?'

'Listen, I have to go in a minute. Tell me what's next on your list and we'll make a plan.'

'I've cancelled the list. It was stupid.'

'It was fun! Don't give up on it. You were doing something with your life at last.'

When I hang up, I count to fifty-seven inside my head. Then I dial 999.

A woman says, 'Emergency services. Which service do you require?'

I don't say anything.

The woman says, 'Is there an emergency?'

I say, 'No.'

She says, 'Can you confirm that there is no emergency? Can you confirm your address?'

I tell her where Mum lives. I confirm there's no emergency. I wonder if Mum'll get sent some kind of bill. I hope so.

I dial directory enquiries and get the number for the Samaritans. I dial it very slowly.

A woman says, 'Hello.' She has a soft voice, maybe Irish. 'Hello,' she says again.

Because I feel sorry for wasting her time, I say, 'Everything's a pile of crap.'

And she makes a little 'Uh-huh' sound in the back of her throat, which makes me think of Dad. He made exactly that sound six weeks ago, when the consultant at the hospital asked if we under-stood the implications of what he was telling us. I remember thinking how Dad couldn't possibly have understood, because he was crying too much to listen.

'I'm still here,' the woman says.

I want to tell her. I press the receiver to my ear, because to talk about something as important as this you have to be hunched up close.

But I can't find words that are good enough.

'Are you still there?' she says.

'No,' I say, and I put the phone down.

Six

Dad takes my hand. 'Give me the pain,' he says.

I'm lying on the edge of a hospital bed, in a knee-chest posi-tion with my head on a pillow. My spine is parallel to the side of the bed.

There are two doctors and a nurse in the room, although I can't see them because they're behind me. One of the doctors is a student. She doesn't say much, but I guess she's watching as the other one finds the right place on my spine and marks the spot with a pen. He prepares my skin with antiseptic solution. It's very cold. He starts at the place where he's going to put the needle in and works outwards in concentric circles, then he drapes towels across my back and puts sterile gloves on.

'I'll be using a twenty-five-gauge needle,' he tells the student. 'And a five-millilitre syringe.'

On the wall behind Dad's shoulder is a painting. They change the paintings in the hospital a lot, and I've never seen this one before. I stare at it very hard. I've learned all sorts of distraction techniques in the last four years.

In the painting, it's late afternoon in some English field and the sun is low in the sky. A man struggles with the weight of a plough. Birds swoop and dive.

Dad turns in his plastic chair to see what I'm looking at, lets go of my hand and gets up to inspect the picture.

Down at the bottom of the field, a woman runs. She holds her skirt with one hand so that she can run faster.

'*The Great Plague Reaches Eyam*,' Dad announces. 'A cheery little picture for a hospital!'

The doctor chuckles. 'Did you know,' he says, 'there are still over three thousand cases of bubonic plague a year?'

'No,' Dad says, 'I didn't.'

'Thank goodness for antibiotics, eh?'

Dad sits down and scoops my hand back into his. 'Thank goodness.'

The woman scatters chickens as she runs, and it's only now that I notice her eyes reaching out in panic towards the man.

The plague, the great fire and the war with the Dutch all happened in 1666. I remember it from school. Millions were hauled off in carts, bodies swept into lime pits and nameless graves. Over three hundred and forty years later, everyone who lived through it is gone. Of all the things in the picture, only the sun remains. And the earth. That thought makes me feel very small.

'Brief stinging sensation coming up,' the doctor says.

Dad strokes my hand with his thumb as waves of static heat push into my bones. It makes me think of the words 'for ever', of how there are more dead than living, of how we're surrounded by ghosts. This should be comforting, but isn't.

'Squeeze my hand,' Dad says.

'I don't want to hurt you.'

'When your mother was in labour with you, she held my hand for fourteen hours and didn't dislocate any fingers! There's no way you're going to hurt me, Tess.'

It's like electricity, as if my spine got jammed in a toaster and the doctor's digging it out with a blunt knife.

'What do you reckon Mum's doing today?' I ask. My voice sounds different. Held in. Tight.

'No idea.'

'I asked her to come.'

'Did you?' Dad sounds surprised.

'I thought you could hang out in the café together afterwards.'

He frowns. 'That's a strange thing to think.'

I close my eyes and imagine I'm a tree drenched in sunlight, that I have no desire beyond the rain. I think of silver water splashing my leaves, soaking my roots, travelling up my veins.

The doctor reels off statistics to the student. He says, 'Approximately one in a thousand people who have this test suffer some minor nerve injury. There's also a slight risk of infection, bleeding, or damage to the cartilage.' Then he pulls out the needle. 'Good girl,' he says. 'All done.'

I half expect him to slap me on the rump, as if I'm an obedient horse. He doesn't. Instead, he waves three sterile tubes at me. 'Off to the lab with these.' He doesn't even say goodbye, just slides quietly out of the room, student in tow. It's as if he's suddenly embarrassed that any of this intimacy happened between us.

But the nurse is lovely. She talks to us as she dresses my back with gauze, then comes round the side of the bed and smiles down at me.

'You need to lie still for a while now, sweetheart.'

'I know.'

'Been here before, eh?' She turns to Dad. 'What're you going to do with yourself?'

'I'll sit here and read my book.'

She nods. 'I'm right outside. You know what to look for when you get home?'

He reels it off like a professional. 'Chill, fever, stiff neck or headache. Drainage or bleeding, any numbness or loss of strength below the puncture site.'

The nurse is impressed. 'You're good!'

When she goes out, Dad smiles at me. 'Well done, Tess. All over now, eh?'

'Unless the lab results are bad.'

'They won't be.'

'I'll be back to having lumbar punctures every week.'

'Shush! Try and sleep now, baby. It'll make the time go more quickly.'

He picks up his book, settles back in his chair.

Pinpricks of light like fireflies bat against my eyelids. I can hear my own blood coursing, like hooves pounding the street. The grey light outside the hospital window thickens.

Seven

'Get up! Get up!' Cal shouts. I pull the duvet over my head, but he yanks it straight off again. 'Dad says if you don't get up right now, he's coming upstairs with a wet flannel!'

I roll over, away from him, but he skips round the bed and stands over me, grinning. 'Dad says you should get up every morning and do something with yourself.'

I kick him hard and pull the duvet back over my head. 'I don't give a shit, Cal! Now piss off out of my room.'

I'm surprised at how little I care when he goes.

Noise invades – the thunder of his feet on the stair, the clatter of dishes from the kitchen as he opens the door and doesn't shut it behind him. Even the smallest sounds reach me – the slosh of milk onto cereal, a spoon spinning in air. Dad tutting as he wipes Cal's school shirt with a cloth. The cat lapping the floor.

The hall closet opens and Dad gets Cal's coat for him. I hear the zip, the button at the top to keep his neck warm. I hear the kiss, then the sigh – a great wave of despair washing over the house.

'Go and say goodbye,' Dad says.

Cal bounds up the stairs, pauses a moment outside my door, then comes in, right over to the bed.

'I hope you die while I'm at school!' he hisses. 'And I hope it bloody hurts! And I hope they bury you somewhere horrible like the fish shop or the dentist's!'

Goodbye, little brother, I think. Goodbye, goodbye.

Dad'll be left in the messy kitchen in his dressing gown and slippers, needing a shave and rubbing his eyes as if surprised to find himself alone. In the last few weeks he's established a little morning routine. After Cal leaves, he makes himself a coffee, then he tidies the kitchen table, rinses the dishes and puts the washing machine on. This takes approximately twenty minutes. After that he comes and asks me if I slept well, if I'm hungry and what time I'm going to get up. In that order.

When I tell him, 'No, no and never,' he gets dressed, then goes back downstairs to his computer, where he taps away for hours, surfing the web for information to keep me alive. I've been told there are five stages of grief, and if that's true, then he's stuck in stage one: denial.

Strangely, his knock at my door is early today. He hasn't had his coffee or tidied up. What's going on? I lie very still as he comes in, shuts the door quietly behind him and kicks his slippers off.

'Shove up,' he says. He lifts a corner of the duvet.

'Dad! What're you doing?'

'Getting into bed with you.'

'I don't want you to!'

He puts his arm around me and pins me there. His bones are hard. His socks rub against my bare feet.

'Dad! Get out of my bed!'

'No.'

I push his arm off and sit up to look at him. He smells of stale smoke and beer and looks older than I remember. I can hear his heart too, which I don't think is supposed to happen.

'What the hell are you doing?'

'You never talk to me, Tess.'

'And you think this'll help?'

He shrugs. 'Maybe.'

'Would you like it if I came into your bed when you were asleep?'

'You used to when you were small. You said it was unfair that you had to sleep by yourself. Every night me and Mum let you in because you were lonely.'

I'm sure this isn't true because I don't remember it. He may have gone mad.

'Well, if you're not getting out of my bed, then I will.'

'Good,' he says. 'I want you to.'

'And you're just going to stay there, are you?'

He grins and snuggles down under the duvet. 'It's lovely and warm.'

My legs feel weak. I didn't eat much yesterday and it seems to have made me transparent. I clutch the bedpost, hobble over to the window and look out. It's still early: the moon's fading into a pale grey sky.

Dad says, 'You haven't seen Zoey for a while.'

'No.'

'What happened that night you went clubbing? Did you two fall out?'

Down in the garden, Cal's orange football looks like a deflated planet on the grass, and next door, that boy is out there again. I press my palms against the window. Every morning he's outside doing something – raking or digging or fiddling about. Right now he's hacking brambles from the fence and chucking them in a pile to make a bonfire.

'Did you hear me, Tess?'

'Yes, but I'm ignoring you.'

'Perhaps you should think about going back to school. You'd see some of your other friends then.'

I turn to look at him. 'I don't have any other friends – and before you suggest it, I don't want to make any. I'm not interested in rubberneckers wanting to get to know me so they'll get sympathy at my funeral.'

He sighs, pulls the duvet close under his chin and shakes his head at me. 'You shouldn't talk that way. Cynicism is bad for you.'

'Did you read that somewhere?'

'Being positive strengthens the immune system.'

'So it's my fault I'm sick then, is it?'

'You know I don't think that.'

'Well, you're always acting as if everything I do is wrong.'

He struggles to sit up. 'I don't!'

'Yeah, you do. It's like I'm not dying properly. You're always coming in my room telling me to get out of bed or pull myself together. Now you're telling me to go back to school. It's ridiculous!'

I stomp across the room, grab his slippers and shove my feet into them. They're way too big, but I don't care. Dad leans on his elbows to look at me. He looks as if I hit him.

'Don't go. Where are you going?'

'Away from you.'

I enjoy slamming the door. He can have my bed. Let him. He can lie there and rot.

Eight

The boy looks surprised when I stick my head over the fence and call him. He's older than I thought, perhaps eighteen, with dark hair and the shadow of a beard.

'Yeah?'

'Can I burn some things on your fire?'

He shambles up the path towards me, wiping a hand across his forehead as if he's hot. His fingernails are dirty and he has bits of leaf in his hair. He doesn't smile.

I lift up the two shoeboxes so he can see them. Zoey's dress is draped across my shoulder like a flag.

'What's in them?'

'Paper mostly. Can I bring them round?'

He shrugs as if he doesn't care either way, so I walk through our side gate and step over the low wall that separates the two houses, across his front garden and down the side of his house. He's already there, holding the gate open for me. I hesitate.

'I'm Tessa.'

'Adam.'

We walk in silence down his garden path. I bet he thinks I've just been chucked by my boyfriend, that these are love letters. I bet he thinks, No wonder she got dumped, with that skeleton face and bald head.

The fire is disappointing when we get there, just a smouldering pile of leaves and twigs, with a few hopeful flames licking at the edges.

'The leaves were damp,' he says. 'Paper'll get it going again.'

I open one of the boxes and tip it upside down.

From the day I noticed the first bruise on my spine, to the day only two months ago when the hospital officially gave up on me, I kept a diary. Four years of pathetic optimism burns well – look at it flare! All the get-well cards I ever received curl at the edges, crisp right up and flake to nothing. Over four long years you forget people's names.

There was a nurse who used to draw cartoons of the doctors and put them by the bed to make me laugh. I can't remember her name either. Was it Louise? She was quite prolific. The fire spits, embers spark away into the trees.

'I'm unburdening myself,' I tell Adam.

But I don't think he's listening. He's dragging a clump of bramble across the grass towards the fire.

It's the next box I hate the most. Me and Dad used to trawl through it together, scattering photos over the hospital bed.

'You will get well again,' he'd tell me as he ran a finger over my eleven-year-old image, self-conscious in my school uniform, first day of secondary school. 'Here's one of you in Spain,' he'd say. 'Do you remember?'

I looked thin and brown and hopeful. I was in remission for the first time. A boy whistled at me on the beach. My dad took a picture, said I'd never want to forget my first whistle.

But I do.

I have a sudden desire to rush back home and get more stuff. My clothes, my books.

I say, 'Next time you have a fire, can I come round again?'

Adam stands on one end of the bramble with his boot and folds the other end into the fire. He says, 'Why do you want to get rid of everything?'

I squash Zoey's dress into a tight ball; it feels small in my fist. I throw it at the fire and it seems to catch light before it even reaches the flames. Airborne and still, melting into plastic.

'Dangerous dress,' Adam says, and he looks right at me, as if he knows something.

All matter is comprised of particles. The more solid something is, the closer the particles are held together. People are solid, but inside is liquid. I think perhaps standing too close to a fire can alter the particles of your body, because I feel strangely dizzy and light. I'm not quite sure what's wrong with me – maybe it's not eating properly – but I seem to not be grounded inside my body. The garden turns suddenly bright.

Like the sparks from the fire, which drift down onto my hair and clothes, the law of gravity says that all falling bodies must fall to the ground.

It surprises me to find myself lying on the grass, to be looking up at Adam's pale face haloed by clouds. I can't work it out for a minute.

'Don't move,' he says. 'I think you fainted.'

I try and speak but my tongue feels slow and it's so much easier to lie here.

'Are you diabetic? Do you need sugar? I've got a can of Coke here if you want some.'

He sits down next to me, waits for me to lean up, then hands me the drink. My head buzzes as the sugar hits my brain. How light I feel, more ghostly than before, but so much better. We both look at the fire. The stuff from my boxes has all burned away; even the boxes themselves are just charred remains. The dress has turned to air. The ashes are still hot though, bright enough to attract a moth, a stupid moth dancing towards them. It crackles as its wings fizz and turn to dust. We both watch the space where it was.

I say, 'You do a lot of gardening, don't you?'

'I like it.'

'I watch you. Through my window, when you're digging and stuff.'

He looks startled. 'Do you? Why?'

'I like watching you.'

He frowns, as if he's trying to work that out, seems about to speak for a moment, but looks away instead, his eyes travelling the garden.

'I'm planning a vegetable patch in that corner,' he says. 'Peas, cabbage, lettuce, runner beans. Everything really. It's for my mum more than me.'

'Why?'

He shrugs, looks up at the house as if mentioning her might bring her to the window. 'She likes gardens.'

'What about your dad?'

'No. It's just me and my mum.'

I notice a thin trickle of blood on the back of his hand. He sees me looking and wipes it away on his jeans.

'I should probably get on,' he says. 'Will you be all right? You can keep the Coke if you want.'

He walks next to me as I make my way slowly up the path. I'm very happy that my photos and diary are burned, that Zoey's dress has gone. It feels as if different things will happen.

I turn to Adam at the gate.

I say, 'Thank you for helping.'

He says, 'Any time.'

He has his hands in his pockets. He smiles, then looks away, down at his boots. But I know he sees me.

Nine

'I don't know why they've sent you here,' the receptionist says.

'We were asked to come,' Dad tells her. 'Dr Ryan's secretary phoned and asked us to come.'

'Not here,' she says. 'Not today.'

'Yes, here,' he tells her. 'Yes, today.'

She huffs at him, turns to her computer and scrolls down. 'Is it for a lumbar puncture?'

'No, it's not.' Dad sounds increasingly pissed off. 'Is Dr Ryan even running a clinic today?'

I sit down in the waiting area and let them get on with it. The usual suspects are here – the hat gang in the corner plugged into their portable chemo and talking about diarrhoea and vomiting; a boy clutching his mum's hand, his fragile new hair at the same stage as mine; and a girl with no eyebrows pretending to read a book. She's pencilled fake eyebrows in above the line of her glasses. She sees me staring and smiles, but I'm not having any of that. It's a rule of mine not to get involved with dying people. They're bad news. I made friends with a girl here once. Her name

51

was Angela and we e-mailed each other every day, then one day she stopped. Eventually her mum phoned my dad and told him Angela had died. Dead. Just like that, without even telling me. I decided not to bother with anyone else.

I pick up a magazine, but don't even have time to open it before Dad taps me on the shoulder. 'Vindicated!' he says.

'What?'

'We were right, she was wrong.' He waves cheerily at the receptionist as he helps me stand up. 'Stupid woman doesn't know her arse from her elbow. Apparently we're now allowed straight through to the great man's office!'

Dr Ryan has a splash of something red on his chin. I can't help staring at it as we sit opposite him at his desk. I wonder – is it pasta sauce, or soup? Did he just finish an operation? Maybe it's raw meat.

'Thank you for coming,' he says, and he shuffles his hands on his lap.

Dad edges his chair closer to me and presses his knee against mine. I swallow hard, fight the impulse to get up and walk out. If I don't listen, then I won't know what he's going to say, and maybe then it won't be true.

But Dr Ryan doesn't hesitate, and his voice is very firm. 'Tessa,' he says, 'it's not good news, I'm afraid. Your recent lumbar puncture shows us that your cancer has spread to your spinal fluid.'

'Is that bad?' I ask, making a little joke.

He doesn't laugh. 'It's very bad, Tessa. It means you've relapsed in your central nervous system. I know this is very difficult to hear, but things are progressing more quickly than we first thought.'

I look at him. 'Things?'

He shifts on his chair. 'You've moved further along the line, Tessa.'

There's a big window behind his desk, and out of it I can see the tops of two trees. I can see their branches, their drying leaves, and a bit of sky.

'How much further along the line have I moved?'

'I can only ask you how you're feeling, Tessa. Are you more tired, or nauseous? Do you have any leg pain?'

'A bit.'

'I can't judge it, but I'd encourage you to do the things you want to do.'

He has some slides with him to prove the point, passes them round like holiday snaps, pointing out little splashes of darkness, lesions, sticky blasts floating loose. It's as if a child with a brush and too much enthusiasm has been set free with a tin of black paint inside me.

Dad's trying unsuccessfully not to cry. 'What happens now?' he asks, and big silent tears fall out of his eyes and plonk onto his lap. The doctor hands him a tissue.

Outside the window, the first rain of the day spatters against the glass. A leaf caught by a gust of wind rips, then flares red and gold as it falls.

The doctor says, 'Tessa may respond to intensive intrathecal medication. I would suggest methotrexate and hydrocortisone for four weeks. If it's successful, her symptoms should improve and we can continue with a maintenance programme.'

The doctor keeps talking and Dad keeps listening, but I stop hearing any of it.

It's really going to happen. They said it would, but this is quicker than anyone thought. I really won't ever go back to school. Not ever. I'll never be famous or leave anything worthwhile behind. I'll never go to college or have a job. I won't see my brother grow up. I won't travel, never earn money, never drive, never fall in love or leave home or get my own house.

It's really, really true.

A thought stabs up, growing from my toes and ripping through me, until it stifles everything else and becomes the only thing I'm thinking. It fills me up, like a silent scream. I've been ill for so long, puffed up and sick, with patchy skin, flaky fingernails, disappearing hair and a feeling of nausea that permeates to my bones. It's not fair. I don't want to die like this, not before I've even lived properly. It seems so clear to me. I feel almost hopeful, which is mad. I want to live before I die. It's the only thing that makes sense.

That's when the room comes sharply back into focus.

The doctor's going on about drug trials now, how they probably won't help me, but might help others. Dad's still quietly crying, and I stare out the window and wonder why the light seems to be fading so quickly. How late is it? How long have we been sitting here? I look at my watch – three thirty and the day is almost ending. It's October. All those kids recently returned to classrooms with new bags and pencil cases will be looking forward to half term already. How quickly it goes. Halloween soon, then firework night. Christmas. Spring. Easter. Then there's my birthday in May. I'll be seventeen.

How long can I stave it off? I don't know. All I know is that I have two choices – stay wrapped in blankets and get on with dying, or get the list back together and get on with living.

Ten

Dad says, 'Hey, you're up!' Then he notices the mini-dress I'm wearing and his lips tighten. 'Let me guess. You're seeing Zoey?'

'Anything wrong with that?'

He pushes my vitamins to me across the kitchen table. 'Don't forget these.' Usually he brings them up on a tray, but he won't have to bother today. You'd think that'd make him happy, but he just sits there watching me swallow pill after pill.

Vitamin E helps the body recover from post-irradiation anaemia. Vitamin A counters the effects radiation has on the intestine. Slippery elm replaces the mucous material lining all the hollow tubes in my body. Silica strengthens the bones. Potassium, iron and copper build up the immune system. Aloe vera is for general healing. And garlic – well, Dad read somewhere that the properties of garlic are not yet properly understood. He calls it vitamin X. All washed down with unprocessed orange juice and a teaspoon of unrefined honey. Yum, yum.

I slide the tray back in Dad's direction with a smile. He stands up, takes it to the sink and clunks it down. 'I thought,' he says, turning on the tap and swirling water round the bowl, 'that you were feeling some nausea and pain yesterday.'

'I'm fine. Nothing hurts today.'

'Don't you think it might be wise to rest?'

Which is dangerous territory, so I change the subject rapidly and turn my attention to Cal, who is mashing his cornflakes into a soggy pile. He looks just as glum as Dad.

'What's wrong with you?' I say.

'Nothing.'

'It's Saturday! Aren't you supposed to be glad about that?'

He looks fiercely at me. 'You don't remember, do you?'

'Remember what?'

'You said you'd take me shopping in half term. You said you'd bring your credit card.' He closes his eyes very tightly. 'I knew you bloody wouldn't!'

'Calm down!' Dad says in that warning voice he uses when Cal begins to lose it.

'I did say that, Cal, but I can't today.'

He looks at me furiously. 'I want you to!'

So then I have to, because it's in the rules. Number two on my list is simple. I must say yes to everything for one whole day. Whatever it is and whoever asks it of me.

I look down at Cal's hopeful face as we step out through the gate and suddenly feel a lurch of fear.

'I'm going to text Zoey,' I tell him. 'Tell her we're on our way.'

He tells me he hates Zoey, which is tough, because I need her.

Her energy. The fact that things always happen when she's around.

Cal says, 'I want to go to the playground.'

'Aren't you a bit old for that?'

'No. It'll be fun.'

I often forget he's just a kid, that there's a bit of him that still likes swings and roundabouts and all that stuff. Not much to harm us in the park though, and Zoey texts back to say fine, she was going to be late anyway and will meet us there.

I sit on a bench and watch Cal climb. It's a spider's web of ropes and he looks so small up there.

'I'm going higher!' he shouts. 'Shall I go right to the top?'

'Yes,' I shout back, because I promised myself. It's in the rules.

'I can see inside planes!' he yells. 'Come and look!'

It's difficult climbing in a mini-dress. The whole web of ropes swings and I have to kick my shoes to the ground. Cal laughs at me. 'Right to the top!' he orders. It's really bloody high, and some kid with a face like a bus is shaking the ropes at the bottom. I haul myself up, even though my arms ache. I want to see inside planes too. I want to watch the wind and catch birds in my fist.

I make it. I can see the top of the church, and the trees that line the park and all the conker pods ready to burst. The air is clean and the clouds are close, like being on a very small mountain. I look down at all the upturned faces.

'High, isn't it?' Cal says.

'Yes.'

'Shall we go on the swings next?'

'Yes.'

Yes to everything you say, Cal, but first I want to feel the air circle my face. I want to watch the curve of the earth as we slowly shift round the sun.

'I told you it would be fun.' Cal's face is shining with good humour. 'Let's go on *everything* else!'

There's a queue at the swings, so we go on the seesaw. I'm still heavier than him, still his big sister, and I can slam my legs on the ground so he bounces high and screams with laughter as he falls back hard on his bum. He'll have bruises, but he doesn't care. Say yes, just say yes.

We go everywhere – the little house at the top of the ladder in the sandpit, where we just fit in. The motorbike on a giant spring, which veers drunkenly to one side when I sit on it, so I scrape my knee on the ground. There's a wooden beam and we pretend we're gymnasts, an alphabet snake to walk, a hopscotch, some monkey bars. Then back to the swings, where a queue of mums with their bits of tissue and fat-faced babies tut at me as I beat Cal to the only available one. My dress flashes thigh. It makes me laugh. It makes me lean back and swing even higher. Maybe if I swing high enough, the world will be different.

I don't see Zoey arrive. When Cal points her out, she's leaning against the entrance to the playground watching us. She might've been there for ages. She's wearing a crop top and a skirt that only just covers her bum.

'Morning,' she says as we join her. 'I see you started without me.'

I feel myself blush. 'Cal wanted me to go on the swings.'

'And you had to say yes, of course.'

'Yes.'

She looks thoughtfully at Cal. 'We're going to the market,' she tells him. 'We're going to buy things and talk about periods, so you're going to be really bored.'

He looks up at her crossly, his face smeared with dirt. 'I want to go to the magic shop.'

'Good. Off you go then. See you later.'

'He has to come with us,' I tell her. 'I promised him.'

She sighs and walks off. Cal and me find ourselves following.

Zoey was the only girl at school who wasn't afraid of my illness. She's still the only person I know who walks down the street as if muggings never happen, as if people never get stabbed, buses never mount pavements, illness never strikes. Being with her is like being told they got it wrong and I'm not dying, someone else is, and it's all a mistake.

'Wiggle,' she calls over her shoulder. 'Move those hips, Tessa!'

This dress is very short. It shows every shiver and fold. A car hoots. A group of boys look long and hard, at my breasts, at my arse.

'Why do you have to do what she says?' Cal asks.

'I just do.'

Zoey's delighted. She waits for us to catch up and links arms with me. 'You're forgiven,' she says.

'For what?'

She leans in conspiratorially. 'For being so horrid about your crap shag.'

'I wasn't!'

'Yeah, you were. But it's OK.'

'It's rude to whisper!' Cal says.

She pushes him ahead of us, pulls me closer to her as we walk. 'So,' she says. 'How far are you prepared to go? Would you get a tattoo if I told you to?'

'Yes.'

'Would you take drugs?'

'I *want* to take drugs!'

'Would you tell that man you love him?'

The man she points to is bald and older than my dad. He's coming out of the newsagent's ripping cellophane from a packet of fags and letting it flutter from his hand to the ground.

'Yes.'

'Go on then.'

The man taps a fag from the box, lights it and blows smoke into the air. I walk up to him and he turns, half smiling, maybe expecting someone he knows.

'I love you,' I say.

He frowns, then notices Zoey giggling. 'Piss off,' he says. 'Bloody idiot.'

It's hilarious. Me and Zoey hold onto each other and laugh a lot. Cal grimaces at us in despair. 'Can we just go now?' he says.

The market's heaving. People everywhere jostling, like the day is full of emergencies. Fat old women with their shopping baskets shove past me; parents with buggies take up all the room.

Standing here with the grey light of this day around me is like being in a dream, as if I'm not moving at all, as if the pavement is sticky and my feet made of lead. Boys stalk past me, hoods up, faces blank. Girls I used to go to school with meander by. They don't recognize me now; it's been so long since I've been in a classroom. The air is thick with the smell of hotdogs, burgers and onions. Everything's for sale – boiling chickens hanging by their feet, trays of tripe and offal, half-sides of pig, their cracked ribs exposed. Material, wool, lace and curtains. At the toy stall, dogs yap and do somersaults and wind-up soldiers clang cymbals. The stallholder smiles at me, points to a giant plastic doll sitting mute in her cellophane.

'Only a tenner, love.'

I turn away, pretend not to hear.

Zoey looks at me sternly. 'You're supposed to be saying yes to everything. Next time, buy it – whatever it is. OK?'

'Yes.'

'Good. Back in a minute.' And she disappears amongst the crowd.

I don't want her to go. I need her. If she doesn't come back, my day will amount to a turn round the playground and a couple of wolf whistles on the way to the market.

'You all right?' Cal says.

'Yeah.'

'You don't look it.'

'I'm fine.'

'Well, I'm bored.'

Which is dangerous, because obviously I'll have to say yes to him if he asks to go back home.

'Zoey'll be back in a minute. Maybe we could get the bus across town. We could go to the magic shop.'

Cal shrugs, shoves his hands in his pockets. 'She won't want to do that.'

'Look at the toys while you're waiting.'

'The toys are crap.'

Are they? I used to come here with Dad and look at them. Everything used to gleam.

Zoey comes back looking agitated. 'Scott's a lying bastard,' she says.

'Who?'

'Scott. He said he worked on a stall, but he's not here.'

'Stoner Boy? When did he tell you that?'

She looks at me as if I'm completely insane and walks off again. She goes over to a man behind the fruit stall and leans over boxes of bananas to talk to him. He looks at her breasts.

A woman comes up to me. She's carrying several plastic bags. She looks right at me and I don't look away.

'Ten pork chops, three packs of smoked bacon and a boiling chicken,' she whispers. 'You want them?'

'Yes.'

She passes a bag over, then picks at her scabby nose while I find some money. I give her five pounds and she digs around in her pocket and gives me two pounds change. 'That's a bargain,' she says.

Cal looks a little afraid as she walks away. 'Why did you do that?'

'Shut up,' I tell him, because nowhere in the rules does it say I have to be glad about what I do. I wonder, since I only have twelve pounds left, if I'm allowed to change the rules so that I can only say yes to things that are free. The bag drips blood at my feet. I wonder if I have to keep everything I buy.

Zoey comes back, notices the bag and peels it from me. 'What the hell's in here?' She peers inside. 'It looks like bits of dead dog!' She chucks the whole lot in a bin, then turns back to me, smiling. 'I've found Scott. He was here after all. Jake's with him. Come on.'

As we edge our way through the crowd, Zoey tells me that she's seen Scott a few times since we went round to their house. She doesn't look at me as she tells me this.

'Why didn't you say so?'

'You've been out of action for over four weeks! Anyway, I thought you'd be pissed off.'

It's quite shocking to see them in daylight, standing behind a stall that sells torches and toasters, clocks and kettles. They look older than I remember.

Zoey goes round the back to talk to Scott. Jake nods at me.

'All right?' he says.

'Yeah.'

'Doing some shopping?'

He looks different – sweaty and vaguely embarrassed. A woman comes up behind me, and Cal and I have to step out of the way for her to get to the stall. She buys four batteries. They cost a pound. Jake puts them in a plastic bag for her and takes her money. She goes away.

'Do you want some batteries?' he asks. He doesn't quite look me in the eyes. 'You don't have to pay.'

There's something about the way he says it, as if he's doing me an enormous favour, as if he's sorry for me and wants to show he's a decent bloke – it tells me that he knows. Zoey's told him. I can see the guilt and pity in his eyes. He shagged a dying girl and now he's afraid. I might be contagious; my illness brushed his shoulder and may lie in wait for him.

'Do you want some then?' He picks up a packet of batteries and waves them at me.

'Yes,' comes out of my mouth. The disappointment of the word has to be swallowed down hard as I take his stupid batteries and put them in my bag.

Cal nudges me hard in the ribs. 'Can we go now?'

'Yes.'

Zoey has her arm round Scott's waist. 'No!' she says. 'We're going back to their place. They get a lunch break in half an hour.'

'I'm taking Cal across town.'

Zoey smiles as she comes over. She looks lovely, as if Scott's warmed her up. 'Aren't you supposed to say yes?'

'Cal asked first.'

She frowns. 'They've got some ketamine back at their place. It's all arranged. Bring Cal if you want. They'll have something for him to do, a PlayStation or something.'

'You told Jake.'

'Told him what?'

'About me.'

'I didn't.'

She blushes, and has to chuck her cigarette down and stamp it out so that she doesn't have to look at me.

I can just imagine how she did it. She went round to their house and made them strap a joint together and she insisted on having first toke, inhaling long and hard as they both watched her. Then she shuffled down next to Scott and said, 'Hey, do you remember Tessa?'

And then she told them. She might even have cried. I bet Scott put his arm round her. I bet Jake grabbed the joint and inhaled so deeply that he didn't have to think about it.

I grab Cal's hand and steer him away. Away from Zoey, away from the market. I pull him down the steps at the back of the stalls and onto the towpath that follows the canal.

'Where are we going?' he whines.

'Shut up.'

'You're scaring me.'

I look down at his face and I don't care.

I have this dream sometimes that I'm walking round at home, just in and out of rooms, and no one in my family recognizes me. I pass Dad on the stairs and he nods at me politely, as if I've come to clean the house, or it's really a hotel. Cal stares at me suspiciously as I go into my bedroom. Inside, all my things have gone and another girl is there instead of me, a girl wearing a flowered dress, with bright lips and cheeks as firm as apples. That's my parallel life, I think. The one where I'm healthy, where Jake would be glad to have met me.

In real life, I drag my brother along the towpath towards the café that overlooks the canal.

'It'll be good,' I tell him. 'We're going to have ice cream and hot chocolate and Coke.'

'You're not supposed to have sugar. I'm telling Dad.'

I grip his hand even harder. A man is standing on the path a little further up, between us and the café. He's wearing pyjamas and looking at the canal. A cigarette ripens in his mouth.

Cal says, 'I want to go home.'

But I want to show him the rats on the towpath, the leaves ripped screaming from trees, the way people avoid what's difficult, the way this man in pyjamas is more real than Zoey, trotting up behind us with her big gob and silly blonde hair.

'Go away,' I tell her without even turning round.

She grabs my arm. 'Why does everything have to be such a big deal with you?'

I push her off. 'I don't know, Zoey. Why do you think?'

'It's not like it's a secret. Loads of people know you're ill. Jake didn't mind, but now he thinks you're a complete weirdo.'

'I *am* a complete weirdo.'

She looks at me with narrowed eyes. 'I think you like being sick.'

'You think?'

'You can't bear to be normal.'

'Yeah, you're right, it's great. Want to swap?'

'Everybody dies,' she says, like it's something she's only just thought of and wouldn't mind for herself.

Cal tugs at my sleeve. 'Look,' he says.

The man in pyjamas has waded into the canal. He's splashing about in the shallows and smacking at the water with his hands. He looks at us blankly, then smiles, showing several gold teeth. I feel my spine tingle.

'Fancy a swim, ladies?' he calls. He's got a Scottish accent. I've never been to Scotland.

'Get in with him,' Zoey says. 'Why don't you?'

'Are you telling me to?'

She grins at me maliciously. 'Yes.'

I glance at the tables outside the café. People are gazing this way. They'll think I'm a junkie, a psycho, a head case. I roll up my dress and tuck it in my knickers.

'What are you doing?' Cal hisses. 'Everyone's looking!'

'Pretend you're not with me then.'

'I will!' He sits stubbornly on the grass as I take off my shoes.

I dip in my big toe. The water's so cold that my whole leg creeps with numbness.

Zoey touches my arm. 'Don't, Tess. I didn't mean it. Don't be stupid.'

Doesn't she get it at all?

I launch myself up to my thighs and ducks quack away in alarm. It's not deep, a bit muddy, probably with all sorts of crap in the bottom. Rats swim in this water. People chuck in tin cans and shopping trolleys and needles and dead dogs. The soft mud squelches between my toes.

Gold Tooth waves, laughs as he wades towards me, slapping his sides. 'You're a good girl,' he says. His lips are blue and his gold teeth glint. He has a gash on his head and fresh blood oozes from his hairline towards his eyes. This makes me feel even colder.

A man comes out of the café waving a tea towel. 'Hey!' he shouts. 'Hey, get out of there!'

He's wearing an apron and his stomach wobbles as he leans down to help me. 'Are you crazy?' he says. 'You could get sick from that water.' He turns to Zoey. 'Are you with her?'

'I'm sorry,' she says. 'I couldn't stop her.' She swings her hair about so he'll understand it's not her fault. I hate that.

'She's not with me,' I tell him. 'I don't know her.'

Zoey's face slams shut and the café man turns back to me, confused. He lets me use his tea towel to dry my legs. Then he tells me I'm crazy. He tells me all young people are junkies. As he shouts, I watch Zoey walk away. She gets smaller and smaller until she disappears. The café man asks where my parents are; he asks if I know the man with gold teeth, who is now clambering up the opposite bank and laughing raucously to himself. The café man tuts a lot, but then he walks with me back up the path to the café and makes me sit down and brings me a cup of tea. I put three sugars in it and take little sips. Lots of people are staring at me. Cal looks rather scared and small.

'What are you doing?' he whispers.

I'm going to miss him so much it makes me want to hurt him.

It also makes me want to take him home and give him to Dad before I lose us both. But home is dull. I can say yes to anything there, because Dad won't ask me to do anything real.

The tea warms my belly. The sky changes from dull grey to sunny and back again in a moment. Even the weather can't decide what to do and is lurching from one ridiculous event to another.

'Let's get a bus,' I say.

I stand up, hold onto the table edge and step back into my shoes. People pretend not to look at me, but I can feel their gaze. It makes me feel alive.

Eleven

'Is it true?' Cal asks as we walk to the bus stop. 'Do you like being ill?'

'Sometimes.'

'Is that why you jumped in the water?'

I stop and look at him, at his clear blue eyes. They're flecked with grey like mine. There are photos of him and me at the same age and there isn't a single difference between us.

'I jumped because I've made a list of things to do. Today I have to say yes to everything.'

He thinks about this, takes a few seconds to work out the implications, then grins broad and wide. 'So whatever I ask you to do, you have to say yes?'

'Got it in one.'

We get the first bus that comes. We sit upstairs at the back.

'OK,' Cal whispers. 'Stick your tongue out at that man.'

He's delighted when I do.

'Now make a V sign at that woman on the pavement, then blow kisses at those boys.'

'It'd be more fun if you did it with me.'

We pull faces, wave at everyone, say *bogey*, *bum* and *willy* at the tops of our voices. By the time we ring the bell to get off the bus, we're alone on the top deck. Everyone hates us, but we don't care.

'Where are we going?' Cal asks.

'Shopping.'

'Have you got your credit card? Will you buy me stuff?'

'Yes.'

First we buy a radio-controlled HoverCopter. It's capable of mid-air launch and can fly up to ten metres high. Cal chucks the packaging in the bin outside the shop and makes it fly ahead of us in the street. We walk behind it, dazzled by its multi-coloured lights, all the way to the lingerie shop.

I make Cal sit on a seat inside with all the men waiting for their wives. There's something so lovely about removing my dress, not for an examination, but for a soft-voiced woman who measures me for a lacy and very expensive bra.

'Lilac,' I tell her when she asks about colour. 'And I want the matching knickers as well.' After I pay, she presents them to me in a classy bag with silver handles.

I buy Cal a talking moneybox robot next. Then jeans for me. I get the same slim-legged pre-washed pair Zoey has.

Cal gets a PlayStation game. I get a dress. It's emerald and black silk and is the most expensive thing I've ever bought. I blink at myself in the mirror, leave my wet dress behind in the changing room and rejoin Cal.

'Cool,' he says when he sees me. 'Is there any money left for a digital watch?'

I get him an alarm clock as well, one that will project the time three-dimensionally onto his bedroom ceiling.

Boots next. Zipped leather with little heels. And a holdall from the same shop to put all our things in.

After a visit to the magic shop we have to buy a suitcase with wheels to put the holdall in. Cal enjoys steering it, but it crosses my mind that if we buy more stuff, we'll have to buy a car to carry the suitcase. A truck for the car. A ship for the truck. We'll buy a harbour, an ocean, a continent.

The headache begins in McDonald's. It's like someone suddenly scalps me with a spoon and digs about inside my brain. I feel dizzy and sick as the world presses in. I take some paracetamol, but know it'll only take the edge off.

Cal says, 'You OK?'

'Yes.'

He knows I'm lying. He's full of food and as satisfied as a king, but his eyes are scared. 'I want to go home.'

I have to say yes. We both pretend it's not because of me.

I stand on the pavement and watch him hail a cab, holding onto the wall to keep myself steady. I will not end this day with a transfusion. I will not have their obscene needles in me today.

In the taxi, Cal's hand is small and friendly and fits neatly into mine. I try to savour the moment. He doesn't often volunteer to hold my hand.

'Will we get into trouble?' he says.

'What can they do?'

He laughs. 'So can we have this kind of day again?'

'Sure.'

'Can we go ice-skating next time?'

'All right.'

He babbles on about white-water rafting, says he fancies horse riding, wouldn't mind having a go at bungee jumping. I look out of the window, my head pounding. Light bounces off walls and faces and comes in at me bright and close. It feels like a hundred fires burning.

Twelve

I know I'm in a hospital as soon as I open my eyes. They all smell the same, and the line hooked into my arm is achingly familiar. I try to sit up in bed, but my head crashes and bile rises in my throat.

A nurse rushes over with a cardboard bowl, but she's too late. Most of it goes over me and the sheets.

'Never mind,' she says. 'We'll soon have that cleaned up.'

She wipes my mouth, then helps me roll onto my side so that she can untie my nightgown.

'Doctor'll be here soon,' she says.

Nurses never tell you what they know. They're hired for their cheeriness and the thickness of their hair. They need to look alive and healthy, to give the patients something to aim for.

She chats as she helps me on with a fresh gown, tells me she used to live near the ocean in South Africa, says, 'The sun is closer to the earth there, and it's always hot.'

She whisks the bed sheets from under me and conjures up fresh ones. 'I get such cold feet in England,' she says. 'Now, let's roll you back again. Ready? That's it, all done. Ah, and what good timing – the doctor's here.'

He's bald and white and middle-aged. He greets me politely and drags a chair over from under the window to sit by the bed. I keep hoping that in some hospital somewhere in this country I'll bump into the perfect doctor, but none of them are ever right. I want a magician with a cloak and wand, or a knight with a sword, someone fearless. This one is as bland and polite as a salesman.

'Tessa,' he says, 'do you know what hypercalcaemia is?'

'If I say no, can I have something else?'

He looks bemused, and that's the trouble – they never quite get the joke. I wish he had an assistant. A jester would be good, someone to tickle him with feathers while he delivers his medical opinion.

He flips through the chart on his lap. 'Hypercalcaemia is a condition where your calcium levels become very high. We're giving you bisphosphonates, which will bring those levels down. You should be feeling much less confused and nauseous already.'

'I'm always confused,' I tell him.

'Do you have any questions?'

He looks expectantly at me and I hate to disappoint him, but what could I possibly ask this ordinary little man?

He tells me the nurse will give me something to help me sleep. He stands up and gives a nod goodbye. This is the point where the jester would lay a trail of banana skins to the door, then come and sit with me on the bed. Together we'd laugh at the doctor's backside as he scurries away.

It's dark when I wake up and I can't remember anything. It freaks me out. For maybe ten seconds I struggle with it, kicking against the twisted sheets, convinced I've been kidnapped or worse.

It's Dad who rushes to my side, smooths my head, whispers my name over and over like a magic spell.

And then I remember. I jumped in a river, I persuaded Cal to join me on a ridiculous spending spree and now I'm in hospital. But the moment of forgetting makes my heart beat fast as a rabbit's, because I actually forgot who I was for a minute. I became no one, and I know it'll happen again.

Dad smiles down at me. 'Do you want some water?' he says. 'Are you thirsty?'

He pours me a glass from the jug, but I shake my head at it and he sets it back down on the table.

'Does Zoey know I'm here?'

He fumbles in his jacket and takes out a packet of cigarettes. He goes over to the window and opens it. Cold air edges in.

'You can't smoke in here, Dad.'

He shuts the window and puts the cigarettes back in his pocket. 'No,' he says. 'I suppose not.' He comes back to sit down, reaches for my hand. I wonder if he too has forgotten who he is.

'I spent a lot of money, Dad.'

'I know. It doesn't matter.'

'I didn't think my card would actually do all that. In every shop I thought they'd refuse it, but they never did. I got receipts though, so we can take it all back.'

'Hush,' he says. 'It's OK.'

'Is Cal all right? Did I freak him out?'

'He'll survive. Do you want to see him? He's out in the corridor with your mother.'

Never, in the last four years, have all three of them visited me at the same time. I feel suddenly frightened.

They walk in so seriously, Cal clutching Mum's hand, Mum looking out of place, Dad holding open the door. All three of them stand by the bed gazing down at me. It feels like a premonition of a day that will come. Later. Not now. A day when I won't be able to see them looking, to smile, or to tell them to stop freaking me out and sit themselves down.

Mum pulls a chair close, leans over and kisses me. The familiar smell of her – the washing powder she uses, the orange oil she sprays at her throat – makes me want to cry.

'You had me scared!' she says, and she shakes her head as if she simply can't believe it.

'I was scared too,' Cal whispers. 'You collapsed in the taxi and the man thought you were drunk.'

'Did he?'

'I didn't know what to do. He said we'd have to pay extra if you puked.'

'Did I puke?'

'No.'

'So did you tell him to piss off?'

Cal smiles, but it wavers at the edges. 'No.'

'Do you want to come and sit on the bed?'

He shakes his head.

'Hey, Cal, don't cry! Come and sit on the bed with me, come on. We'll try and remember all the things we bought.'

But he sits on Mum's lap instead. I don't think I've ever seen him do this. I'm not sure Dad has either. Even Cal seems surprised. He turns into her shoulder and sobs for real. She strokes his back, sweeping circles with her hand. Dad looks out of the window. And I spread my fingers out on the sheet in front of me. They're very thin and white, like vampire hands that could suck everyone's heat away.

'I always wanted a velvet dress when I was a kid,' Mum says. 'A green one with a lacy collar. My sister had one and I never did, so I understand about wanting lovely things. If you ever want to go shopping again, Tessa, I'll go with you.' She waves her hand at the room extravagantly. 'We'll all go!'

Cal pulls away from her shoulder to look at her. 'Really? Me as well?'

'You as well.'

'I wonder who'll be paying!' Dad says wryly from his perch on the window ledge.

Mum smiles, dries Cal's tears with the back of her hand, then kisses his cheek. 'Salty,' she says. 'Salty as the sea.'

Dad watches her do this. I wonder if she knows he's looking.

She launches into a story about her spoiled sister Sarah and a pony called Tango. Dad laughs and tells her she can hardly complain of a deprived childhood. She teases him then, telling us how she turned her back on a wealthy family in order to slum it by marrying Dad. And Cal practises a coin trick, palming a pound from one hand to the other, then opening his fist to show us it's vanished.

It's lovely listening to them talk, their words gliding into each other. My bones don't ache so much with the three of them so close. Perhaps if I keep really still, they won't notice the pale moon outside the window, or hear the meds trolley come rattling down the corridor. They could stay the night. We could be rowdy, telling jokes and stories until the sun comes up.

But eventually Mum says, 'Cal's tired. I'll take him home now and put him to bed.' She turns to Dad. 'I'll see you there.'

She kisses me goodbye, then blows another kiss from the door. I actually feel it land on my cheek.

'Smell you later,' Cal says.

And then they're gone.

'Is she staying at ours?' I ask Dad.

'It seems to make sense just for tonight.'

He comes over, sits on the chair and takes my hand. 'You know,' he says, 'when you were a baby, me and Mum used to lie awake at night watching you breathe. We were convinced you'd forget how to do it if we stopped looking.' There's a shift in his hand, a softening of the contours of his fingers. 'You can laugh at me, but it's true. It gets easier as your children get older, but it never goes away. I worry about you all the time.'

'Why are you telling me this?'

He sighs. 'I know you're up to something. Cal told me about some list you've made. I need to know about it, not because I want to stop you, but because I want to keep you safe.'

'Isn't that the same thing?'

'No, I don't think so. It's like you're giving the best of yourself away, Tess. To be left out of that hurts so much.'

His voice trails off. Is that really all he wants? To be included? But how can I tell him about Jake and his narrow single bed? How can I tell him it was Zoey who told me to jump, and that I had to say yes? Drugs are next. And after drugs, there are still seven things left to do. If I tell him, he'll take it away. I don't want to spend the rest of my life huddled in a blanket on the sofa with my head on Dad's shoulder. The list is the only thing keeping me going.

Thirteen

I thought it was morning, but it isn't. I thought the house was this quiet because everyone had got up and gone out. It's only six o'clock though, and I'm stuck with the muffled light of dawn.

I get a packet of cheese nibbles from the kitchen cupboard and turn on the radio. Following a pile-up several people have been trapped in their cars overnight on the M3. They had no access to toilet facilities, and food and water had to be delivered to them by the emergency services. Gridlock. The world is filling up. A Tory MP cheats on his wife. A body is found in a hotel. It's like listening to a cartoon. I turn it off and get a choc-ice from the freezer. It makes me feel vaguely drunk and very cold. I get my coat off the peg and creep about the kitchen listening for leaves and shadows and the soft sound of dust falling. This warms me up a bit.

It's seventeen minutes past six.

Maybe something different will be out in the garden – wild buffalo, a spaceship, mounds of red roses. I open the back door really slowly, begging the world to bring me something startling and new. But it's all horribly familiar – empty flowerbeds, soggy grass and low grey cloud.

I text Zoey one word: DRUGS!!

She doesn't text back. She's at Scott's, I bet, hot and happy in his arms. They came to visit me at the hospital, sat together on one chair like they got married and I missed it. They brought me some plums and a Halloween torch from the market.

'I've been helping Scott on the stall,' Zoey said.

All I could think was how quickly the end of October had come, and how the weight of Scott's arm across her shoulder was slowing her down. A week has gone by since then. Although she's texted me every day, she doesn't seem interested in my list any more.

Without her, I guess I'll just stand here on the step and watch the clouds gather and burst. Water will run in rivulets down the kitchen window and another day will begin to collapse around me. Is that living? Is it even anything?

A door opens and shuts next door. There's the heavy tread of boots on mud. I walk across and stick my head over the fence.

'Hello again!'

Adam puts his hand to his chest as if I gave him a heart attack. 'Jesus! You scared me!'

'Sorry.'

He's not dressed for gardening. He's wearing a leather jacket and jeans and he's carrying a motorcycle helmet.

'Are you going out?'

'Yeah.'

We both look at his bike. It's down by the shed, tied up. It's red and silver. It looks as if it'd bolt if you let it free.

'It's a nice bike.'

He nods. 'I just got it fixed.'

'What was wrong with it?'

'It got knocked over and the forks got twisted. Do you know about bikes?'

I think about lying, but it's the kind of lie that would catch you out very quickly. 'Not really. I've always wanted to go on one though.'

He gives me an odd look. It makes me wonder what I look like. Yesterday I looked like a smack-head because my skin seemed to be turning yellow. I put earrings in last night to try and counteract the effect, but I forgot to check my face this morning. Anything could've happened during the night. I feel a bit uncomfortable with him looking at me like that.

'Listen,' he says. 'There's something I should probably tell you.'

I can tell by the discomfort in his voice what it'll be, and I want to save him from it.

'It's all right,' I say. 'My dad's a real blabbermouth. Even strangers look at me with pity these days.'

'Really?' He looks startled. 'It's just I hadn't seen you around for a while, so I asked your brother if you were OK. It was him who told me.'

I look at my feet, at a patch of lawn in front of my feet, at the gap between the grass and the bottom of the fence.

'I thought you had diabetes. You know, when you fainted that time. I didn't realize.'

'No.'

'I'm sorry. I mean, I was very sorry when he told me.'

'Yes.'

'It felt important to tell you I know.'

'Thanks.'

Our words sound very loud. They take up all the room in my head and sit there echoing back at me.

Eventually I say, 'People tend to get a bit freaked when they find out, like they just can't bear it.' He nods, as if he knows this. 'But it's not as if I'm going to drop dead this very second. I've got a whole list of things I'm going to do first.'

I didn't know I was going to tell him this. It surprises me. It also surprises me when he smiles.

'Like what?' he says.

I'm certainly not telling him about Jake or about jumping in the river. 'Well, drugs are next.'

'Drugs?'

'Yeah, and I don't mean aspirin.'

He laughs. 'No, I didn't think you did.'

'My friend's going to get me some E.'

'Ecstasy? You should take mushrooms, they're better.'

'They make you hallucinate, don't they? I don't want skeletons rushing at me.'

'You'll feel dreamy, not trippy.'

That's not very reassuring because I don't think my dreams are like other people's. I end up in desolate places that are hard to get back from. I wake up hot and thirsty.

'I can get you some if you want,' he says.

'You can?'

'Today if you like.'

'Today?'

'No time like the present.'

'I promised my friend I wouldn't do anything without her.'

He raises an eyebrow. 'That's a lot to promise.'

I look away and up to the house. Dad'll be up soon and straight onto his computer. Cal will be off to school. 'I could ring her, see if she can come over.'

He zips up his jacket. 'All right.'

'Where are you going to get them from?'

A slow smile lifts the edges of his mouth. 'One day I'll take you out on the bike and show you.' He backs off down the path, still smiling. I'm held by his eyes, pale green in this early light.

Fourteen

'Where do you reckon he gets them from, Zoey?'

She yawns hugely. 'Legoland?' she says. 'Toytown?'

'Why are you being so horrible?'

She turns on the bed and looks at me. 'Because he's boring and ugly and you've got me, so I don't know why you're even interested. You shouldn't have asked him for drugs. I told you I'd get them.'

'You haven't exactly been around.'

'Last time I looked, you were flat on your back in hospital and I was visiting you!'

'And last time I looked, I was only there because you told me to jump in a river!'

She sticks her tongue out, so I turn back to the window. Adam got home ages ago, went inside for half an hour, then came back out and started raking leaves. I thought he'd have knocked on the door by now. Maybe we're supposed to go to him.

Zoey comes to stand beside me and we watch him together. Every time he loads leaves onto the wheelbarrow, dozens of them fly off again in the wind and settle back on the lawn.

'Hasn't he got anything better to do?'

I knew she'd think that. She doesn't have much patience for anything she has to wait for. If she planted a seed, she'd have to dig it back up and look at it every day to see if it was growing yet.

'He's gardening.'

She gives me a withering look. 'Is he retarded?'

'No!'

'Shouldn't he be at college or something?'

'I think he looks after his mum.'

She looks at me with plotting eyes. 'You fancy him.'

'I don't.'

'You do. You're secretly in love with him. You know stuff about him you couldn't possibly know if you didn't care.'

I shake my head, try to put her off the scent. She'll play with it now, make it bigger than it would have been without her.

'Do you stand here every day spying on him?'

'No.'

'I bet you do. I'm going to ask him if he fancies you back.'

'No, Zoey!'

She runs to the door laughing. 'I'm going to ask him if he wants to marry you!'

'Please, Zoey. Don't mess it up.'

She walks slowly back across the room, shaking her head. 'Tessa, I thought you understood the rules! Never let a bloke into your heart – it's fatal.'

'What about you and Scott?'

'That's different.'

'Why?'

She smiles. 'That's just sex.'

'No, it's not. When you visited me at the hospital, you could barely drag your eyes from his face.'

'Rubbish!'

'It's true.'

Zoey used to live her life as if the human race was about to become extinct, like nothing really mattered. But around Scott, she goes all soft and warm. Doesn't she know this about herself?

She's looking at me so seriously that I grab her face and kiss it, because I want her to smile again. Her lips are soft and she smells nice. It crosses my mind that it might be possible to suck some of her good white cells into me in this way, but she pushes me off before I have a chance to test my theory.

'What did you do that for?'

'Because you're spoiling it. Now go and ask Adam if he's got the mushrooms.'

'You go.'

I laugh at her. 'We'll both go.'

She wipes her lips with her sleeve and looks confused. 'OK, fine. Your bedroom's starting to smell weird anyway.'

When Adam sees us coming across the lawn, he puts down his rake and walks over to meet us at the fence. I feel a bit dizzy as he gets closer. The garden seems brighter than before.

'This is my friend Zoey.'

He nods at her.

'I've heard *so* much about you!' she tells him. And she sighs, a sound that makes her seem small and helpless. Every boy I ever knew thought Zoey was gorgeous.

'Is that right?'

'Oh yes! Tessa talks about you all the time!'

I give her a quick kick to shut her up, but she dodges me and swishes her hair about.

'Did you get them?' I ask, wanting to distract him from her.

He reaches into his jacket pocket, pulls out a small plastic bag and passes it to me. Inside are small dark mushrooms. They look half formed, secret, not quite ready for the world.

'Where did you get them?'

'I picked them.'

Zoey snatches the bag from me and holds it up. 'How do we know they're right? They could be toadstools!'

'They're not,' he says. 'They're not Death Caps or Destroying Angels either.'

She frowns, passes them back to him. 'I don't think we'll bother. We're better off with Ecstasy.'

'Do both,' he tells her. 'These now and E another day.'

She turns to me. 'What do you think?'

'I think we should take them.'

But then, I've got nothing to lose.

Adam grins. 'Good,' he says. 'Come over and I'll make some tea with them.'

* * *

It's so clean in his kitchen it looks like something from a show home; there's not even any washing up on the draining board. It's strange how everything's the reverse of our house. Not just the mirror-image room, but the tidiness and the quiet.

Adam pulls out a chair for me at the table and I sit down.

'Is your mum in?' I ask.

'She's sleeping.'

'Isn't she well?'

'She's fine.'

He goes over to the kettle and switches it on, gets some cups from the cupboard and puts them next to the kettle.

Zoey screws her face up at him behind his back, then grins at me as she takes off her coat.

'This house is just like yours,' she says. 'Except backwards.'

'Sit down,' I tell her.

She picks up the mushrooms from the table, opens the bag and sniffs. 'Yuk! Are you sure these are right?'

Adam takes them from her and carries them over to the teapot. He tips the whole lot in and pours boiling water on them. She follows him and stands watching behind his shoulder.

'That doesn't look like enough. Do you actually know what you're doing?'

'I'm not having any,' he tells her. 'We'll go somewhere when they kick in. I'll look after you both.'

Zoey rolls her eyes at me as if that's the most pathetic thing she's ever heard.

'I have done drugs before,' she tells him. 'I'm sure we don't need a babysitter.'

I watch his back as he stirs the pot. The chink of spoon reminds me of bed time, when Dad makes me and Cal cocoa; there's the same thoroughness in the stirring.

'You mustn't laugh at us if we do anything silly,' I say.

He smiles at me over his shoulder. 'You're not going to.'

'We might,' Zoey says. 'You don't know us. We might go completely crazy. Tessa's capable of anything now she's got her list.'

'Is that right?'

'Shut up, Zoey!' I tell her.

She sits back down at the table. 'Oops,' she says, though she doesn't look sorry at all.

Adam brings the cups over and puts them in front of us. They're wreathed in steam and smell disgusting – of cardboard and wet nettles.

Zoey leans over and sniffs at her cup. 'It looks like gravy!'

He sits down beside her. 'It's fine. Trust me. I put a cinnamon stick in to sweeten it up.'

Which makes her roll her eyes at me again.

She takes a tentative sip, swallows it down with a grimace.

'All of it,' Adam says. 'The sooner you drink it, the sooner you'll get high.'

I don't know what will happen next, but there's something very calm about him, which seems to be contagious. His voice is the one clear thing. Drink it, he says. So we sit in his kitchen and drink brown swill and he watches us. Zoey holds her nose and takes great disgusted gulps. I just swig it down. It doesn't really matter what I eat or drink, because nothing tastes good any more.

We sit for a bit, talking about rubbish. I can't really concentrate. I keep waiting for something to happen, for something to alter. Adam explains how you can tell the mushrooms are right by their pointed caps and spindly stems. He says they grow in clumps, but only in late summer and autumn. He tells us they're legal, that you can buy them dried in certain shops. Then, because nothing is happening yet, he makes us all a normal cup of tea. I don't really want mine, just wrap my hands round it to keep myself warm. It feels very cold in this kitchen, colder than outside. I think about asking Zoey to go and get my coat from next door, but when I try to speak, my throat constricts, as if little hands are strangling me from inside.

'Is it supposed to hurt your neck?'

Adam shakes his head.

'It feels as if my windpipe's shrinking.'

'It'll stop.' But a flicker of fear crosses his face.

Zoey glares at him. 'Did you give us too much?'

'No! It'll be all right – she just needs some air.'

But doubt has crept into his voice. I bet he's thinking the same as me – that I'm different, that my body reacts differently, that maybe this was a mistake.

'Come on, let's get you outside.'

I stand up and he leads me down the hallway to the front door.

'Wait on the step – I'll get you a coat.'

The front of the house is in shadow. I stand on the step, trying to breathe deeply, trying not to panic. At the bottom of the step is a path leading to the front driveway and Adam's mum's car. On either side of the path is grass. For some reason the grass seems different today. It's not just the colour, but the shortness of it, stubbled like a shaved head. As I look, it becomes increasingly obvious that both step and path are safe places to be, but that the grass is malevolent.

I hold onto the doorknocker to make sure I don't slip down. As I clench it, I notice that the front door has a hole in it that looks like an eye. All the wood in the door leads to this hole in spirals and knots, so it seems as if the door is sliding into itself, gathering and coming back round again. It's a slow and subtle movement. I watch it for ages. Then I put my eye to the hole, but it's cloudy in there, so I step back inside the hallway and close the door, and look through the hole from the other direction. The world is very different from in here, the driveway elongated into a thread.

'How's your throat?' Adam asks as he reappears in the hallway and hands me a coat.

'Have you ever looked through here?'

'Your pupils are huge!' he says. 'We should go out now. Put the coat on.'

It's a parka with fur round the hood. Adam does the zip up for me. I feel like an Inuit child.

'Where's your friend?'

For a minute I don't know who he's talking about; then I remember Zoey and my heart floods with warmth.

'Zoey! Zoey!' I call. 'Come and see this.'

She's smiling as she comes along the hallway, her eyes deep and dark as winter.

'Your eyes!' I tell her.

She looks at me in wonder. 'Yours too!'

We peer at each other until our noses touch.

'There's a rug in the kitchen,' she whispers, 'that's got a whole world in it.'

'It's the same with the door. Things change shape if you look through it.'

'Show me.'

'Excuse me,' Adam says. 'I don't want to spoil the moment, but does anyone fancy a ride?'

He gets car keys from his pocket and shows them to us. They're amazing.

He brushes Zoey away from the door and we step outside. He points the keys at the car and it beeps in recognition. I tread very cautiously down the step and along the path, warn Zoey to do the same, but she doesn't hear me. She dances across the grass and seems to be fine, so maybe things are different for her.

I get in the front of the car next to Adam; Zoey sits in the back.

We wait for a minute, then Adam says, 'Well, what do you think?'

But I'm not telling him any of that.

I notice how careful he is as he reaches for the steering wheel, as if tempting some rare animal to feed from his hand.

He says, 'I love this car.'

I know what he means. Being in here is like sitting inside a fine watch.

'It was my dad's. My mum doesn't like me driving it.'

'Perhaps we should just stay here then!' Zoey calls from the back. 'Won't that be fun!'

Adam turns round to look at her. He speaks very slowly. 'I'm going to take you somewhere,' he says. 'I'm just saying she won't be very happy about it.'

Zoey flings herself down across the back seat and shakes her head at the roof in disbelief.

'Watch out with your shoes!' he yells.

She sits up again very quickly and thrusts a finger at him.

'Look at you!' she says. 'You look like a dog that's about to shit itself somewhere it shouldn't!'

'Shut up,' he says, and it's completely shocking to me, because I didn't know that voice was in him.

Zoey sinks back away from him. 'Just drive the car, man,' she mutters.

I don't even realize he's started the engine. It's so quiet and expensive in here, you can't hear it at all. But as we glide down the driveway and out of the gate, the houses and gardens in our street slide by, and I'm glad. This trip will open doors for me. My dad says musicians write all their best songs when they're high. I'm going to discover something amazing. I know I will. I'll bring it back with me too. Like the Holy Grail.

I open the window and hang out, my arms as well, the whole top half of me dangling. Zoey does the same in the back. Air rushes at me. I feel so awake. I see things I've never seen before, my fingers drawing in other lives – the pretty girl gazing at her boyfriend and wanting so much from him. The man at the bus stop raking his hair, each flake of skin shimmering as it falls to the ground, leaving pieces of himself all over this earth. The baby crying up at him, understanding the brevity and hopelessness of it all.

'Look, Zoey,' I say.

I point to a house with its door open, a glimpse of hallway, a mother kissing her daughter. The girl hesitates on the doorstep. I know you, I think. Don't be afraid.

Zoey has pulled herself almost out of the car by heaving on the roof. Her feet are on the back seat, and her face has appeared alongside my window. She looks like a mermaid on the prow of a ship.

'Get back in the bloody car!' Adam shouts. 'And get your feet off the bloody seat!'

She sinks back inside, hooting with laughter.

They call this stretch of road Mugger Mile. My dad's always reading bits out of the local paper about it. It's a place of random acts of violence, of poverty and despair. But as we pick up speed and other lives whip by, I see how beautiful the people are. I will die first, I know, but they'll all join me one by one.

We cut through the back streets. The plan, Adam says, is to go to the woods. There's a café and a park and no one will know us.

'You can go crazy there and not be recognized,' he says. 'It's not too far either, so we'll be back in time for tea.'

'Are you insane?' Zoey yells from the back. 'You sound like Enid Blyton! I want everyone to know I'm high and I don't want any bloody tea!'

She heaves herself out of the window again, blowing kisses at every passing stranger. She looks like Rapunzel escaping, her hair snapping in the wind. But then Adam slams on the brakes and Zoey bangs her head hard against the roof.

'Jesus!' she screams. 'You did that on purpose!'

She slumps down in the back seat, rubbing her head and moaning softly.

'Sorry,' Adam says. 'We need petrol.'

'Wanker,' she says.

He gets out of the car, walks round the back to the nozzles and pumps. Zoey appears to be suddenly asleep, slumped in the back sucking her thumb. Maybe she's got a concussion.

'You OK?' I ask.

'He's after you!' she hisses. 'He's trying to get rid of me so he can have you all to himself. You mustn't let him!'

'I don't think that's true.'

'Like you'd notice!'

She stuffs her thumb back in her mouth and turns her head from me. I leave her to it, get out of the car and walk over to speak to the man at the window. He has a scar like a silver river running from his hairline all the way down his forehead to the bridge of his nose. He looks like my dead uncle Bill.

He leans forward over his little desk. 'Number?' he says.

'Eight.'

He looks confused. 'No, not eight.'

'OK, I'll be three.'

'Where's your car?'

'Over there.'

'The Jag?'

'I don't know.'

'You don't know?'

'I don't know its name.'

'Jesus Christ!'

The glass between us warps to accommodate his anger. I back away in amazement and awe.

'I think he's a magician,' I tell Adam as he approaches from behind and puts his hand on my shoulder.

'I think you're right,' he whispers. 'Best get back in the car.'

Later, I wake up in a wood. The car has stopped and Adam isn't there. Zoey is asleep, spread out on the back seat like a child. Through the car window, the light filtering through the trees is ghostly and thin. I can't tell if it's day or night. I feel very peaceful as I open the door and step outside.

There are plenty of trees, all different kinds, deciduous and evergreen. It's so cold it must be Scotland.

I walk about for a bit, touching the bark, greeting the leaves. I realize that I'm hungry, really, dangerously hungry. If a bear turns up, I'll wrestle it to the ground and bite off its head. Maybe I should build a fire. I'll lay traps and dig holes and the next animal that comes by will end up on a spit. I'll make a shelter with sticks and leaves, and live here for ever. There are no microwaves or pesticides. No fluorescent pyjamas or clocks that glow in the dark. No TV, nothing made of plastic. No hairspray or hair dye or cigarettes. The petrochemical factory is far away. In this wood I'm safe. I laugh quietly to myself. I can't believe I didn't think of this before. This is the secret I came for.

Then I see Adam. He seems smaller and suddenly far away.

'I've discovered something!' I yell.

'What are you doing?' His voice is tiny and perfect.

I don't answer, because it's obvious and I don't want him to look stupid. Why else would I be up here collecting twigs, leaves and so on?

'Get down!' he yells.

But the tree wraps its arms about me and begs me not to. I try to explain this to Adam, but I'm not sure he hears me. He's taking off his coat. He starts to climb.

'You need to get down!' he shouts. He looks very religious coming up through the branches, higher and higher, like a sweet monk come to save me. 'Your dad's going to kill me if you break anything. Please, Tessa, come down now.'

He's close, his face reduced to just the light behind his eyes. I bend down to lick the coldness from him. His skin is salty.

'Please,' he says.

It doesn't hurt at all. We sail down together, catching great armfuls of air. At the bottom we sit in a nest of leaves and Adam holds me like a baby.

'What were you doing?' he says. 'What the hell were you doing up there?'

'Collecting materials for a shelter.'

'I think your friend was right. I really wish I hadn't given you so much.'

But he hasn't given me anything. Apart from his name and the dirt under his fingernails, I barely know him at all. I wonder if I should trust him with my secret.

'I'm going to tell you something,' I say. 'And you have to promise not to tell anyone. OK?'

He nods, though he looks uncertain. I sit up next to him and make sure he's looking at me before I begin. Colours and lights blaze across him. He's so luminous I can see his bones, and the world behind his eyes.

'I'm not sick any more.' I'm so excited it's difficult to speak. 'I need to stay here in this wood. I need to keep away from the modern world and all its gadgets and then I won't be sick. You can stay with me if you want. We'll build things, shelters and traps. We'll grow vegetables.'

Adam's eyes are full of tears. Looking at him cry is like being pulled from a mountain.

'Tessa,' he says.

Above his shoulder there's a hole in the sky, and through it, a satellite's static chatter makes my teeth tremble. Then it disappears and there's only yawning emptiness.

I put my finger on his lips. 'No,' I tell him. 'Don't say anything.'

Fifteen

'I'm on line,' Dad says, pointing at his laptop. 'Do you want to do your restless pacing somewhere else?'

The light from the computer flickers in his glasses. I sit down on the chair opposite him.

'That's annoying as well,' he says, without looking up.

'Me sitting here?'

'No.'

'Me tapping the table?'

'Listen,' he says, 'there's a doctor here who's developed a system called bone breathing. Ever heard of that?'

'No.'

'You have to imagine your breath as a warm colour, then breathe in through the left foot, up the leg to the hip and then out the same way. Seven times, then the right leg the same. Want to give it a try?'

'No.'

He takes off his glasses and looks at me. 'It's stopped raining. Why don't you take a blanket and sit in the garden? I'll let you know when the nurse gets here.'

'I don't want to.'

He sighs, puts his glasses back on and goes back to his laptop. I hate him. I know he watches me leave. I hear his small sigh of relief.

All the bedroom doors are shut, so it's gloomy in the hallway. I go up the stairs on all fours, sit at the top and look down. The gloom has movement to it. Maybe I'm beginning to see things other people can't. Like atoms. I bump down on my bum and crawl back up again, enjoying the squash of carpet beneath my knees. There are thirteen stairs. Every time I count them it's the same.

I curl up at the foot of the stairs. This is where the cat sits when she wants to trip people over. I've always wanted to be a cat. Warm and domesticated when you want to be, wild when you don't.

The doorbell rings. I curl myself tighter.

Dad comes out to the hallway. 'Tessa!' he says. 'For Christ's sake!'

Today's nurse is new. She's wearing a tartan skirt and is stout as a ship. Dad looks disappointed.

'This is Tessa,' he says, and points at me where I lie on the carpet.

The nurse looks shocked. 'Did she fall?'

'No, she's refused to leave the house for nearly two weeks, and it's sending her crazy.'

She comes over and looks down at me. Her breasts are huge and wobble as she holds out her hand to pull me up. Her hand's as big as a tennis racket. 'I'm Philippa,' she says, as if that explains anything.

She leads me into the lounge and helps me to a seat, lowers herself squarely down opposite me.

'So,' she says, 'not feeling too good today?'

'Would you be?'

Dad shoots me a warning glance. I don't care.

'Any shortness of breath or nausea?'

'I'm on anti-emetics. Have you actually read my case file?'

'Excuse her,' Dad says. 'She's had a bit of leg pain recently, nothing else. The nurse who saw her last week said she was doing well. Sian, I think her name was – she's aware of the medication regime.'

I snort through my nose. He tries to make it sound casual, but it doesn't wash with me. Last time Sian was here he offered her supper and made a right idiot of himself.

'The team tries to provide continuity,' Philippa says, 'but it's not always possible.' She turns back to me, dismissing Dad and his sorry love life.

'Tessa, you've got quite a bit of bruising on your arms.'

'I climbed a tree.'

'It suggests your platelets are low. Have you got any major activities planned for this week?'

'I don't need a transfusion!'

'We'll do a blood test anyway, to be on the safe side.'

Dad offers her coffee, but she declines. Sian would've said yes.

'My dad can't cope,' I tell Philippa as he goes out to the kitchen in a sulk. 'He does everything wrong.'

She helps me off with my shirt. 'And how does that make you feel?'

'It makes me laugh.'

She gets gauze and antiseptic spray from her medical case, puts on sterile gloves and holds my arm up so she can clean around the portacath. We both wait for it to dry.

'Have you got a boyfriend?' I ask her.

'I've got a husband.'

'What's his name?'

'Andy.'

She looks uncomfortable saying his name out loud. I see different people all the time and they never introduce themselves properly. They like knowing all about me though.

'Do you believe in God?' I ask her.

She sits back in her chair and frowns. 'What a question!'

'Do you?'

'Well, I suppose I'd like to.'

'What about heaven? Do you believe in that?'

She rips a sterile needle from its package. 'I think heaven sounds nice.'

'That doesn't mean it exists.'

She looks at me sternly. 'Well, let's hope it does.'

'I think it's a great big lie. When you're dead, you're dead.'

I'm beginning to get to her now: she's looking flustered. 'And what happens to all that spirit and energy?'

'It turns to nothing.'

'You know,' she says, 'there are support groups, places you can meet other young people in the same position as you.'

'No one's in the same position as me.'

'Is that how it feels?'

'That's how it is.'

I lift my arm so she can draw blood through the portacath. I'm half robot, with plastic and metal embedded under my skin. She draws blood into a syringe and discards it. It's such a waste, that first syringe tainted with saline. Over the years, nurses must have thrown a body-full of my blood away. She draws a second syringe, transfers it to a bottle and scribbles my name in blue ink on the label.

'That's you done,' she says. 'I'll ring in an hour or so and let you know the results. Anything else before I go?'

'No.'

'Have you got enough meds? Do you want me to drop into the GP's and pick up any repeat prescriptions?'

'I don't need anything.'

She heaves herself out of the chair and looks down at me solemnly.

'The community team offer a lot of support that you might not be aware of, Tessa. We can help you get back to school, for instance, even if it's only part-time, even if it's only for a few weeks. It might be worth thinking about trying to normalize your situation.'

I laugh right up at her. 'Would you go to school if you were me?'

'I might get lonely here by myself all day.'

'I'm not by myself.'

'No,' she says. 'But it's tough on your dad.'

She's a cow. You're not supposed to say things like that. I stare at her. She gets the message then.

'Goodbye, Tessa. I'm going to pop into the kitchen and have a word, then I'll be off.'

Despite the fact that she's fat already, Dad offers her fruitcake and coffee, and she accepts! The only thing we should be offering guests are plastic bags to wrap around their shoes. We should have a giant X marked on the gate.

I steal a fag from Dad's jacket and go upstairs and lean out of Cal's window. I want to see the street. There's a view through the trees to the road. A car passes. Another car. A person.

I blow smoke out into the air. Every time I inhale I can hear my lungs crackle. Maybe I've got TB. I hope so. All the best poets had TB; it's a mark of sensibility. Cancer's just humiliating.

Philippa comes out of the front door and stands by the step. I flick ash on her hair, but she doesn't notice, just says goodbye in that booming voice of hers and waddles off up the path.

I sit on Cal's bed. Dad'll come up in a minute. While I wait, I get a pen and write, *Parachutes, cocktails, stones, lollipops, buckets, zebras, sheds, cigarettes, cold tap water*, on the wallpaper above Cal's bed. Then I smell my armpits, the skin on my arm, my fingers. I stroke my hair backwards, forwards, like a rug.

Dad's taking ages. I go for a walk round the room. At the mirror I pull out a single hair. It's growing back much darker, and

107

strangely curly, like pubic hair. I examine it, let it fall. I like being able to spare one to the carpet.

There's a map of the world on Cal's wall. Oceans and deserts. He's got the solar system staked out on his ceiling. I lie on his bed to look at it properly. It makes me feel tiny.

It's literally five minutes later when I open my eyes and go downstairs to see what's keeping Dad. He's already scarpered, left some stupid note by his laptop.

I phone him. 'Where are you?'

'You were asleep, Tess.'

'But where are you?'

'I just came out for a quick coffee. I'm in the park.'

'The park? Why would you go there? We've got coffee at home.'

'Tess! Come on, I just need a bit of space. Turn the TV on if you're lonely. I'll be back soon.'

A woman cooks breaded chicken. Three men press a buzzer as they compete for fifty thousand pounds. Two actors argue about a dead cat. One of them makes a joke about stuffing it. I sit hunched. Mute. Stunned by how crap TV is, how little we all have to say.

I text Zoey. WHERE R U? She texts back that she's at college, but that's a lie because she doesn't have classes on Fridays.

I wish I had a mobile number for Adam. I'd text, DID U DIE?

He should be outside digging in manure, peat and rotting vegetation. I looked up November in Dad's Reader's Digest *Book of Gardening* and it suggests that this is the perfect time for conditioning the soil. He should also be thinking about planting a hazel bush, since they provide an attractive addition to any garden. I thought a filbert might be nice. They have large heart-shaped nuts.

He hasn't been out there for days though.

And he promised me a motorbike ride.

Sixteen

He's uglier than I remember. It's as if he warmed up in my memory. I don't know why that should be. I think how Zoey would snort with derision if she knew I'd come knocking on his door, and that thought makes me want to never let her know. She says ugly people give her a headache.

'You're avoiding me,' I tell him.

He looks surprised for a second, but covers it up pretty quick. 'I've been busy.'

'Is that right?'

'Yeah.'

'So it's not because you think I'm contagious? Most people start acting as if they can catch cancer from me in the end, or as if I've done something to deserve it.'

He looks alarmed. 'No, no! I don't think that.'

'Good. So when are we going out on your bike then?'

He shuffles his feet on the step and looks embarrassed. 'I haven't actually got a full licence. You're not supposed to take passengers without it.'

I can think of a million reasons why going on the back of Adam's bike might be a bad idea. Because we might crash. Because it might not be as good as I hope. Because what will I tell Zoey? Because it's what I really want to do more than anything. But I'm not going to let the lack of a full licence be one of them.

'Have you got a spare helmet?' I ask him.

That slow smile again. I love that smile! Did I think he was ugly just now? No, his face is transformed.

'In the shed. I've got a spare jacket too.'

I can't help smiling back. I feel brave and certain. 'Come on then. Before it rains.'

He shuts the door behind him. 'It's not going to rain.'

We go round the side of the house and get the stuff from the shed. But just as he helps me zip into the jacket, just as he tells me his bike is capable of ninety miles per hour and the wind will be cold, the back door opens and a woman steps into the garden. She's wearing a dressing gown and slippers.

Adam says, 'Go back inside, Mum, you'll get cold.'

But she keeps walking down the path towards us. She has the saddest face I've ever seen, like she drowned once and the tide left its mark there.

'Where are you going?' she says, and she doesn't look at me at all. 'You didn't say you were going anywhere.'

'I won't be long.'

She makes a funny little sound in the back of her throat. Adam looks up sharply. 'Don't, Mum,' he says. 'Go and have your bath and get dressed. I'll be back before you know it.'

She nods forlornly, begins to walk up the path, then stops as if she remembered something, and turns and looks at me for the first time, a stranger in her garden.

'Who are you?' she says.

'I live next door. I came to see Adam.'

The sadness in her eyes deepens. 'Yes, that's what I thought.'

Adam goes over to her and grips her gently by the elbows. 'Come on,' he says. 'You should go back inside.'

She allows herself to be helped up the path and walked to the back door. She goes up the step and then she turns and looks at me again. She doesn't say anything, and neither do I. We just look at each other, and then she goes through the door and into her kitchen. I wonder what happens then, what they say to each other.

'Is she OK?' I ask as Adam walks back out into the garden.

'Let's get out of here,' he says.

It's not what I imagined, not like cycling fast downhill, or even sticking your head out of a car window on the motorway. It's more elemental, like being on a beach in the winter when the wind howls in off the sea. The helmets have plastic visors. I've got mine down, but Adam's got his up; he did it very deliberately.

He said, 'I like to feel the wind in my eyes.'

He told me to lean when we go round corners. He told me that since it was my first time he wouldn't go top speed. But that could mean anything. Even at half speed, we might take off. We might fly.

We leave the streets and lampposts and houses. We leave the shops and the industrial estate and the wood yard, and we go beyond some kind of boundary where things belong to the town and are understood. Trees, fields, space appears. I shelter behind the curve of his back, and I close my eyes and wonder where he's taking me. I imagine horses in the engine, their manes flying, their breath steaming, their nostrils flaring as they gallop. I heard a story once about some nymph, snatched by a god and taken somewhere dark and dangerous on the back of a chariot.

Where we end up is somewhere I didn't expect – a muddy car park off the dual carriageway. There are two large trucks parked here, a couple of cars and a hotdog stand.

Adam turns off the ignition, kicks the stand down with his foot and takes off his helmet.

'You should get off first,' he says.

I nod, can barely speak, left my breath behind on the road somewhere. My knees are shaking and it takes a lot of effort to swing my leg over the bike and stand up. The earth feels very still. One of the lorry drivers winks at me out of his cab window. He holds a steaming cup of tea in one hand. Over at the hotdog stand, a girl with her hair in a ponytail passes a bag of chips across the counter to a man with a dog. I'm different from them all. It's as if we flew here and everyone else is completely ordinary.

Adam says, 'This isn't the place. Let's get something to eat, then I'll show you.'

He seems to understand that I can't quite talk yet and doesn't wait for an answer. I walk slowly after him, listen to him order two hotdogs with onion rings. How did he know that would be my idea of a perfect lunch?

We stand and eat. We share a Coke. It seems astonishing to me that I'm here, that the world opened up from the back of a bike, that the sky looked like silk, that I saw the afternoon arrive, not white, not grey, not quite silver, but a combination of all three. Finally, when I've thrown my wrapper in the bin and finished the Coke, Adam says, 'Ready?'

And I follow him through a gate at the back of the hotdog stand, across a ditch and into a thin little wood. A mud path threads through and out to the other side, where space opens up. I hadn't realized how high we were. It's amazing, the whole town down there like someone laid it at our feet, and us high up, looking down at it all.

'Wow!' I say. 'I didn't know this view was here.'

'Yeah.'

We sit together on a bench, our knees not quite touching. The ground's hard beneath my feet. The air's cold, smelling of frost that didn't quite make it, of winter to come.

'This is where I come when I need to get away,' he says. 'I got the mushrooms from here.'

He gets out his tobacco tin and opens it up, puts tobacco in a paper and rolls it. He has dirty fingernails and I shiver at the thought of those hands touching me.

'Here,' he says. 'This'll warm you up.'

He passes me the cigarette and I look at it while he rolls himself another one. It looks like a pale slim finger. He offers me a

114

light. We don't say anything for ages, just blow smoke at the town below.

He says, 'Anything could be happening down there, but up here you just wouldn't know it.'

I know what he means. It could be pandemonium in all those little houses, everyone's dreams in a mess. But up here feels peaceful. Clean.

'I'm sorry, about earlier with my mum,' he says. 'She's a bit hard to take sometimes.'

'Is she ill?'

'Not really.'

'What's up with her then?'

He sighs, runs a hand through his hair. 'My dad was killed in a road accident eighteen months ago.'

He flicks his cigarette across the grass and we both watch the orange glow. It feels like minutes until it goes out.

'Do you want to talk about it?'

He shrugs. 'There's not that much to say. My mum and dad had a fight, he stomped off to the pub and forgot to look when he crossed the road. Two hours later the police were knocking on the door.'

'Shit!'

'Ever seen a scared policeman?'

'No.'

'It's terrifying. My mum sat on the stairs and covered her ears with her hands, and they stood in the hallway with their hats off and their knees shaking.' He laughs through his nose, a soft sound with no humour to it. 'They were only a bit older than me. They hadn't got a clue how to handle it.'

'That's horrible!'

'It didn't help. They took her to see my dad's body. She wanted to, but they shouldn't have let her. He was pretty mashed up.'

'Did you go?'

'I sat outside.'

I understand now why Adam's different from Zoey, or any of the kids I knew at school. It's a wound that connects us.

He says, 'I thought moving from our old house would help, but it hasn't really. She's still on a million tablets a day.'

'And you look after her?'

'Pretty much.'

'What about your life?'

'I don't really have a choice.'

He turns on the bench so that he's facing me. He looks as if he's really seeing me, as if he knows something about me that even I don't know.

'Are you afraid, Tessa?'

No one's ever asked me that before. Not ever. I look at him to check he's not taking the piss or asking out of politeness, but he returns a steady gaze. So I tell him how I'm afraid of the dark, afraid of sleeping, afraid of webbed fingers, of small spaces, of doors.

'It comes and goes. People think if you're sick you become fearless and brave, but you don't. Most of the time it's like being stalked by a psycho, like I might get shot any second. But sometimes I forget for hours.'

116

'What makes you forget?'

'People. Doing stuff. When I was with you in the wood, I forgot for a whole afternoon.'

He nods very slowly.

There's a silence then. Just a little one, but it has shape to it, like a cushion round a sharp box.

Adam says, 'I like you, Tessa.'

When I swallow, my throat hurts. 'You do?'

'That day you came round to chuck your stuff on the fire, you said you wanted to get rid of all your things. You told me you watch me from your window. Most people don't talk that way.'

'Did it freak you out?'

'The opposite.' He looks at his feet as if they'll give him a clue. 'I can't give you what you want though.'

'What I want?'

'I'm only just coping. If anything happened between us, it's kind of like, what would be the point?' He shifts on the bench. 'This is coming out all wrong.'

I feel strangely untouchable as I stand up. I can feel myself closing some kind of internal window. It's the one that controls temperature and feelings. I feel crisp as a winter leaf.

'I'll see you around,' I say.

'You're going?'

'Yeah, I've got stuff to do in town. Sorry, I didn't realize what the time was.'

'You have to go right now?'

'I'm meeting friends. They'll be waiting for me.'

He fumbles around on the grass for the crash helmets. 'Well, let me take you.'

'No, no, it's OK. I'll get one of them to pick me up. They've all got cars.'

He looks stunned. Ha! Good! That'll teach him to be the same as everyone else. I don't even bother saying goodbye.

'Wait!' he says.

But I won't. I won't look back at him either.

'The path might be slippery!' he shouts. 'It's beginning to rain.'

I said it would rain. I knew it would.

'Tessa, let me give you a lift!'

But if he thinks I'm climbing on that bike with him, he can think again.

I made a fatal error thinking he could save me.

Seventeen

I start with assault, shove my elbow hard into a woman's back as I get on the bus. She spins round, crazy-eyed.

'Ow!' she yelps. 'Watch where you're going!'

'It was him!' I tell her, pointing to the man behind me. He doesn't hear, is too busy carrying a screaming child and yelling into his phone to know I just slandered him. The woman sidesteps me. 'Arsehole!' she tells him.

He hears that.

In the commotion, I dodge the fare and find myself a seat at the back. Three crimes in under one minute. Not bad.

I rifled through the pockets of Adam's motorbike jacket on the way down the hill, but all I found was a cigarette lighter and a bent old rollie, so I couldn't have paid for the bus anyway. I decide to go for crime number four and light it up. An old bloke turns round and jabs a finger at me. 'Put that out!' he says.

'Piss off,' I tell him, which I believe might count as violent behaviour in a court of law.

I'm good at this. Time for a little murder now, with a round of the Dying Game.

The man three seats in front is feeding takeaway noodles to the small boy on his lap. I give myself three points for the food colouring creeping along the child's veins.

In the opposite aisle, a woman ties a scarf about her throat. One point for the lump on her neck, raw and pink as a crab's claw.

Another point for the bus exploding as it brakes at the lights. Two for the great globs of melting plastic from the seats splitting the air.

A counsellor I saw at the hospital said it's not my fault. She reckoned there must be loads of sick people secretly wishing malevolence upon the healthy.

I told her my dad says cancer is a sign of treachery, since the body's doing something without the knowledge or consent of the mind. I asked if she thought the game might be a way for my mind to get its own back.

'Possibly,' she said. 'Do you play it a lot?'

The bus sweeps past the cemetery, the iron gates open. Three points for the dead slowly prising open the lids of their coffins. They want to hurt the living. They can't stop. Their throats have turned to liquid and their fingers glint under the weak autumn sun.

Maybe that's enough. There are too many people on the bus now. Down the aisles, they blink and shift. 'I'm on the bus,' they say as their mobiles chirrup. It'll just depress me if I kill them all off.

I force myself to look out of the window. We're in Willis Avenue already. I used to go to school along here. There's the mini mart!

I'd forgotten it even existed, though it was the first place in town to sell Slush Puppies. Zoey and me used to get one every day in the summer on the way home from school. They sell other stuff too – fresh dates and figs, halva, sesame bread and Turkish delight. I can't believe I let the mini mart slip my mind.

Left at the video shop, and a man wearing a white apron stands in the doorway of the Barbecue Café sharpening his knife. A rack of lamb slowly rotates in the window behind him. Dinner money bought a kebab and chips there two years ago or, if you're Zoey, it bought a kebab and chips plus a cigarette from under the counter.

I miss her. I get off the bus in the market square and phone her. She sounds like she's underwater.

'Are you in a swimming pool?'

'I'm in the bath.'

'On your own?'

'Of course I'm on my own!'

'You texted me that you were at college. I knew it was a lie.'

'What do you want, Tessa?'

'Breaking the law.'

'What?'

'It's number four on my list.'

'And how are you planning on doing that?'

Before, she'd have had an idea. But now, because of Scott, she's lost her definition. It's like their edges got blurred together.

'I was thinking of killing the Prime Minister. I quite fancy starting a revolution.'

'Funny.'

'Or the Queen. We could get a bus to Buckingham Palace.'

Zoey sighs. She doesn't even bother to hide it. 'I've got stuff to do. I can't be with you every day.'

'I haven't seen you for ten days!' There's a silence. It makes me want to hurt her. 'You promised you'd do everything with me, Zoey. I've only done three things on the list. At this rate I'm not going to get it all done in time.'

'Oh, for God's sake!'

'I'm at the market. Come and meet me, it'll be fun.'

'At the market? Is Scott there?'

'I don't know, I've only just got off the bus.'

'I'll meet you in twenty minutes,' she says.

There's sun in my teacup and it's very easy sitting outside this café watching it shine.

'I think you're a vampire,' Zoey says. 'You've sucked all my energy away,' and she pushes her plate to one side and rests her head on the table.

I like it here – the candy-striped awning above us, the view across the square to the water fountain. I like the tang of rain in the air and the row of birds lining the wall over by the dustbins.

'What kind of birds are they?'

Zoey opens one eye to look. 'Starlings.'

'How do you know?'

'I just do.'

I'm not sure I believe her, but I write it down on my napkin anyway. 'What about the clouds? Do you know what they're called?'

She groans, shifts her head on the table.

'Do you think stones have names, Zoey?'

'No! Neither do raindrops, or leaves, or any of the other mad things you keep going on about.'

She makes a nest with her arms and hides her face from me completely. She's been grouchy ever since she got here and it's beginning to piss me off. This is supposed to be making me feel better.

Zoey shifts in her chair. 'Aren't you freezing?'

'No.'

'Can we just go and rob a bank, or whatever it is we're supposed to be doing?'

'Will you teach me to drive?'

'Can't you ask your dad?'

'I did, but it's not working out.'

'It'd take a million years, Tessa! I'm probably not even allowed. I've only just learned myself.'

'Since when did you care about what was allowed?'

'Do we have to talk about this now? Come on, let's go.'

She scrapes her chair back, but I'm not ready yet. I want to watch that black cloud drive towards the sun. I want to watch the sky turn from grey to charcoal. The wind'll pick up and all the leaves will rip off the trees. I'll race about catching them. I'll make hundreds of wishes.

Three women appear, hauling buggies and children across the square towards us.

'Quick!' they cry. 'In here, quick, before it rains again.'

They shiver and laugh as they squeeze past us to an empty table. 'Who wants what?' they cry. 'What do we want?' They sound just like the starlings.

Zoey stretches, blinks at the women as if wondering where they came from. They make a great fuss taking off coats and plonking babies in high chairs, wiping noses with bits of tissue and ordering juice and fruitcake.

'My mum used to bring me to this café when she was pregnant with Cal,' I tell Zoey. 'She was completely addicted to milkshakes. We used to come every day until she got so fat her entire lap disappeared. I had to sit on a stool by her side to watch the telly.'

'Oh my God!' Zoey snarls. 'Being with you is like being in a horror movie!'

I look at her properly for the first time. She hasn't made any effort; is just wearing shapeless jogging pants and a sweatshirt. I don't think I've ever seen her without make-up before. Her spots are really obvious.

'Are you all right, Zoey?'

'I'm cold.'

'Did you think the market was on today? Were you expecting to see Scott?'

'No!'

'Good, because you don't look great.'

She glares at me. 'Shoplifting,' she says. 'Let's just get it over with.'

Eighteen

Morrisons is the biggest supermarket in the shopping centre. It's nearly school kicking-out time and it's busy.

'Take a basket,' Zoey says. 'And watch out for store detectives.'

'What do they look like?'

'They look as if they're at work!'

I walk slowly, savouring the details. It's ages since I've been in a supermarket. At the deli they have little saucers on top of the counter. I take two pieces of cheese and an olive, realize I'm starving, so help myself to a handful of cherries at the fruit bar. I munch on them as I walk.

'How can you eat so much?' Zoey says. 'I feel sick just looking at you.'

She instructs me to put things that I don't want in the basket – normal things like tomato soup and cream crackers.

'And in your coat,' she says, 'you put the things you *do* want.'

'Like what?'

She looks exasperated. 'I don't bloody know! There's a whole shop full of stuff. Take your pick.'

I choose a slim bottle of vampire-red nail varnish. I'm still wearing Adam's jacket. It's got lots of pockets. It slips in easily.

'Great!' Zoey says. 'Law successfully broken. Can we go now?'

'Is that it?'

'Technically.'

'That's not anything! A runner from the café would have been more exciting.'

She sighs, checks her mobile. 'Five more minutes then.' She sounds like my dad.

'And what about you? Are you just going to watch?'

'I'm your lookout.'

The assistant at the pharmacy is discussing chesty coughs with a customer. I don't think she's going to miss this tube of Relief Body Moisturizer or this small jar of Crème de Corps Nutritif. In the basket go crispbreads. In my pocket goes Hydrating Face Cream. Tea bags for the basket. Signs of Silk Skin Treatment for me. It's a bit like strawberry picking.

'I'm good at this!' I tell Zoey.

'Great!'

She's not even listening. Some lookout she is. She's fiddling about at the pharmacy counter.

'Chocolate aisle next,' I tell her.

But she doesn't answer, so I leave her to it.

It's not exactly Belgium, but the confectionery section has miniature boxes of truffles tied with sweet little ribbons. They're only £1.99, so I nick two boxes and shove them in my pocket. A biker's jacket is very good for thieves. I wonder if Adam knows this.

At the end aisle, by the freezers, my pockets are bulging. I'm wondering how long Ben and Jerry's Phish Food would last in a coat when two girls I used to go to school with walk by. They stop when they see me, bend their heads close together and whisper. I'm just about to text Zoey to let her know she needs to help me out when they come over.

'Are you Tessa Scott?' the blonde one says.

'Yeah.'

'Do you remember us? We're Fiona and Beth.' She makes it sound as if they only come in a pair. 'You left in Year Eleven, didn't you?'

'Ten.'

They both look at me expectantly. Don't they realize that they come from another planet – somewhere that spins much more slowly than mine – and that I have absolutely nothing to say to them?

'How's it going?' Fiona says. Beth nods, as if she agrees entirely with this question. 'Are you still having all that treatment?'

'Not any more.'

'So you're better?'

'No.'

I watch them understand. It starts in their eyes and spreads down their cheeks to their mouths. It's all so predictable. They won't ask any more questions, because there are no polite ones left. I want to give them permission to leave, but I don't know how to.

'I'm here with Zoey,' I say, because the silence goes on for

127

too long. 'Zoey Walker. She was in the year above us.'

'Really?' Fiona nudges her friend. 'That's weird. She's the one I was telling you about.'

Beth brightens at this, relieved that normal communication has resumed. 'Is she helping you shop?' She sounds as if she's talking to a four-year-old.

'Not exactly.'

'Hey, look!' Fiona says. 'There she is. Do you know who I mean now?'

Beth nods. 'Oh, *her*!'

I'm beginning to wish I hadn't said anything. I've got a horrible feeling about this. But it's too late now.

Zoey doesn't look at all pleased to see them. 'What're you doing here?'

'Talking to Tessa.'

'What about?'

'This and that.'

Zoey looks at me suspiciously. 'Are you ready to go?'

'Yeah.'

'Before you do' – Fiona touches Zoey's sleeve – 'is it true you've been seeing Scott Redmond?'

Zoey hesitates. 'What's it to you? You know him?'

Fiona snorts, a soft noise with her nose. 'Everyone knows him,' and she rolls her eyes at Beth. 'I mean *everyone*.'

Beth laughs. 'Yeah, he went out with my sister for about half an hour.'

Zoey's eyes glitter. 'Is that right?'

'Hey, listen,' I say. 'Fascinating as this is, we've got to go now. I have to collect the invites for my funeral.'

That shuts them up. Fiona looks astonished. 'Really?'

'Yeah.' I grab Zoey's arm. 'It's a shame I can't be there myself – I like parties. Text me if you think of any good hymns!'

We leave them looking completely bewildered. Me and Zoey go round the corner and stand in the kitchenware section, surrounded by cutlery and stainless steel.

'They're just idiots, Zoey. They don't know anything.'

She feigns interest in a pair of sugar tongs. 'I don't want to talk about it.'

'Let's do something wild to cheer ourselves up. Let's do as many illegal things as we can in an hour!'

Zoey smiles reluctantly. 'We could burn Scott's house down.'

'You shouldn't believe what they say, Zoey.'

'Why not?'

'Because you know him better than they do.'

I've never seen Zoey cry, not ever. Not when she got her GCSE results, not even when I told her my terminal diagnosis. I always thought she was incapable, like a Vulcan. But she's crying now. In the supermarket. She's trying to hide it, swinging her hair to cover her face.

'What? What is it?'

'I have to go and find him,' she says.

'Now?'

'I'm sorry.'

It feels very cold watching her cry, like how could she like

Scott so much? She's only known him a few weeks.

'We haven't finished breaking the law yet.'

She nods; tears slip down her face. 'Just dump the basket and walk out when you're done. I'm sorry. I can't help it. I have to go.'

I've been here before with exactly this view. Her retreating back, her hair swinging gold as she gets further and further away from me.

Maybe I'll burn *her* house down instead.

It's no fun without her though, so I put the basket down in a 'I can't believe I forgot my purse' kind of way and stand scratching my head for a moment, before walking towards the doors. But just before I get there I'm grabbed by the wrist.

I thought Zoey said store detectives would be easy to spot. I thought they'd be dressed badly in a suit and tie, that they wouldn't wear a coat because they're inside all day.

This man's wearing a denim jacket and has close-cropped hair. He says, 'Are you going to pay for the items inside your jacket?' He says, 'I have reason to believe you have concealed items from aisles five and seven about your person. This was witnessed by a member of our staff.'

I take the nail varnish from my pocket and hold it out to him. 'You can have it back.'

'You need to come with me now.'

Heat spreads from my neck to my face to my eyes. 'I don't want it.'

'You intended to leave the store without paying,' he says, and he pulls me by the arm.

We walk down an aisle towards the back of the shop. Everyone can see me and their gaze burns. I'm not sure he's allowed to pull me like this. He might not be a store detective at all: he could be trying to get me somewhere lonely and quiet. I dig my heels in and grab hold of a shelf. It's difficult to breathe.

He hesitates. 'Are you OK? Do you have asthma or something?'

I shut my eyes. 'No, I'm . . . I don't want . . .'

I can't finish. Too many words falling off my tongue.

He frowns at me, gets out his pager and asks for assistance. Two little kids sitting in a trolley stare at me as they're wheeled past. A girl my age saunters by, saunters back again smirking.

The woman who scurries up is wearing a name badge. Her name's Shirley and she frowns at me. 'I'll take it from here,' she says to the man and waves him away. 'Come on.'

Behind the fish counter is a secret office. You wouldn't know it was there if you were ordinary. Shirley shuts the door behind us. It's the kind of room you get in police dramas on TV – small and airless, with a table and two chairs, lit by a fluorescent strip that flickers from the ceiling.

'Sit down,' Shirley says. 'Empty your pockets.'

I do as she tells me. The things I stole look shabby and cheap on the table between us.

'Well,' she says, 'I'd call that evidence, wouldn't you?'

I try crying, but she doesn't fall for it. She passes me a tissue, though she can barely be bothered. She waits for me to blow my nose and points out the bin when I've finished.

'I need to ask you some questions,' she says. 'Starting with your name.'

It takes ages. She wants all the details – age, address, Dad's phone number. She even wants to know Mum's name, though I don't see why that's of any importance.

'You have a choice,' she says. 'We can call your father, or we can call the police.'

I decide to do something desperate. I take off Adam's jacket and begin to undo my shirt. Shirley merely blinks. 'I'm not very well,' I tell her. I slip my shirt off one shoulder and raise my arm to show her the metal disc under my armpit. 'It's a portacath, an access disc for medical treatments.'

'Please put your shirt back on.'

'I want you to believe me.'

'I do believe you.'

'I've got acute lymphoblastic leukaemia. You can phone up the hospital and ask them.'

'Please put your shirt back on.'

'Do you even know what acute lymphoblastic leukaemia is?'

'No, I'm afraid I don't.'

'It's cancer.'

But the c-word doesn't scare her and she calls my dad anyway.

There's a place under our fridge at home where there's always a puddle of fetid water. Every morning Dad wipes it up with antiseptic household cleaning wipes. Over the course of the day, the water creeps back. The wooden boards are beginning to buckle with damp. One night, when I couldn't sleep, I saw three cockroaches scuttle for cover as I flicked on the light. The next day Dad bought glue traps and baited them with banana. We've never caught a single cockroach though. Dad says I'm seeing things.

Even when I was a really little kid, I recognized the signs – the butterflies that crisped up in jam jars, Cal's rabbit eating its own babies.

There was a girl at my school who was crushed falling off her pony. Then the boy from the fruit shop collided with a taxi. Then my uncle Bill got a brain tumour. At his funeral, all the sandwiches curled at the edges. For days afterwards, the grave earth wouldn't come off my shoes.

When I noticed the bruises on my spine, Dad took me to a doctor. The doctor said I shouldn't be this tired. The doctor said lots of things. At night, the trees bang on my window like they're trying to get in. I'm surrounded. I know it.

When Dad turns up, he crouches next to my chair, cups my chin in his hands and makes me look right at him. He looks sadder than I've ever seen him.

'Are you all right?'

He means medically, so I nod. I don't tell him about the spiders blooming on the window ledge.

He stands up then and eyes Shirley behind her desk. 'My daughter's not well.'

'She mentioned it.'

'And doesn't that make any difference? Are you people so insensitive?'

Shirley sighs. 'Your daughter was found to be concealing items with the intention of leaving the shop without paying.'

'How do you know she wasn't going to pay?'

'The items were hidden about her person.'

'But she didn't leave.'

'Intention to steal is a crime. At this stage we have the option of giving your daughter a warning. We've had no dealings with her before, and I'm not obliged to call the police if I hand her back into your care. I do need to be very certain, however, that you will deal with the matter most seriously.'

Dad looks at her as if he's been asked a very difficult question and needs to think about the answer.

'Yes,' he says. 'I'll do that.' Then he helps me to stand up.

Shirley stands up too. 'Do we have an understanding then?'

He looks confused. 'I'm sorry. Do I need to give you money or something?'

'Money?'

'For the things she took?'

'No, no, you don't.'

'So I can take her home?'

'You will relay to her the seriousness of this matter?'

Dad turns to me. He speaks slowly, as if I'm suddenly stupid. 'Put your coat on, Tessa. It's cold outside.'

He hardly even waits for me to get out of the car before shoving me up the path and through the front door. He pushes me into the lounge. 'Sit down,' he says. 'Go on.'

I sit on the sofa and he sits opposite me in the armchair. The journey home seems to have wound him up. He looks mad and breathless, as if he hasn't slept for weeks and is capable of anything.

'What the hell are you doing, Tessa?'

'Nothing.'

'You call shoplifting nothing? You disappear all afternoon, you don't leave me a note or anything, and you think it doesn't matter?'

He wraps his arms about himself as if he's cold and we sit like this for a bit. I can hear the clock ticking. On the coffee table next to me is one of Dad's car magazines. I fiddle with one corner, folding and unfolding it into a triangle as I wait for what's going to happen next.

When he speaks, he does it very carefully, as if he wants to get the words just right. 'There are some things you're entitled to,' he says. 'There are some rules we can stretch for you, but there are some things that you can want all you like and you're still not having.'

When I laugh, it sounds like glass falling from somewhere very high. It surprises me. It's also surprising to find myself folding Dad's magazine in half and tearing out the front page – the red car, the pretty girl with white teeth. I scrunch it up and throw it on the floor. I rip page after page, slamming them onto the coffee table one after the other, until the whole magazine is spread out between us.

We stare at the torn pages together, and I'm heaving for breath and I want so much for something to happen, something huge like a volcano exploding in the garden. But all that happens is that Dad hugs himself closer, which is what he always does when he gets upset: you just get this kind of blank from him, as if he turns into some kind of nothing.

And then he says, 'What happens if anger takes you over, Tessa? Who will you be then? What will be left of you?'

And I say nothing, just look at the lamplight slanting across the sofa and splashing the carpet to congeal at my feet.

Nineteen

There's a dead bird on the lawn, its legs thin as cocktail sticks. I'm sitting in the deck chair under the apple tree watching it.

'It definitely moved,' I tell Cal.

He stops juggling and comes over to look. 'Maggots,' he says. 'It can get so hot inside a dead body that the ones in the middle have to move to the edges to cool down.'

'How the hell do you know that?'

He shrugs. 'Internet.'

He nudges the bird with his shoe until its stomach splits. Hundreds of maggots spill onto the grass and writhe there, stunned by sunlight.

'See?' Cal says, and he squats down and pokes at them with a stick. 'A dead body is its own eco-system. Under certain conditions it only takes nine days for a human to rot down to the bones.' He looks at me thoughtfully. 'That won't happen to you though.'

'No?'

'It's more when people are murdered and left outside.'

'What will happen to me, Cal?'

I have a feeling that whatever he says will be right, like he's some grand magician touched by cosmic truth. But he only shrugs and says, 'I'll find out and let you know.'

He goes off to the shed to get a spade. 'Guard the bird,' he says.

Its feathers ruffle in the breeze. It's very beautiful, black with a sheen of blue, like oil on the sea. The maggots are rather beautiful too. They panic on the grass; searching for the bird, for each other.

And that's when Adam walks across the lawn.

'Hi,' he says. 'How are you?'

I sit up in my deckchair. 'Did you just climb over the fence?'

He shakes his head. 'It's broken down the bottom.'

He's wearing jeans, boots, a leather jacket. He's got something behind his back. 'Here,' he says. He holds out a bunch of wild green leaves to me. Amongst them are bright orange flowers. They look like lanterns or baby pumpkins.

'For me?'

'For you.'

My heart hurts. 'I'm trying not to acquire new things.'

He frowns. 'Perhaps living things don't count.'

'I think they might count more.'

He sits down on the grass next to my chair and puts the flowers between us. The ground is wet. It will seep into him. It will make him cold. I don't tell him this. I don't tell him about the maggots either. I want them to creep into his pockets.

Cal comes back with a gardening trowel.

'You planting something?' Adam asks him.

138

'Dead bird,' he says, and he points to the place where it lies.

Adam leans over. 'That's a rook. Did your cat get it?'

'Don't know. I'm going to bury it though.'

Cal walks over to the back fence, finds a spot in the flowerbed and starts to dig. The earth is wet as cake mix. Where the spade meets little stones, it sounds like shoes on gravel.

Adam plucks bits of grass and sieves them between his fingers. 'I'm sorry about what I said the other day.'

'It's OK.'

'It didn't come out right.'

'Really, it's OK. We don't have to talk about it.'

He nods very seriously, still threading grass, still not looking at me. 'You are worth bothering with.'

'I am?'

'Yeah.'

'So you want to be friends?'

He looks up. 'If you do.'

'And you're sure there's a point to it?'

I enjoy watching him blush, the confusion in his eyes. Maybe Dad's right and I'm turning to anger.

'I think there's a point,' he says.

'Then you're forgiven.'

I hold my hand out and we shake on it. His hand is warm.

Cal comes over, smeared in dirt, spade in hand. He looks like a demented boy undertaker. 'The grave's ready,' he says.

Adam helps him roll the rook onto the spade. It's stiff and looks heavy. Its injury is obvious – a red gash at the back of its neck. Its head lolls drunkenly as they carry it between them over to the hole. Cal talks to it as they walk. 'Poor bird,' he says. 'Come on, time to rest.'

I wrap my blanket round my shoulders and follow them across the grass to watch them tip it in. One eye shines up at us. It looks peaceful, even grateful. Its feathers are darker now.

'Should we say something?' Cal asks.

'*Goodbye, bird?*' I suggest.

He nods. 'Goodbye, bird. Thank you for coming. And good luck.'

He scoops mud over it, but leaves the head uncovered, as if the bird might like to take a last look around. 'What about the maggots?' he says.

'What about them?'

'Won't they suffocate?'

'Leave an air hole,' I tell him.

He seems happy with this suggestion, crumbles earth over the bird's head and pats it down. He makes a hole for the maggots with a stick.

'Get some stones, Tess, then we can decorate it.'

I do as I'm told and wander off to look. Adam stays with Cal. He tells him that rooks are very sociable, that this rook will have many friends, and they'll be grateful to Cal for burying it with so much care.

I think he's trying to impress me.

These two white stones are almost perfectly round. Here is a snail's shell, a red leaf. A soft grey feather. I hold them in my hand.

They're so lovely that I have to lean against the shed and close my eyes.

It's a mistake. It's like falling into darkness.

There's earth on my head. I'm cold. Worms burrow. Termites and woodlice come.

I try and focus on good things, but it's so hard to scramble out. I open my eyes to the rough fingers of the apple tree. A spider's web quivering silver. My warm hands clutching the stones.

But all that is warm will go cold. My ears will fall off and my eyes will melt. My mouth will be clamped shut. My lips will turn to glue.

Adam appears. 'You all right?' he says.

I concentrate on breathing. In. Out. But breathing brings the opposite when you become aware of it. My lungs will dry up like paper fans. Out. Out.

He touches my shoulder. 'Tessa?'

No taste or smell or touch or sound. Nothing to look at. Total emptiness for ever.

Cal runs up. 'What's wrong?'

'Nothing.'

'You look weird.'

'I got dizzy bending down.'

'Shall I get Dad?'

'No.'

'Are you sure?

'Finish the grave, Cal. I'll be OK.'

I give him the things I collected and he runs off. Adam stays.

141

A blackbird flies low over the fence. The sky is griddled pink and grey. Breathe. In. In.

Adam says, 'What is it?'

How can I tell him?

He reaches out and touches my back with the flat of his hand. I don't know what this means. His hand is firm, moving in gentle circles. We agreed to be friends. Is this what friends do?

His heat comes through the weave of the blanket, through my coat, my jumper, my T-shirt. Through to my skin. It hurts so much that thoughts are difficult to find. My body becomes all sensation.

'Stop it.'

'What?'

I shrug him off. 'Can't you just go away?'

There's a moment. It has a sound in it, as if something very small got broken.

'You want me to go?'

'Yes. And don't come back.'

He walks across the grass. He says goodbye to Cal and goes back through the broken bit of fence. Except for the flowers by the chair, it's as if he's never been here at all. I pick them up. Their orange heads nod at me as I give them to Cal.

'These are for the bird.'

'Cool!'

He lays them on the damp earth and we stand together looking down at the grave.

Twenty

Dad's taking ages to discover I'm missing. I wish he'd hurry up because my left leg's gone to sleep and I need to move before I get gangrene or something. I shuffle to a squatting position, grab a jumper from the shelf above me and push it down with one hand amongst the shoes so that I have a better place to sit. The wardrobe door creaks open a fraction as I settle. It sounds very loud for a moment. Then it stops.

'Tess?' The bedroom door eases open and Dad tiptoes across the carpet. 'Mum's here. Didn't you hear me call?'

Through the crack in the wardrobe door I see the confusion on his face as he realizes that the bundle on my bed is only the duvet. He lifts it up and looks underneath, as if I might've shrunk into someone very small since he last saw me at breakfast.

'Shit!' he says, and he rubs a hand across his face as if he doesn't understand, walks over to the window and looks out at the garden. Beside him, on the ledge, is a green glass apple. I was given it for being a bridesmaid at my cousin's wedding. I was twelve and recently diagnosed. I remember people telling me how lovely I looked with my bald head wrapped in a floral headscarf, when all the other girls had real flowers in their hair.

Dad picks up the apple and holds it up to the morning. There are swirls of cream and brown in there that look like the core of a real apple; an impression of pips, blown in by the glassmaker. He spins it slowly in his hand. I've looked at the world through that green glass many times – it looks small and calm.

I don't think he should be touching my things though. I think he should be dealing with Cal, who's yelling up the stairs about the aerial coming out of the back of the TV. I also think he should go down and tell Mum that the only reason he's asked her round is because he wants her back. Getting involved in matters of discipline goes against all her principles, so he's hardly looking for advice in that area.

He puts down the apple and goes to the bookshelf, runs a finger along the spines of my books, like they're piano keys and he's expecting a tune. He twists his head to look up at the CD rack, picks one out, reads the cover, then puts it back.

'Dad!' Cal yells from downstairs. 'The picture's completely fuzzy and Mum's useless!'

Dad sighs, moves towards the door, but can't resist the temptation to pull the duvet straight as he passes. He reads my wall for a bit – all the things I'm going to miss, all the things I want. He shakes his head at it, then bends down and picks up a T-shirt from the floor, folds it and places it on my pillow. And that's when he notices my bedside drawer is slightly open.

Cal's getting closer. 'I'm missing my programmes!'

'Go back down, Cal! I'm coming now.'

But he isn't. He's sitting on the edge of my bed and sliding the drawer open with one finger. Inside are pages and pages of words I've written about my list. My thoughts on the things I've already done – sex, yes, drugs, breaking the law – and my plans for the rest. It's going to freak him out if he reads what I intend to do for number five today. There's the rustle of paper, the shift of the elastic band. It sounds very loud. I struggle to sit up in order to jump out of the wardrobe and wrestle him to the ground, but Cal saves me by opening the bedroom door. Dad fumbles the papers back into the drawer, slams it shut.

'Can't I have any peace?' he says. 'Not even for five minutes?'

'Were you looking at Tessa's stuff?'

'Is it any business of yours?'

'It is if I tell her.'

'Oh for God's sake, give me a break!' Dad's footsteps pound down the stairs. Cal follows him.

I clamber out of the wardrobe and rub life back into my legs. I can feel the curdle of sluggish blood at my knee, and my foot has gone completely dead. I hobble over to the bed and plonk myself down just as Cal comes back in.

He looks at me in surprise. 'Dad said you weren't here.'

'I'm not.'

'Yeah, you are!'

'Keep your voice down. Where's he gone?'

Cal shrugs. 'He's in the kitchen with Mum. I hate him. He just called me a bugger and then he said the f-word.'

145

'Are they talking about me?'

'Yeah, and they won't let me watch the telly!'

We creep down the stairs and peer over the banister. Dad's perched on a bar stool in the middle of the kitchen. He looks clumsy up there digging around in his trouser pocket for his cigarettes and lighter. Mum stands with her back against the fridge watching him.

'When did you start smoking again?' she says. She's wearing jeans and has tied her hair back so that strands of it hang loose around her face. She looks young and pretty as she passes him a saucer.

Dad lights the cigarette and blows smoke across the room. 'I'm sorry, it looks like I got you here under false pretences.' He looks confused for a moment, as if he doesn't know what to say next. 'I just thought you could talk some sense into her.'

'Where do you reckon she's gone this time?'

'Knowing her, she's probably on her way to the airport!'

Mum chuckles, and it's strange because it makes her seem more alive than Dad somehow. He smiles grimly at her from his stool, runs a hand over his hair. 'I'm bloody knackered.'

'I can see that.'

'The boundaries change all the time. One minute she doesn't want anyone near her, then she wants to be held for hours. She won't leave the house for days, then disappears when I'm least expecting it. This list of hers is doing my head in.'

'You know,' Mum says, 'the only really right thing anyone could do would be to make her well again, and none of us can do that.'

He looks at her very intently. 'I'm not sure how much more I can manage by myself. Some mornings I can hardly bear to open my eyes.'

Cal nudges me. 'Shall I gob at him?' he whispers.

'Yeah. Get it in his cup.'

He gathers spit in his mouth and gobs it out hard. His aim's rubbish. It barely makes it through the door; most of it just slimes down his chin and onto the hall carpet.

I roll my eyes at him and gesture for him to follow me. We go back upstairs to my room.

'Sit on the floor by the door,' I tell him. 'Put your hands over your face and don't let either of them in.'

'What're you going to do?'

'I'm getting dressed.'

'Then what are you going to do?'

I take off my pyjamas, step into my best knickers and ease myself into the silk dress I bought on my shopping spree with Cal. I rub the fizz of pins and needles from my feet and pull on my strappy shoes.

Cal says, 'Do you want to see my Megazord? You'll have to come to my room because it's defending a city and if I move it, everyone will die.'

I get my coat from the back of the chair. 'I'm in a bit of a hurry actually.'

He peeps at me between his fingers. 'That's your adventuring dress!'

'Yeah.'

He stands up, blocking the door. 'Can I come?'

'No.'

'Please. I hate it here.'

'No.'

I leave my phone because they can trace you from that. I stuff the papers from the drawer in my coat pocket. I'll chuck them in a bin somewhere later. See, Dad, how things disappear in front of your eyes?

Before I send him downstairs, I bribe Cal. He knows exactly how many magic tricks he can buy with a tenner, and understands he'll get written out of my will if he ever squeals I was here.

I wait until I hear him down there, then I follow slowly behind. I pause on the turn of the stair, not only for breath, but also to look through the window over the flat of the lawn, to brush a finger along the wall, to encircle a spindle of the banisters, to smile at the photos at the top of the stairs.

In the kitchen, Cal squats on the floor in front of Mum and Dad and simply stares at them.

'Did you want something?' Dad says.

'I want to listen.'

'Sorry, it's grown-up talk.'

'I want something to eat then.'

'You've just had half a packet of biscuits.'

'I've got some chewing gum,' Mum says. 'Do you want a bit of that?' She looks in her jacket pocket and hands it over.

Cal stuffs the gum in his mouth, chews it thoughtfully, then says, 'When Tessa dies, can we go on holiday?'

Dad manages to look vicious and surprised at the same time. 'That's a terrible thing to say!'

'I don't even remember going to Spain. It's the only time I've been in an aeroplane and it was so long ago, it might not even be true.'

Dad says, 'That's enough!' and he goes to stand up, but Mum stops him.

'It's all right,' she says, and she turns to Cal. 'Tessa's been sick for a long time, hasn't she? You must feel really left out sometimes.'

He grins. 'Yeah. Some mornings I can hardly bear to open my eyes.'

Twenty-one

Zoey comes to the door, her hair a mess. She's wearing the same clothes as last time I saw her.

'Coming to the seaside?' I jangle the car keys at her.

She peers past me to Dad's car. 'Did you come here on your own?'

'Yeah.'

'But you can't drive!'

'I can now. It's number five on my list.'

She frowns. 'Have you actually had any lessons?'

'Sort of. Can I come in?'

She opens the door wider. 'Wipe your feet, or take your shoes off.'

Her parents' house is always incredibly tidy, like something from a catalogue. They're out at work so much I guess they never get a chance to make it messy. I follow Zoey into the lounge and sit on the sofa. She sits opposite me on the edge of the armchair and folds her arms at me.

'So your dad lent you the car, did he? Even though you're not insured and it's completely illegal?'

'He doesn't exactly know I've got it, but I'm really good at driving! You'll see. I'd pass my test if I was old enough.'

She shakes her head at me as if she just can't believe how stupid I am. She should be proud of me. I got away without Dad even noticing. I remembered to check the mirrors before turning on the ignition, then clutch down, into first, clutch up, accelerator down. I managed three times round the block and only stalled twice, which was my best ever. I navigated the roundabout and even got into third gear along the main road to Zoey's house. And now she's sitting there glaring at me, like it's all some terrible mistake.

'You know,' I say as I stand and zip my coat back up, 'I thought if I made it as far as here without crashing, the only difficult thing left would be the dual carriageway. It didn't cross my mind that you'd be a pain in the arse.'

She shuffles her feet on the floor, as if rubbing something out. 'Sorry. It's just I'm kind of busy.'

'Doing what?'

She shrugs. 'You can't assume everyone's free just because you are.'

I feel something growing inside me as I look at her, and I realize in one absolutely clear moment that I don't like her at all.

'You know what?' I say. 'Forget it. I'll do the list by myself.'

She stands up, swings her stupid hair about and tries to look offended. It's a trick that works with guys, but it makes no difference to the way I feel about her.

'I didn't say I wouldn't come!'

But she's bored of me, it's obvious. She wishes I'd hurry up and die so she can get on with her life.

'No, no, you stay here,' I tell her. 'Everything always turns out crap with you around anyway!'

She follows me out into the hallway. 'No, it doesn't!'

I turn on the mat. 'I meant for me. Haven't you ever noticed how any shit that's falling always lands on my head, never yours?'

She frowns. 'When? When does that happen?'

'All the time. I sometimes wonder if you're only friends with me so you can keep being the lucky one.'

'Christ!' she says. 'Can you stop going on about yourself for even a minute?'

'Shut up!' I tell her. And it feels so good that I say it again.

'No,' she says. '*You* shut up,' but her voice is barely a whisper, which is weird. She takes one small step away, stops as if she's about to say something else, thinks better of it and runs up the stairs.

I don't follow her. I wait in the hall for a bit, feeling the thickness of the carpet under my feet. I listen to the clock. I count sixty ticks, then I go into the lounge and turn on the TV. I watch amateur gardening for seven minutes. I learn that in a sunny south-facing plot you can grow apricots, even in England. I wonder if Adam knows this. But then I get bored with aphids and red spider mites and the drone of the silly man's voice, so I turn it off and text Zoey: SORRY.

I look out of the window to see if the car's still there. It is. The sky's murky, the clouds really low down and the colour of sulphur.

152

I've never driven in rain, which is a bit worrying. I wish it was still October. It was warm then, as if the world had forgotten autumn was supposed to happen next. I remember looking at the leaves fall past the hospital window.

Zoey texts back. ME 2.

She comes downstairs and into the lounge. She's wearing a turquoise mini-dress and loads of bangles. They snake up her arm and jingle as she walks over and gives me a hug. She smells nice. I lean against her shoulder and she kisses the top of my head.

Zoey laughs as I start the car and immediately stall. I try again, and as we kangaroo down the road, I tell her how Dad took me out driving five times and I just couldn't get it right. The feet were so hard – the slight tipping of toes from the clutch, the equal but opposite push on the accelerator.

'That's it!' he kept yelling. 'Feel the biting point?'

But I couldn't feel anything, not even when I took off my shoes.

We got tired, both of us. Each session was shorter than the one before, until we stopped going out at all, and neither of us even mentioned it.

'I doubt he'll notice the car's missing till lunchtime,' I tell her. 'And even then, what's he going to do? Like you said, I'm immune to the rules.'

'You're a complete hero,' she says. 'You're fantastic!'

And we laugh like old times. I'd forgotten how much I like laughing with Zoey. She isn't critical of my driving like Dad was. She isn't scared as I scrape into third gear, or when I forget to indicate to turn left at the end of her road. I'm a much better driver with her watching.

'You're not bad. Your old man taught you something at last.'

'I love it,' I tell her. 'Think how much fun it would be to drive across Europe. You could take a gap year from college and come with me.'

'I don't want to,' she says, and she picks up the map and goes quiet.

'We don't need a map.'

'Why not?'

'Think of it as a road movie.'

'Bollocks,' she says, and she stabs a finger at the window.

There's a gang of boys on bikes blocking the road ahead. They've got their hoods up, cigarettes shielded. The sky's a really strange colour and there's hardly anyone else about. I slow right down.

'What shall I do?'

'Reverse,' Zoey says. 'They're not going to move.'

I wind down the window. 'Oi!' I yell. 'Move your arses!'

They turn languid, shift lazily to the edge of the road and grin as I blow kisses at them.

Zoey looks stunned. 'What's got into you?'

'Nothing – I just haven't learned reversing yet.'

We get caught in traffic on the main road. I watch snatches of other people's lives through the window. A baby cries in its car seat, a man drums his fingers on the steering wheel. A woman picks her nose. A child waves.

'Amazing, isn't it?' I say.

'What?'

'I'm me and you're you, and all of them out there are them. And we're all so different and equally unimportant.'

'Speak for yourself.'

'It's true. Don't you ever think that when you look in a mirror? Don't you ever imagine your own skull?'

'No, actually, I don't.'

'I don't know my seven and eight times tables and I hate beetroot and celery. You don't like your acne or your legs, but in the great scheme of things, none of it matters.'

'Shut up, Tessa! Stop going on about crap.'

So I do, but in my head I know that I have minty breath from toothpaste, and hers is sour from smoke. I have a diagnosis. She has two parents who live together. I got out of my bed this morning and there was sweat on the sheets. I'm driving now. It's my face in the car mirror, my smile, my bones they'll burn or bury. It'll be my death. Not Zoey's. Mine. And for once, it doesn't feel so bad.

We don't speak. She just stares out of the window and I drive. Out of town, onto the dual carriageway. The sky gets darker and darker. It's great.

But eventually Zoey starts complaining again.

'This is the worst drive I've ever been on,' she says. 'I feel sick. Why aren't we arriving anywhere?'

'Because I'm ignoring the road signs.'

She looks at me, amazed. 'Why would you do that? I want to be somewhere.'

I push my foot hard down on the accelerator. 'OK.'

Zoey yelps, braces her arms against the dashboard. 'Slow down! You've only just learned to bloody drive!'

Thirty. Thirty-five. So much power in my hands.

'Slow down. That was thunder!'

Rain spots the windscreen. The shine of it on the glass makes everything blur and reflect. It looks like electricity, and not water at all.

I count silently in my head until lightning breaks across the sky.

'One kilometre away,' I tell her.

'Pull over!'

'What for?'

Rain hits the roof of the car hard now and I don't know where the wipers are. I fumble with the light switches, the horn, the ignition. I forget the car's in fourth gear and immediately stall.

'Not here!' Zoey yells. 'We're on a dual carriageway! Do you want to die?'

I put the car back in neutral. I don't feel scared at all. Water runs down the windscreen in waves, and the cars behind us beep and flash as they pass, but I very calmly check my mirrors, turn on the ignition, then into first gear and away. I even find the wipers as I slip through second gear and into third.

Zoey's face is alive with panic. 'You're mad. Let me drive!'

'You're not insured.'

'Neither are you!'

The storm's louder now, with no space between thunder and

156

lightning. Other cars have put their lights on, even though it's day-time. I can't seem to find ours though.

'Please!' Zoey shouts. 'Please pull over!'

'A car's a safe place to be. Cars have rubber tyres.'

'Slow down!' she yells. 'We're going to have an accident. Have you never heard of stopping distances?'

No. Instead, I've discovered a fifth gear I didn't even know existed. We're really speeding along now and the sky is alight with proper forked lightning. I've never seen it close up before. When Dad took us to Spain, there was an electric storm over the sea, which we watched from the balcony of the hotel. But it didn't feel real, more like something arranged for the tourists. This one's right above us and is completely fantastic.

Zoey doesn't think so though. She's cowering in her seat. 'Cars are made of metal!' she shrieks. 'We could get hit any second! Pull over!' I feel sorry for her, but she's wrong about the lightning.

She stabs at the window with a frantic finger. 'There's a garage, look. Pull in there, or I'm going to throw myself out the door.'

I fancy some chocolate anyway, so I pull in. We're going a bit fast, but I manage to find the brake. We slide dramatically across the forecourt and come to a stop surrounded by petrol pumps and fluorescent lights. Zoey closes her eyes. Funny how I'd rather be out on the road with mine wide open.

'I don't know what your game is,' she hisses, 'but you nearly killed both of us.'

She opens her door, gets out, slams it shut and marches off to the shop. For a moment I think of leaving without her, but before

I can think about it properly, she stomps back again and opens my door. She smells different, cold and fresh. She yanks a wet tail of hair from her mouth.

'I haven't got any money. I need cigarettes.'

I pass her my bag. I feel very happy suddenly. 'Can you get me some chocolate while you're there?'

'After I've had a cigarette,' she says, 'I'm going to the toilet. When I get back, you're going to let me drive.'

She slams the door shut and walks back across the forecourt. It's still raining heavily and she cowers under it, winces at the sky as thunder rumbles again. I've never seen her afraid before and I feel a sudden rush of love for her. She can't handle it like I can. She's not used to it. The whole world could roar and it wouldn't freak me out. I want an avalanche at the next junction. I want black rain to fall and a plague of locusts to buzz out of the glove compartment. Poor Zoey. I can see her now in the garage, innocently buying sweets and fags. I'll let her drive, but only because I choose to. She can't control me any more. I'm beyond her.

Twenty-two

Four twenty and the sea is grey. So is the sky, although the sky is slightly lighter and not moving so fast. The sea makes me dizzy – something about the never-ending movement and how no one could stop it even if they wanted to.

'It's crazy being here,' Zoey says. 'How did I let you persuade me?'

We're sitting on a bench on the sea front. The place is practically deserted. Far away across the sand a dog barks at the waves. Its owner is the tiniest dot on the horizon.

'I used to come here on holiday every summer,' I tell her. 'Before Mum left. Before I got sick. We used to stay at the Crosskeys Hotel. Every morning we'd get up, have breakfast and spend the day on the beach. Every single day for two weeks.'

'Fun, fun, fun!' Zoey says, and she slumps down on the bench and pulls her coat closer across her chest.

'We didn't even go up to the hotel for lunch. Dad made sandwiches, and we'd buy packets of Angel Delight for pudding. He'd mix it with milk on the beach in a Tupperware dish. The sound of the fork whisking against a bowl was so weird amongst the noise of the seagulls and the waves.'

Zoey looks at me long and hard. 'Did you forget to take some kind of important medication today?'

'No!' I grab her arm, pull her up. 'Come on, I'll show you the hotel we used to stay in.'

We walk along the promenade. Below us, the sand is covered in cuttlefish. They're heavy and scarred as if they've been flung against each other with every tide. I make a joke about picking them up and selling them to a pet shop for the budgies, but really it's strange. I don't remember that happening when I used to come here.

'Maybe it's an autumn thing,' Zoey says. 'Or pollution. The whole crazy planet's dying. You should think yourself lucky you're getting out of here.'

Zoey says she needs to pee, and she goes down the steps onto the beach and crouches there. I can't quite believe she's doing this. There's hardly anyone about, but usually she'd really care about somebody seeing her. Her pee gushes a hole in the sand and disappears, steaming. She looks very primeval as she hitches herself up and makes her way back to me.

We stand for a bit looking at the sea together. It rushes, whitens, retreats.

'I'm glad you're my friend, Zoey,' I say, and I take her hand in mine and hold it tight.

We walk along to the harbour. I almost tell her about Adam and the motorbike ride and what happened on the hill, but it feels

160

too difficult, and really I don't want to talk about it. I get lost in remembering this place instead. Everything's so familiar – the souvenir hut with its buckets and spades and racks of postcards, the whitewashed walls of the ice-cream parlour and the giant pink cone glinting outside. I'm even able to find the alley near the harbour that's a short cut through to the hotel.

'It looks different,' I tell her. 'It used to be bigger.'

'But it's the right place?'

'Yeah.'

'Great, so can we go back to the car now?'

I open the gate, walk up the little path. 'I wonder if they'll let me look at the room we used to stay in.'

'Christ!' mutters Zoey, and she plonks herself on the wall to wait.

A middle-aged woman opens the door. She looks kind and fat and is wearing an apron. I don't remember her. 'Yes?'

I tell her that I used to come here as a child, that we had the family room every summer for two weeks.

'And are you looking for a room for tonight?' she asks.

Which hadn't actually crossed my mind, but suddenly sounds like a wonderful idea. 'Can we have the same one?'

Zoey comes marching up the path behind me, grabs my arm and spins me round. 'What the hell are you doing?'

'Booking a room.'

'I can't stay here, I've got college tomorrow.'

'You've always got college,' I tell her. 'And you've got lots more tomorrows.'

I think this sounds rather eloquent and it certainly seems to shut Zoey up. She slouches back to the wall and sits there gazing at the sky.

I turn back to the woman. 'Sorry about that,' I say. I like her. She isn't at all suspicious. Perhaps I look fifty today, and she thinks Zoey's my terrible teenage daughter.

'There's a four-poster bed in there now,' she says, 'but it's still en-suite.'

'Good. We'll take it.'

We follow her upstairs. Her bottom is huge and sways as she walks. I wonder what it would be like having her for a mother.

'Here we go,' she says as she opens the door. 'We've completely re-decorated, so it probably looks different.'

It does. The four-poster bed dominates the room. It's high and old-fashioned and draped with velvet.

'We get lots of honeymooners here,' the woman explains.

'Fantastic!' Zoey snarls.

It's difficult to see the sunny room I used to wake up in every summer. The bunk beds have gone, replaced by a table with a kettle and tea things. The arched window is familiar though, and the same fitted wardrobe lines one wall.

'I'll leave you to it,' the woman says.

Zoey kicks off her shoes and hauls herself onto the bed. 'This room is seventy pounds a night!' she says. 'Do you actually have any money on you?'

'I just wanted to look.'

'Are you insane?'

I climb up beside her on the bed. 'No, but it's going to sound stupid out loud.'

She props herself up on one elbow and looks at me suspiciously. 'Try me.'

So I tell her about the last summer I ever came here, how Mum and Dad were arguing more than ever. I tell her how at breakfast one morning, Mum wouldn't eat, said she was sick of sausages and tinned tomatoes and that it would've been cheaper to go to Benidorm.

'Go then,' Dad said. 'Send us a postcard when you get there.'

Mum took my hand and we came back upstairs to the room. 'Let's hide from them,' she said. 'Won't that be fun?' I was really excited. She'd left Cal with Dad. It was me she'd chosen.

We hid in the wardrobe.

'No one will find us here,' she said.

And nobody did, although I wasn't sure anyone was actually looking. We sat there for ages, until eventually Mum crept out to get a pen from her bag, then came back and wrote her name very carefully on the inside of the wardrobe door. She passed me the pen and I wrote my name next to hers.

'There,' she said. 'Even if we never come back, we'll always be here.'

Zoey eyes me doubtfully. 'Is that it? End of story?'

'That's it.'

'You and your mum wrote your names in a cupboard and we had to drive forty miles for you to tell me?'

'Every few years we disappear, Zoey. All our cells are replaced by others. Not a single bit of me is the same as when I was last in this room. I was someone else when I wrote my name in there, someone healthy.'

Zoey sits up. She looks furious. 'So, if your signature's still there you'll be miraculously cured, will you? And if it isn't, then what? Didn't you hear that woman say they'd re-decorated?'

I don't like her shouting at me. 'Can you look in the wardrobe and see, Zoey?'

'No. You made me come here and I didn't want to. I feel like crap, and now this – a stupid cupboard! You're unbelievable.'

'Why are you so angry?'

She scrambles off the bed. 'I'm leaving. You're doing my head in looking for signs all the time.' She gets her coat from where she dumped it by the door and yanks it on. 'You go on and on about yourself, like you're the only one in the world with anything wrong. We're all in the same boat, you know. We're born, we eat, we shit, we die. That's it!'

I don't know how to be when she's yelling this loud. 'What's wrong with you?'

'Same question,' she shouts, 'right back to you!'

'There's nothing wrong with me, apart from the obvious.'

'Then I'm fine too.'

'No, you're not. Look at you.'

'Look at me, what? What do I look like?'

'Sad.'

She falters by the door. 'Sad?'

There's a terrible stillness. I notice a small tear in the wallpaper above her shoulder. I notice finger marks grimed on the light switch. Somewhere down in the house, a door opens and shuts. As Zoey turns to face me, I realize that life is made up of a series of moments, each one a journey to the end.

When she finally speaks, her voice is heavy and dull. 'I'm pregnant.'

'Oh my God!'

'I wasn't going to tell you.'

'Are you sure?'

She sinks down into the chair next to the door. 'I did two tests.'

'Did you do them right?'

'If the second window turns pink and stays pink, then you're pregnant. It stayed pink twice.'

'Oh my God!'

'Would you stop saying that?'

'Does Scott know?'

She nods. 'I couldn't find him that day at the supermarket and he wouldn't answer his phone all weekend, so I went round to his house yesterday and made him listen. He hates me. You should have seen the look on his face.'

'Like what?'

'Like I'm an idiot. Like how can I be so stupid? He's definitely seeing someone else. Those girls were right.'

I want to walk over and stroke her shoulders, the tough curve of her spine. I don't though, because I don't think she'd want me to.

'What will you do?'

She shrugs, and in that shrug I see her fear. She looks about twelve. She looks like a kid on a boat, travelling on some big sea with no food or compass.

'You could have it, Zoey.'

'That's not even funny.'

'It wasn't meant to be. Have it. Why not?'

'I'm not having it because of you!'

I can tell this isn't the first time she's thought this. 'Get rid of it then.'

She moans softly as she leans her head against the wall behind her and stares hopelessly up at the ceiling.

'I'm over three months,' she says. 'Do you think that's too late? Do you think they'll even let me have an abortion?' She wipes the first tears from her eyes with her sleeve. 'I'm so stupid! How could I have been so stupid? My mum's going to find out now. I should've gone to a chemist and got the morning-after pill. I wish I'd never met him!'

I don't know what to say to her. I don't know if she'd even hear me if I could think of anything. She feels very far away sitting on that chair.

'I just want it gone,' she says. Then she looks right at me. 'Do you hate me?'

'No.'

'Will you hate me if I get rid of it?'

I might.

'I'm going to make a cup of tea,' I tell her.

There are shortbread biscuits on a plate and little sachets of

166

sugar and milk. This really is a very nice room. I look out of the window while I wait for the kettle to boil. Two boys are playing football on the promenade. It's raining and they've got their hoods up. I don't know how they can see the ball. Zoey and me were down there just now, in the cold and the wind. I held Zoey's hand.

'There are daily boat trips from the harbour,' I tell her. 'Maybe they go somewhere warm and far away.'

'I'm going to sleep,' she says. 'Wake me up when it's over.'

But she doesn't move from the chair and she doesn't close her eyes.

A family walk past the window. A dad pushing a buggy and a small girl in a pink shiny mac clutching her mum's hand in the rain. She's wet, maybe cold, but she knows she'll be home and dry soon. Warm milk. Children's TV. Maybe a biscuit and early pyjamas.

I wonder what her name is. Rosie? Amber? She looks like her name would have a colour in it. Scarlett?

I don't really mean to. I don't even think about it first. I simply walk across the room and open the wardrobe door. I startle the coat hangers and they chink together. The smell of damp wood fills me.

'Is it there?' Zoey asks.

The inside of the door is glossy white. A total re-paint. I touch it with my fingers, but it stays the same. It's so bright it makes the room waver at the edges. Every few years we disappear.

Zoey sighs and leans back in her chair. 'You shouldn't've looked.'

I shut the wardrobe door and go back to the kettle.

I count as I pour water onto the tea bags. Zoey's over three months pregnant. A baby needs nine months to grow. It'll be born in May, same as me. I like May. You get two bank holiday weekends. You get cherry blossom. Bluebells. Lawnmowers. The drowsy smell of new-cut grass.

It's one hundred and fifty-four days until May.

Twenty-three

Cal comes trotting up from the bottom of the dark garden, his hand outstretched. 'Next,' he says.

Mum opens the box of fireworks on her lap. She looks as if she's choosing a chocolate, delicately picking one out, then reading the label before passing it over.

'Enchanted Garden,' she tells him.

He rushes back to Dad with it. The tops of his wellies slap against each other as he runs. Moonlight filters through the apple tree and splashes the grass.

Mum and me have brought chairs from the kitchen and we're sitting together by the back door. It's cold. Our breath like smoke. Now winter is here, the earth smells wet, as if life is hunkering down, things crouching low, preserving energy.

Mum says, 'Do you know how truly horrible it is when you go off and don't tell anyone where you are?'

Since she's the great disappearing expert of all time, I laugh at that. She looks surprised, obviously doesn't get the irony. 'Dad says you slept for two days solid when you got back.'

'I was tired.'

'He was terrified.'

'Were you?'

'We both were.'

'Enchanted Garden!' Dad announces.

There's a sudden crackle, and flowers made of light bloom into the air, expand, then sink and fade across the grass.

'Ahhh,' Mum says. 'That was lovely.'

'That was boring,' Cal cries as he comes galloping back to us.

Mum opens the box again. 'How about a rocket? Would a rocket be any better?'

'A rocket would be excellent!' Cal runs round the garden to celebrate before handing it over to Dad. Together they push the stick into the ground. I think of the bird, of Cal's rabbit. Of all the creatures that have died in our garden, their skeletons jostling together under the earth.

'Why the seaside?' Mum asks.

'I just fancied it.'

'Why Dad's car?'

I shrug. 'Driving was on my list.'

'You know,' she says, 'you can't go around doing just what you like. You have to think about the people who love you.'

'Who?'

'The people who love you.'

'Loud one,' Dad says. 'Hands over ears, ladies.'

The rocket launches with a single *boom*, so loud its energy expands inside me. Sound waves break in my blood. My brain feels tidal.

Mum's never said she loves me. Not ever. I don't think she ever will. It would be too obvious now, too full of pity. It would embarrass both of us. Sometimes I wonder at the quiet things that must have passed between us before I was born, when I was curled small and dark inside her. But I don't wonder very often.

She shifts uncomfortably on her chair. 'Tessa, are you planning on killing anyone?' She sounds casual, but I think she might mean it.

'Of course not!'

'Good.' She looks genuinely relieved. 'So what's next on your list then?'

I'm surprised. 'You really want to know?'

'I really do.'

'OK. Fame's next.'

She shakes her head in dismay, but Cal, who has turned up for the next firework, thinks it's hilarious. 'See how many drinking straws you can stuff in your mouth,' he says. 'The world record's two hundred and fifty-eight.'

'I'll think about that,' I tell him.

'Or you could get tattooed all over your body like a leopard. Or we could push you up the motorway in your bed.'

Mum regards him thoughtfully. 'Twenty-one-shot Cascade,' she says.

We count them. They shoot up with a soft *phut*, burst into clusters of stars, then drift slowly down. I wonder if the grass will be stained sulphur-yellow, vermilion, aquamarine by morning.

A comet next, to appease Cal's desire for action. Dad lights it and it whizzes up above the roof, trailing a tail of glitter.

Mum bought smoke bombs. They cost £3.50 each and Cal's seriously impressed. He shouts the price to Dad.

'More money than sense,' Dad yells back.

Mum shoves two fingers up at him and he laughs so warmly that she shivers.

'I got two for the price of one,' she tells me. 'That's one advantage of you being ill and us having firework night in December.'

The bombs spray the garden with green smoke. Loads of it. It's as if goblins are about to arrive. Cal and Dad come running from the bottom of the garden, laughing and spluttering.

'That's a ridiculous amount of smoke!' Dad cries. 'It's like being in Beirut!'

Mum smiles, passes him a Catherine wheel. 'Do this one next. It's my favourite.'

He gets a hammer, and she stands up and holds the fence post still while he bangs the nail in. They're laughing together.

'Don't hit my fingers,' she says, and she nudges him with her elbow.

'I will if you do that!'

Cal sits in Mum's seat and rips open a packet of sparklers. 'I bet I'm famous before you,' he tells me.

'I bet you're not.'

'I'm going to be the youngest person ever to join the Magic Circle.'

'Don't you have to be invited?'

172

'They *will* invite me! I've got talent. What can you do? You can't even sing.'

'Hey!' Dad says. 'What's this?'

Mum sighs. 'Both our children want to be famous.'

'Do they?'

'Fame's next on Tessa's list.'

I can tell from Dad's face that he wasn't expecting this. He turns to me, the hammer limp at his side. 'Fame?'

'Yeah.'

'How?'

'I haven't decided.'

'I thought you'd finished with the list.'

'No.'

'I thought after the car, after all that's happened . . .'

'No, Dad, it's not finished.'

I used to believe that Dad could do anything, save me from anything. But he can't, he's just a man. Mum puts her arm around him and he leans in to her.

I stare at them. My mother. My father. His face is in shadow, the edges of her hair are tipped with light. I keep really still. Cal, next to me, keeps really still too.

'Wow!' he whispers.

It hurts more than I could ever have imagined.

In the kitchen, I swill my mouth out with water at the sink and spit it out. My spit looks slimy, is pulled so slowly towards the plug-hole that I have to chase it down with more water from the tap. The sink is cold against my skin.

I turn off the light and watch my family through the window. They stand together on the lawn, sorting through the last of the fireworks. Dad holds each one up and shines the torch at it. They choose one, shut the box, and all three of them walk away down the garden.

Perhaps I'm dead. Perhaps this is all it will be. The living will carry on in their world – touching, walking. And I'll continue in this empty world, tapping soundlessly on the glass between us.

I go out of the front door, shut it behind me and sit on the step. The undergrowth rustles, as if some night creature is trying to hide itself from me, but I don't freak out, don't even move. As my eyes adjust, I can see the fence and the bushes that line it. I can see the street beyond the gate quite clearly, lamplight splashing across the pavement, slanting across other people's cars, reflected back from other people's blank windows.

I can smell onions. Kebabs. If my life was different, I'd be out with Zoey. We'd have chips. We'd be standing on some street corner, licking salty fingers, waiting for action. But instead, I'm here. Dead on the doorstep.

I hear Adam before I see him, the guttural roar of his bike. As he gets closer, the noise vibrates the air, so that the trees seem to dance. He stops outside his gate, switches off the engine and turns off the lights. Silence and darkness descend again as he unclips his helmet, threads it through the handlebars and pushes the bike up the drive.

I mostly believe in chaos. If wishes came true, my bones wouldn't ache as if all the space inside them is used up. There wouldn't be a mist in front of my eyes that I can't brush away.

But watching Adam walk up the path feels like a choice. The universe might be random, but I can make something different happen.

I step over the low wall that separates our front gardens. He's locking the bike to the gate at the side of his house. He doesn't see me. I walk up behind him. I feel very powerful and certain.

'Adam?'

He turns round, startled. 'Shit! I thought you were a ghost!' There's a cold-washed smell to him, as if he's an animal come out of the night. I take a step closer.

'What are you doing?' he says.

'We said we'd be friends.'

He looks confused. 'Yeah.'

'I don't want to be.'

There's space between us, and in that space there's darkness. I take another step, so close that we share a breath. The same one. In and out.

'Tessa,' he says. I know it's a warning, but I don't care.

'What's the worst thing that can happen?'

'It'll hurt,' he says.

'It already hurts.'

He nods very slowly. And it's like there's a hole in time, as if everything stops and this one minute, where we look at each other so close, is spread out between us. As he leans towards me, I feel a strange warmth filtering through me. I forget that my brain is full of every sad face at every window I've ever passed. As he leans

175

closer, I feel only the warmth of his breath on my skin. We kiss very gently. Hardly at all, like we're not sure. Our lips are the only place where we touch.

We stand back and look at each other. What words are there for the look that passes from me to him and back again? Around us all the night things gather and stare. The lost things found again.

'Shit, Tess!'

'It's all right,' I tell him. 'I won't break.'

And to prove it, I push him back against the wall of his house and keep him there. And this time it's not about tenderness. My tongue is in his mouth, searching, meeting his. His arms wrap me warm. His hand is on the back of my neck. I melt there. My hand slides down his back. I press myself closer, but it's not close enough. I want to climb inside him. Live in him. Be him. It's all tongue and longing. I lick him, take small bites on the edges of his lips.

I never realized I was this hungry.

He pulls away. 'Shit,' he says. 'Shit!' And he runs his hand through his hair; it gleams wet, animal dark. The streetlights blaze in his eyes. 'What's happening to us?'

'I want you,' I tell him.

My heart's thumping. I feel absolutely alive.

Twenty-four

Zoey shouldn't've asked me to come. I haven't been able to stop counting since we got through the door. We've been here seven minutes. Her appointment's in six minutes. She got pregnant ninety-five days ago.

I try to think of random numbers, but they all seem to add up to something. Eight – the number of discrete windows across the far wall. One – the equally discreet receptionist. Five hundred – the number of pounds it's costing Scott to get rid of the baby.

Zoey flicks me a nervous smile across the top of her magazine. 'I bet you don't get anything like this on the NHS.'

You don't. The seats are leather, there's a big square coffee table stacked with glossy magazines, and it's so warm that I've had to take my coat off. I thought it'd be full of girls clutching hankies and looking forlorn, but me and Zoey are the only ones here. She's scraped her hair back into a ponytail and she's wearing her baggy sweat pants again. She looks tired and pale.

'Do you want to know which symptoms I'll be most glad to get rid of?' She rests her magazine on her lap and counts them off on her fingers. 'My breasts look like some freaky map, all covered in blue veins. I feel heavy – even my fingers are heavy. I keep throwing up. I've got a constant headache. And my eyes are sore.'

'Anything good?'

She thinks about this for a moment. 'I smell different. I smell quite nice.'

I lean across the coffee table and breathe her in. She smells of smoke, perfume, chewing gum. And something else.

'Fecund,' I tell her.

'What?'

'It means you're fertile.'

She shakes her head at me as if I'm nuts. 'Did your boyfriend teach you that?'

When I don't reply, she goes back to her magazine. Twenty-two pages of hot new gadgets. How to write a perfect love song. Will space travel ever be accessible?

'I saw this film once,' I tell her, 'about a girl who died. When she got to heaven, her sister's still-born baby was already there, and she looked after it until they were all reunited.'

Zoey pretends she hasn't heard. She turns the page as if she's read it.

'That might happen to me, Zoey.'

'It won't.'

'Your baby's so small I could keep it in my pocket.'

'Shut up, Tessa!'

'You were looking at clothes for it the other day.'

Zoey slumps back in her chair and closes her eyes. Her mouth goes slack, as if she's been unplugged. 'Please,' she says. 'Please shut up. You shouldn't've come if you're going to disapprove.'

She's right. I knew it last night when I couldn't sleep. Across the landing, the shower was dripping and something – a cockroach? a spider? – scuttled across the bedroom carpet.

I got up and went downstairs in my dressing gown. I was planning a cup of hot chocolate, maybe some late-night TV. But there, right in the middle of the kitchen, was a mouse stuck to one of Dad's cockroach traps. The only bit of it that wasn't glued to the cardboard was one of its back legs, which it used like a paddle to try and get away from me. It was in agony. I knew I'd have to kill it, but I couldn't think how to do it without causing it more pain. A carving knife? A pair of scissors? A pencil through the back of the head? I could only think of awful endings.

Finally I got an old ice-cream carton out of the cupboard and filled it up with water. I dunked the mouse in and held it down with a wooden spoon. It looked up at me, amazed, as it struggled to breathe. Three tiny air bubbles escaped, one after the other.

I write Zoey's baby a text: HIDE!

'Who's that to?'

'No one.'

She leans over the table. 'Let me see.'

I delete it, show her the blank screen.

'Was it to Adam?'

'No.'

She rolls her eyes. 'You practically have sex in the garden and then you get some kind of perverted kick out of pretending it didn't happen.'

'He's not interested.'

She frowns. 'Of course he's interested. His mum came out and caught you, that's all. He'd happily have shagged you otherwise.'

'It was four days ago, Zoey. If he was interested, he'd have contacted me.'

She shrugs. 'Maybe he's busy.'

We sit with that lie for a minute. My bones poke through my skin, I've got purple blotches under my eyes, and I'm definitely beginning to smell weird. Adam's probably still washing his mouth out.

'Love's bad for you anyway,' Zoey says. 'I'm living proof of that.' She chucks her magazine down on the table and looks at her watch. 'What the hell am I paying for exactly?'

I move seats to be next to her.

'Maybe it's a joke,' she says. 'Maybe they take your money, let you sweat, and hope you get so embarrassed that you just go home.'

I take her hand and hold it between mine. She looks a bit surprised, but doesn't take hers away.

The windows have darkened glass in them so that you can't see the street. When we arrived, it was beginning to snow; people doing their Christmas shopping were all wrapped up against the cold. In here, heat is blasting from the radiators and piped music washes over us. The world out there could've ended, but in here you wouldn't know it.

Zoey says, 'When this is over and it's just you and me again, we'll get back to your list. We'll do number six. Fame, isn't it? I saw this woman on the telly the other day. She's got terminal cancer and she's just done a triathlon. You should do that.'

'She's got breast cancer.'

'So?'

'So it's different.'

'Running and cycling keep her motivated. How different can it be? She's lived much longer than anyone thought she would, and she's really famous.'

'I hate running!'

Zoey shakes her head at me very solemnly, as if I'm being deliberately difficult. 'What about *Big Brother*? They've never had anyone like you on that before.'

'It doesn't start until next summer.'

'So?'

'So think about it!'

And that's when the nurse comes out of a side room and walks towards us. 'Zoey Walker? We're ready for you now.'

Zoey hauls me up. 'Can my friend come?'

'I'm sorry, but it's better if she waits outside. It's just a discussion today, but it's not the type of discussion that's easy to have in front of a friend.'

The nurse sounds very certain of this and Zoey doesn't seem able to resist. She passes me her coat, says, 'Look after this for me,' and goes off with the nurse. The door shuts behind them.

I feel very solid. Not small, but large and beating and alive. It's so tangible, being and not being. I'm here. Soon I won't be. Zoey's baby is here. Its pulse tick-ticking. Soon it won't be. And when Zoey comes out of that room, having signed on the dotted line, she'll be different. She'll understand what I already know – that death surrounds us all.

And it tastes like metal between your teeth.

Twenty-five

'Where are we going?'

Dad takes one hand off the steering wheel to pat me on the knee. 'All in good time.'

'Is it going to be embarrassing?'

'I hope not.'

'Are we going to meet someone famous?'

He looks alarmed for a moment. 'Is that what you meant?'

'Not really.'

We drive through town and he won't tell me. We drive past the housing estates and onto the ring road, and my guesses get completely random. I like making him laugh. He doesn't do it much.

'Moon landing?'

'No.'

'Talent competition?'

'With your singing voice?'

I phone Zoey and see if she wants to have a guess, but she's still freaking out about the operation. 'I have to take a responsible adult with me. Who the hell am I going to ask?'

'I'll come.'

'They mean a proper adult. You know, like a parent.'

'They can't make you tell your parents.'

'I hate this,' she says. 'I thought they'd give me a pill and it would just fall out. Why do I need an operation? It's only the size of a dot.'

She's wrong about that. Last night I got out the Reader's Digest *Book of Family Medicine* and looked up pregnancy. I wanted to know how big babies are in week sixteen. I discovered they're the length of a dandelion. I couldn't stop reading. I looked up bee-stings and hives. Lovely mundane, family illnesses – eczema, tonsillitis, croup.

'You still there?' she says.

'Yeah.'

'Well, I'm going now. Acid liquid is coming up my throat and into my mouth.'

It's indigestion. She needs to massage her colon and drink some milk. It will pass. Whatever she decides to do about the baby, all Zoey's symptoms will pass. I don't tell her this though. Instead, I press the red button on my phone and concentrate on the road ahead.

'She's a very silly girl,' Dad says. 'The longer she leaves it, the worse it will be. Terminating a pregnancy isn't like taking out the rubbish.'

'She knows that, Dad. Anyway, it's nothing to do with you – she's not your daughter.'

'No,' he agrees. 'She's not.'

I write Adam a text. I write, WHERE THE HELL ARE U? Then I delete it.

Six nights ago his mum stood on the doorstep and cried. She said the fireworks were terrifying. She asked why he'd left her when the world was ending.

'Give me your mobile number,' he told me. 'I'll call you.'

We swapped numbers. It was erotic. I thought it was a promise.

'Fame,' Dad says. 'Now, what do we mean by fame, eh?'

I mean Shakespeare. That silhouette of him with his perky beard, quill in hand, was on the front of all the copies of his plays at school. He invented tons of new words and everyone knows who he is after hundreds of years. He lived before cars and planes, guns and bombs and pollution. Before pens. Queen Elizabeth I was on the throne when he was writing. She was famous too, not just for being Henry VIII's daughter, but for potatoes and the Armada and tobacco and for being so clever.

Then there's Marilyn. Elvis. Even modern icons like Madonna will be remembered. Take That are touring again and sold out in milliseconds. Their eyes are etched with age and Robbie isn't even singing, but still people want a piece of them. Fame like that is what I mean. I'd like the whole world to stop what it's doing and personally come and say goodbye to me when I die. What else is there?

'What do you mean by fame, Dad?'

After a minute's thought he says, 'Leaving something of yourself behind, I guess.'

185

I think of Zoey and her baby. Growing. Growing.

'OK,' Dad says. 'Here we are.'

I'm not sure where 'here' is. It looks like a library, one of those square, functional buildings with lots of windows and its own car park with allocated spaces for the director. We pull into a disabled bay.

The woman who answers the intercom wants to know who we've come to see. Dad tries to whisper, but she can't hear, so he has to say it again, louder. 'Richard Green,' he says, and he gives me a sideways glance.

'Richard Green?'

He nods, pleased with himself. 'One of the accountants I used to work with knows him.'

'And that's relevant because . . . ?'

'He wants to interview you.'

I stall on the step. 'An interview? On the radio? But everyone'll hear me!'

'Isn't that the idea?'

'What am I supposed to be interviewed about?'

And that's when he blushes. That's when maybe he realizes that this is the worst idea he's ever had, because the only thing that makes me extraordinary is my sickness. If it wasn't for that, I'd be in school or bunking. Maybe I'd be at Zoey's, fetching her Rennies from the bathroom cabinet. Maybe I'd be lying in Adam's arms.

The receptionist pretends everything's all right. She asks for our names and gives us both a sticker. We obediently attach these to our coats as she tells us that the producer will be with us soon.

'Have a seat,' she says, gesturing to a row of armchairs on the other side of the foyer.

'You don't have to speak,' Dad says as we sit down. 'I'll go in by myself if you want, and you can stay out here.'

'And what would you talk about?'

He shrugs. 'Paucity of teen cancer units, lack of funding for alternative medicine, your dietary needs not being subsidized by the NHS. I could talk for bloody hours. It's my specialist subject.'

'Fundraising? I don't want to be famous for raising a bit of money! I want to be famous for being amazing. I want the kind of fame that doesn't need a surname. Iconic fame. Ever heard of that?'

He turns to me, his eyes glistening. 'And how precisely were we going to manage that?'

The water machine bubbles and drips beside us. I feel sick. I think of Zoey. I think of her baby with all its nails already in place – tiny, tiny dandelion nails.

'Shall I tell the receptionist to cancel?' Dad asks. 'I don't want you to say I forced you.'

I feel ever so slightly sorry for him as he scuffs his shoes on the floor under his chair like a schoolboy. How many miles we miss each other by.

'No, Dad, you don't have to cancel.'

'So you'll go in?'

'I'll go in.'

He squeezes my hand. 'That's great, Tess.'

A woman comes up the stairs and into the lobby. She strides up to us and shakes Dad's hand warmly.

'We spoke on the phone,' she says.

'Yes.'

'And this must be Tessa.'

'That's me!'

She puts her hand out for me to shake, but I ignore it, pretend I can't move my arms. Maybe she'll think it's part of my illness. Her eyes travel in sorrow to my coat, scarf and hat. Perhaps she knows it isn't that cold outside today.

'There isn't a lift,' she says. 'Will you manage the stairs?'

'We'll be fine,' Dad says.

She looks relieved. 'Richard's really looking forward to meeting you.'

She flirts with Dad as we go down to the studio. It crosses my mind that his shambling protectiveness towards me might be attractive to women. It makes them want to save him. From me. From all this suffering.

'The interview will be live,' she tells us. She lowers her voice as we get to the studio door. 'See that red light? It means Richard's on air and we can't go in. In a minute he'll play a trail and the light will turn green.' She says this as if we're bound to be impressed.

'What's Richard's angle?' I ask. 'Is it the whole dying girl thing, or does he have something original planned?'

'Sorry?' Her smile slips; there's a flicker of concern as she looks at Dad for reassurance. Is she only just able to smell something hostile in the air?

'Teen cancer units are rare in hospitals,' Dad says quickly. 'If we could even think about raising awareness, that'd be great.'

The red light outside the studio flips to green. 'That's you!' the producer says, and she opens the door for us. 'Tessa Scott and her father,' she announces.

We sound like dinner party guests, like we came to a ball. But Richard Green is no prince. He half squats above his chair and puts out a fat hand for us to shake in turn. His hand is sweaty, like it needs squeezing out. His lungs wheeze as he sits back down. He stinks of fags. He shuffles papers. 'Take a seat,' he tells us. 'I'll introduce you, then we'll just launch straight in.'

I used to watch Richard Green present the local news at lunch-time. One of the nurses in the hospital used to fancy him. Now I know why he's been relegated to radio.

'OK,' he says. 'Here we go. Be as natural as you can. It'll be very informal.' He turns to the microphone. 'And now I'm honoured to have as my guest in the studio today a very brave young lady called Tessa Scott.'

My heart beats fast as he says my name. Will Adam be listening? Or Zoey? She might be lying on her bed with the radio on. Feeling nauseous. Half asleep.

'Tessa's been living with leukaemia for the last four years and she's come here today with her dad to talk to us about the whole experience.'

Dad leans forward and Richard, perhaps recognizing his willingness, asks him the first question.

'Tell us about when you first realized Tessa was ill,' Richard says.

Dad loves that. He talks about the flu-like illness which lasted for weeks and didn't ever seem to go away. He tells of how our GP didn't routinely pick up the cause because leukaemia is so rare.

'We noticed bruises,' he says. 'Small bleeds on Tessa's back, caused by a reduction of platelets.'

Dad's a hero. He talks about having to give up his job as a financial adviser, of the way our lives disappeared into hospitals and treatment.

'Cancer's not a local illness,' he says, 'but a disease of the whole body. Once Tess made the decision to stop the more aggressive treatments, we decided to manage in a holistic way at home. She's on a special diet. It's expensive to maintain, but I firmly believe it's not the food in your life that brings health, but the life in your food that really counts.'

I'm stunned by this. Does he want people to phone up and pledge money for organic vegetables?

Richard turns to me, his face serious. 'You decided to give up treatment, Tessa? That sounds like a very difficult decision to make at sixteen.'

My throat feels dry. 'Not really.'

He nods as if he's expecting more. I glance at Dad, who winks at me. 'Chemo prolongs your life,' I say, 'but it makes you feel bad. I was having some pretty heavy therapy and I knew if I stopped, I'd be able to do more things.'

'Your dad says you want to be famous,' Richard says. 'That's why you wanted to come on the radio today, isn't it? To grab your fifteen minutes of fame?'

He makes me sound like one of those sad little girls who put an advert in the local paper because they want to be a bridesmaid at someone's wedding, but don't know any brides. He makes me sound like a right twat.

I take a deep breath. 'I've got a list of things I want to do before I die. Being famous is on it.'

Richard's eyes light up. He's a journalist and knows a good story. 'Your dad didn't mention a list.'

'That's because most of the things on it are illegal.'

He was practically asleep talking to Dad, but now he's at the edge of his chair. 'Really? Like what?'

'Well, I took my dad's car and drove off for the day without a licence or having taken my test.'

'Ho, ho!' Richard chuckles. 'There go your insurance premiums, Mr Scott!' He nudges Dad to show he doesn't mean it badly, but Dad simply looks bewildered. I feel a surge of guilt and have to look away.

'One day I said yes to everything that was suggested.'

'What happened?'

'I ended up in a river.'

'There's an advert like that on TV,' Richard says. 'Is that where you got the idea?'

'No.'

'She nearly broke her neck on the back of a motorbike,' Dad

191

interrupts. He wants to get us back onto safe territory. But this was his idea and he can't get out of it now.

'I was almost arrested for shoplifting. I wanted to break as many laws as I could in a day.'

Richard's looking a little edgy now.

'Then there was sex.'

'Ah.'

'And drugs . . .'

'And rock 'n' roll!' Richard says breezily into his microphone. 'I've heard it said that being told you have a terminal illness can be seen as an opportunity to put your house in order, to complete any unfinished business. I think you'll agree, ladies and gents, that here is a young lady who is taking life by the horns.'

We're bundled out pretty sharpish. I think Dad's going to have a go at me, but he doesn't. We walk slowly up the stairs. I feel exhausted.

Dad says, 'People might give money. It's happened before. People will want to help you.'

My favourite Shakespeare play is *Macbeth*. When he kills the king, there are strange happenings across the land. Owls scream. Crickets cry. There's not enough water in the ocean to wash away all the blood.

'If we raise enough money, we could get you to that research institute in the States.'

'Money doesn't do it, Dad.'

'It does! We couldn't possibly afford it without help, and they've had some success with their immunity build-up programme.'

I hold onto the banister. It's made of plastic and is shiny and smooth.

'I want you to stop, Dad.'

'Stop what?'

'Stop pretending I'm going to be all right.'

Twenty-six

Dad sweeps a feather duster across the coffee table, over the mantelpiece and then across all four window ledges. He opens the curtains wider and switches on both lamps. It's as if he's trying to warn the dark away.

Mum, sitting next to me on the sofa, has a face shocked with the familiar. 'I'd forgotten,' she says.

'What?'

'The way you get in such a panic.'

He glares at her suspiciously. 'Is that an insult?'

She takes the duster from him and hands him the glass of sherry she's been swigging and re-filling since breakfast. 'Here,' she says. 'You've got some catching up to do.'

I think she woke up drunk. She certainly woke up in Dad's bed with him. Cal dragged me along the landing to look.

'Number seven,' I told him.

'What?'

'On my list. I was going to travel the world, but I swapped it for getting Mum and Dad back together.'

He grinned at me, as if it was all my doing, when actually they did it all by themselves. We opened our stockings and presents on their bedroom floor while they gazed sleepily down on us. It was like being in a time warp.

Dad goes over to the dining table now and shuffles forks and napkins about. He's decorated the table with crackers and little snowmen made of cotton wool. He's folded serviettes into origami lilies.

'I told them one o'clock,' he says.

Cal groans from behind his *Beano* annual. 'I don't know why you told them anything. They're weird.'

'Shush,' Mum tells him. 'Christmas spirit!'

'Christmas stupid,' he mumbles, and he rolls over on the carpet and stares mournfully up at her. 'I wish it was just us.'

Mum nudges him with her shoe, but he won't smile. She waves the feather duster at him. 'Want some of this?'

'Just try it!' He leaps up, laughing, and dashes across the room to Dad. Mum races after him, but Dad protects him by standing in her way and batting her off with fake karate chops.

'You're going to knock something over,' I tell them, but nobody listens. Instead, Mum shoves the feather duster between Dad's legs and jiggles it about. He grabs it from her and sticks it down her blouse, then chases her round the table.

It's odd how irritating I find it. I wanted them to get back together, but this isn't quite what I meant. I thought they'd be deeper than this.

They're making so much noise we miss the doorbell. There's

a sudden rap on the window.

'Oops,' Mum says. 'Our guests are here!' She looks giddy as she skips off to open the door. Dad adjusts his trousers. He's still smiling as he and Cal follow her out to the hallway.

I stay just where I am on the sofa. I cross my legs. I uncross them. I pick up the TV guide and casually flip through the pages.

'Look who's here,' Mum says as she steers Adam into the lounge. He's wearing a shirt with buttons, and chinos instead of jeans. He's combed his hair.

'Happy Christmas,' he says.

'You too.'

'I got you a card.'

Mum winks at me. 'I'll leave you two alone then.'

Which isn't exactly subtle.

Adam sits on the arm of the chair opposite and watches me open the card. It has a cartoon reindeer on the front with holly wrapped around its antlers. Inside, he's written, *Have a good one!* There are no kisses.

I stand it up on the coffee table between us and we both look at it. I ache with something. It feels thin and old, as if nothing will make it go away.

'About the other night . . .' I say.

He slides himself from the arm of the chair into the seat. 'What about it?'

'Do you think we should talk about it?'

He hesitates, as if this might be a trick question. 'Probably.'

'Because I was thinking maybe you were a bit freaked out.' I dare to look at him. 'Are you?'

But before he can answer, the lounge door opens and Cal comes crashing in.

'You got me juggling clubs!' he announces. He stands in front of Adam looking utterly amazed. 'How did you know I wanted them? They're so cool! Look, I can nearly do it already.'

He's useless. Clubs spin across the lounge in all directions. Adam laughs, picks them up, and then has a go himself. He's surprisingly good, managing seventeen catches before dropping them.

'You reckon you could do it with knives?' Cal asks him. 'Because I saw this man once who juggled with an apple and three knives. He peeled the apple and ate it while he juggled. Could you teach me to do that before I'm twelve?'

'I'll help you practise.'

How easy they are with each other as they flip the clubs between them. How easy it is for them to talk about the future.

Adam's mum comes in and sits next to me on the sofa. We shake hands, which is slightly weird. Her hands are small and dry. She looks tired, as if she's been travelling for days.

'I'm Sally,' she says. 'We've got a present for you too.'

She hands over a carrier bag. Inside is a box of chocolates. It's not even wrapped up. I get it out and turn it over on my lap.

Cal passes her the juggling clubs. 'Want to have a go?' She looks doubtful, but stands up anyway. 'I'll show you what to do,' he says.

197

Adam sits in her place next to me on the sofa. He leans in close and says, 'I'm not freaked out.'

He smiles. I smile back. I want to touch him but I can't, because Dad comes in, sherry bottle in one hand, carving knife in the other, and announces that dinner is served.

There's mountains of food. Dad's cooked turkey, roast and mashed potatoes, five different kinds of vegetables, stuffing and gravy. He's put his Bing Crosby CD on, and antique music about sleigh bells and snow drift over us as we eat.

I thought the adults would sit around discussing mortgages and being generally boring. But because Mum and Dad are a bit pissed, they're gently silly with each other and it's not awkward at all.

Even Sally can't help smiling as Mum tells the story of how her parents thought Dad was too working-class and banned her from seeing him. She talks of private schools and coming-out parties, of how she regularly stole her sister's pony and rode across town to the council estate to visit Dad at night.

He laughs at the memory. 'It was only a little market town, but I lived right on the other side. That poor pony was so knackered on a Saturday, it never won a gymkhana again.'

Mum tops up Sally's wineglass. Cal does a magic trick with the butter knife and his napkin.

Perhaps Sally's medication allows her to touch alternative realities, because it's really obvious how Cal's making the napkin move, but she looks at him in awe.

'Can you do anything else?' she asks.

He's delighted. 'Loads. I'll show you later.'

Adam's sitting opposite me. My foot's touching his under the table. Every bit of me is aware of this. I watch him eat. When he takes a sip of wine, I think of how his kisses might taste.

'Upstairs,' I tell him with my eyes. 'Upstairs now. Let's escape.'

What would they do? What could they do? We could undress, get into my bed.

'Crackers!' Mum cries. 'We forgot to pull the crackers!'

We cross arms and link up, a Christmas cracker chain round the table. Hats and jokes and plastic toys fly through the air as we pull.

Cal reads his joke out. *'What do you call Batman and Robin after they've been run over by a steamroller?'* Nobody knows. *'Flatman and Ribbon!'* he cries.

Everyone laughs, except for Sally. Maybe she's thinking about her dead husband. My joke's rubbish, about a man going into a bar, but it's an iron bar and he gets a headache. Adam's isn't even a joke, but an observation that if the universe had appeared today, all of recorded history would have happened in the last ten seconds.

'That's true,' Cal says. 'Human beings are really trivial compared to the solar system.'

'I think I might try to get a job in a cracker factory,' Mum says. 'Imagine making up jokes all year round, wouldn't that be fun?'

'I could put the bangers in,' Dad says, and he winks at her. They really have drunk way too much.

Sally touches her hair. 'Shall I read mine out?'

We all shush each other. Her eyes are sad as she reads. '*A duck goes into a chemist's to buy some lipstick. The chemist says, "That's fifty-nine pence." The duck says, "Thank you, could you put it on my bill please?"*'

Cal explodes with laughter. He throws himself off his chair onto the floor and waves his legs about. Sally's pleased, reads the joke out again. It *is* funny. It starts as a ripple in my belly, then moves up to my mouth. Sally laughs too, a great gulping sound. She looks surprised to make such a noise, which makes Mum, Dad and Adam start to chuckle. It's such a relief. Such a bloody relief. I can't remember the last time I laughed out loud. Tears roll down my cheeks. Adam passes me his napkin across the table.

'Here.' His fingers brush mine.

I wipe my eyes. Upstairs, upstairs. I want to run my hands along you. And I'm just about to say it out loud, just about to say, 'I've got something for you, Adam, but it's in my bedroom, so you'll have to come and get it,' when there's a rap on the window.

It's Zoey, her face pressed against the glass, like Mary in the Christmas story. She wasn't supposed to be here until tea time, and her parents were meant to be coming with her.

She brings in the cold. She stamps her feet on the carpet in front of us all. 'Merry Christmas, everyone,' she says.

Dad raises his glass to her and wishes her the same. Mum gets up and gives her a hug.

Zoey says, 'Thank you.' Then she bursts into tears.

Mum gets her a chair and some tissues. From somewhere two mince pies appear with a large dollop of brandy butter. Zoey shouldn't really have alcohol, but maybe the butter doesn't count.

'When I looked through the window,' she sniffs, 'it looked like something from an advert. I nearly went home.'

Dad says, 'What's going on, Zoey?'

She stuffs a spoonful of pie and brandy butter into her mouth, chews quickly, then swallows it down. 'What do you want to know?'

'Whatever you want to tell us.'

'Well, my nose is stuffed up and I feel like crap. Do you want to know about that?'

'That's caused by an increase in HCG,' I tell her. 'It's the pregnancy hormone.' There's a moment's silence around the table as everyone looks at me. 'I read it in the Reader's Digest.'

I'm not sure I should have said this out loud. I forgot that Adam, Cal and Sally don't even know Zoey's pregnant. None of them say anything though, and Zoey doesn't seem to mind, just shoves another load of pie into her mouth.

Dad says, 'Has something happened at home, Zoey?'

She carefully reloads her spoon. 'I've told my parents.'

'You told them today?' He sounds surprised.

She wipes her mouth with her sleeve. 'It may have been bad timing.'

'What did they say?'

'They said a million things, all of them terrible. They hate me. Everyone hates me in fact. Except for the baby.'

Cal grins. 'You're having a baby?'

'Yeah.'

'I bet it's a boy.'

She shakes her head at him. 'I don't want a boy.'

Dad says, 'But you do want a baby?' He says this very gently.

Zoey hesitates, as if she's thinking about this for the very first time. Then she smiles at him, her eyes watery and amazed. I've never seen such a look on her face before. 'Yes,' she says. 'I really think I do. I'm going to call her Lauren.'

She's nineteen weeks pregnant, her baby is fully formed and weighs roughly two hundred and forty grammes. If it were born now, it would fit into the palm of my hand. Its stomach would be pink-veined and transparent. If I spoke, it would hear me.

I say, 'I've put your baby on my list.' I probably shouldn't have said this out loud either. I didn't really mean to. Once again, every-one stares at me.

Dad reaches out a hand and touches mine across the table. 'Tessa,' he says.

I hate that. I shrug him off. 'I want to be there.'

Zoey says, 'It's another five months, Tess.'

'So? That's only a hundred and sixty days. But if you don't want me there, I can sit outside and maybe come in afterwards. I want to be one of the first people in the world to ever hold her.'

She stands up and walks round the table. She wraps her arms around me. She feels different. Her tummy's gone all hard and she's very hot.

'Tessa,' she says, 'I *want* you to be there.'

Twenty-seven

The afternoon goes quickly. The table's cleared and the TV's turned on. We all listen to the Queen's speech, then Cal does a few magic tricks.

Zoey spends the afternoon on the sofa with Sally and Mum, going through every detail of her doomed love affair with Scott. She even asks for their advice on childbirth. 'Tell me,' she says, 'does it hurt as much as they say?'

Dad's engrossed in his new book, *Eating Organic*. He occasionally reads out statistics about chemicals and pesticides to anyone who's interested.

Adam mostly talks to Cal. He shows him how to spin the clubs; he teaches him a new coin trick. I keep changing my mind about him. Not if I fancy him or not, but if he likes me. Every now and then his eyes catch mine across the room, but he always looks away before I do.

'He wants you,' Zoey mouths at me at one point. But if it's true, I don't know how to make it happen.

I've spent the afternoon flicking through the book Cal got me,

A Hundred Weird Ways to Meet Your Maker. It's quite funny, but it doesn't stop me feeling as if there's a space inside me that's shrinking. I've sat in this chair in the corner for two hours, and I've separated myself. I know I do it and I know it isn't right, but I don't know how else to be.

By four o'clock it's dark and Dad's switched on all the lights. He brings out bowls of sweets and nuts. Mum suggests a game of cards. I sidle out to the hallway while they rearrange the chairs. I've had enough of stagnant walls and bookshelves. I've had enough of central heating and party games. I get my coat from its hook and go out into the garden.

The cold is shocking. It ignites my lungs, turns my breath to smoke. I put my hood up, pull the drawstring tight under my chin and wait.

Slowly, as if arriving out of mist, everything in the garden comes into focus – the holly bush scratching the shed, a bird on the fence post, its feathers fluffing in the wind.

Indoors they'll be dealing out the cards and passing round the peanuts, but out here, each blade of grass glistens, spiked by frost. Out here, the sky's packed full of stars, like something from a fairy-tale. Even the moon looks stunned.

I squash windfalls under my boots on my way to the apple tree. I touch the twists in the trunk, trying to feel its bruised slate colour through my fingers. A few leaves hang damply in the branches. A handful of withered apples turn to rust.

Cal says that humans are made from the nuclear ash of dead stars. He says that when I die, I'll return to dust, glitter, rain. If that's true, I want to be buried right here under this tree. Its roots will reach into the soft mess of my body and suck me dry. I'll be re-formed as apple blossom. I'll drift down in the spring like confetti and cling to my family's shoes. They'll carry me in their pockets, scatter the subtle silk of me across their pillows to help them sleep. What dreams will they have then?

In the summer they'll eat me. Adam will climb over the fence to steal me, maddened by my scent, by my roundness, the shine and health of me. He'll get his mum to cook me up in a crumble or a strudel and then he'll gorge on me.

I lie on the ground and try to imagine it. Really, really. I'm dead. I'm turning into an apple tree. It's a bit difficult though. I wonder about the bird I saw earlier, if it's flown away. I wonder what they're doing indoors, if they miss me yet.

I turn over and press my face right into the grass; it pushes coldly back at me. I rake my hands through it, bring up my fingers to smell the earth. It smells of leaf mould, worm breath.

'What are you doing?'

I turn round very slowly. Adam's face is upside down. 'I thought I'd come and look for you. Are you all right?'

I sit up and brush the dirt from my trousers. 'I'm fine. I was hot.'

He nods, as if this explains why I have wet leaves stuck to my coat. I look like an idiot, I know I do. I also have my hood tied under my chin like an old woman. I undo it quickly.

His jacket creaks as he sits down next to me. 'Want a rollie?'

I take the cigarette he offers and let him light it. He lights his own and we blow silent smoke across the garden. I can feel him watching me. My thoughts are so clear that I wouldn't be surprised if he could see them blazing above my head like a neon sign outside a fish and chip shop. I fancy you. I fancy you. *Flash. Flash. Flash.* With a neon red heart glowing beside the words.

I lie back on the grass to get away from his gaze. Cold seeps through my trousers like water.

He lies down next to me, right next to me. It hurts and hurts to have him this close. I feel sick with it.

'That's Orion's Belt,' he says.

'What is?'

He points up to the sky. 'See those three stars in a line? Mintaka, Alnilam, Alnitak.' They bloom at the end of his finger as he names them.

'How do you know that?'

'When I was a kid, my dad used to tell me stories about the constellations. If you point binoculars below Orion, you'll see a giant gas cloud where all new stars are born.'

'New stars? I thought the universe was dying.'

'It depends which way you look at it. It's also expanding.' He rolls over onto his side and props himself up with one elbow. 'I've been hearing from your brother about you being famous.'

'And did he tell you it was a complete disaster?'

He laughs. 'No, but now you have to.'

206

I like making him laugh. He has a beautiful mouth and it gives me the chance to look at him. So I tell him about the whole radio station ridiculousness and I make it much funnier than it really was. I sound heroic, an anarchist of the airwaves. Then, because it's going so well, I tell him about taking Dad's car and driving Zoey to the hotel. We lie on the damp grass with the sky massive above us, the moon low and bright, and I tell him about the wardrobe, and how my name has gone from the world. I even tell him about my habit of writing on walls. It's easy to talk in the dark – I never knew that before.

When I've finished, he says, 'You shouldn't worry about being forgotten, Tess.' Then he says, 'Do you reckon they'll miss us if we go next door for ten minutes?'

We both smile.

Flash, flash, goes the sign above my head.

As we go through the broken bit of fence and up the path to his back door, his arm brushes mine. We hardly touch at all, but it's startling.

I follow him into the kitchen. 'I'll just be a minute,' he says. 'I've got a present for you,' and he disappears into the hallway and runs up the stairs.

I miss him as soon as he goes. When he isn't with me, I think I made him up.

'Adam?' It's the first time I've ever called his name. It sounds strange on my tongue, and powerful, as if something will happen if I say it often enough. I go into the hallway and look up the stairs. 'Adam?'

'Up here. Come up if you want.'

So I do.

His room's the same as mine, but backwards. He's sitting on his bed. He looks different, awkward. He has a small silver parcel in his hand.

'I don't even know if you're going to like this.'

I sit next to him. Every night we sleep with only a wall between us. I'm going to knock a hole in the wall behind my wardrobe and make a secret entrance to his world.

'Here,' he says. 'I suppose you better open it.'

Inside the wrapping paper is a bag. Inside the bag is a box. Inside the box is a bracelet – seven stones, all different colours, bound with a silver chain.

'I know you're trying not to acquire new things, but I thought you might like it.'

I'm so startled I can't speak.

He says, 'Shall I help you put it on?'

I hold out my hand and he wraps the chain around my wrist and does up the clasp. Then he threads his fingers with mine. We look down at our hands, together on the bed between us. Mine look different, entangled with his, the new bracelet on my wrist. And his hands are completely new to me.

'Tessa?' he says.

This is his room. With only a wall between my bed and his. We're holding hands. He bought me a bracelet.

'Tessa?' he says again.

When I look at him, it feels like fear. His eyes are green and full of shadows. His mouth is beautiful. He leans towards me and I know. I know.

It hasn't happened yet, but it's going to.

Number eight is love.

Twenty-eight

My heart stumbles. 'I can do that.'

'No,' Adam says. 'Let me.'

Each buckle gets his absolute attention, then he slides my boots off and places them side by side on the floor.

I join him on the rug. I undo his laces, put each of his feet on my lap in turn and pull off his trainers. I stroke his ankles, my hand running under his trousers and up his calves. I'm touching him. I'm touching the soft hair on his legs. I never knew I could be so brave.

We make it a game, like strip poker, but without the cards or dice. I unzip his jacket and let it fall to the floor. He undoes my coat and slides it off my shoulders. He finds a leaf from the garden in my hair. I touch his dark curls, twine their strength through my fingers.

Nothing seems small with him watching, so I take my time with the buttons on his shirt. This last one condenses into a planet under our gaze – milky white and perfectly round.

It's astounding that we both know what to do. I'm not even

having to think about it. I'm not being dragged along. It's not slick or knowing. It's as if we're discovering the path together.

I hold my hands over my head like a child as he peels my jumper off me. My hair, my new short hair, gets caught in static and crackles in the dark. It makes me laugh. It makes me feel as if my body is plump and healthy.

The backs of his fingers brush my breasts through my bra, and he knows, because we're looking at each other, that this is OK. I've been touched by so many people, prodded and poked, examined and operated on. I thought my body was numb, immune to touch.

We kiss again. For minutes. Tiny kisses where he bites my top lip gently, where my tongue edges his mouth. The room seems full of ghosts, of trees, the sky.

Our kisses become deeper. We sink into each other. It's like the first time we kissed – urgent, fierce.

'I want you,' he says.

And I want him right back.

I want to show him my breasts. I want to undo my bra and get them out. I pull him towards the bed. We're still kissing – throats, necks, mouths. The room seems full of smoke, with something burning here between us.

I lie on the bed and buck my hips. I need my jeans off. I want to display myself to him, want him to see me.

'Are you sure about this?' he says.

'Very.'

It's simple.

He unbuckles my jeans. I undo his belt with one hand, like a magic trick. I circle his belly button with my finger, my thumb nudging at his boxers.

The feel of his skin next to mine, the weight of him on top of me, his warmth pressing into me – I didn't know it would feel like this. I didn't understand that when you make love, you actually do *make* love. Stir things. Affect each other. The breath that escapes from me is dazzled. He breathes it in with a gasp.

His hand slides under my hip, I meet it with mine, our fingers lock. I'm not sure whose hand belongs to who.

I'm Tessa.

I'm Adam.

It's utterly beautiful not to know my own edges.

The feel of us under our fingers. The taste of us on our tongues.

And always we watch each other, check with each other, like music, like a dance. Eye to eye.

It builds, this ache between us, changing and swelling. I want him. I want him closer. I can't get near enough. I wrap my legs round his, sweep his back with my hands, trying to pull him further into me.

It's as if my heart springs up and marries my soul, as my whole body implodes. Like a stone falling in a pond, circles and circles of love ripple through me.

Adam shouts for joy.

I gather him and hold him close. I'm amazed at him. At us. This gift.

He strokes my head, my face, he kisses my tears.

I'm alive, blessed to be with him on this earth, at this very moment.

Twenty-nine

Blood spills from my nose. I stand in front of the hall mirror and watch it pour down my chin and through my fingers until my hands are slippery with it. It drips onto the floor and spreads into the weave of the carpet.

'Please,' I whisper. 'Not now. Not tonight.'

But it doesn't stop.

Upstairs, I hear Mum say goodnight to Cal. She closes his bedroom door and goes into the bathroom. I wait, listening to her pee, then the flush of the toilet. I imagine her washing her hands at the sink, drying them on the towel. Perhaps she looks at herself in the mirror, just as I'm doing down here. I wonder if she feels as far away as I do, as dazed by her own reflection.

She closes the bathroom door and comes down the stairs. I step into her path as she appears on the bottom step.

'Oh my God!'

'I've got a nosebleed.'

'It's pumping out of you!' She flaps her arms at me. 'In here, quick!' She pushes me into the lounge. Heavy, dull drops

214

splash the carpet as I walk. Poppies blooming at my feet.

'Sit down,' she commands. 'Lean back and pinch your nose.'

This is the opposite of what you're supposed to do, so I ignore her. Adam'll be here in ten minutes and we're going dancing. Mum stands watching me for a moment, then rushes out of the room. I think maybe she's gone to throw up, but she comes back with a tea towel and thrusts it at me.

'Lean back. Press this against your nose.'

Since my way's not working, I do as she says. Blood leaks down my throat. I swallow as much as I can, but loads of it goes in my mouth and I can't really breathe. I sit forward and spit onto the tea towel. A big clot glistens back at me, alien dark. It's definitely not something that's supposed to be outside my body.

'Give that to me,' Mum says.

I hand it over and she looks at it closely before wrapping it up. Her hands, like mine, are smeared with blood now.

'What am I going to do, Mum? He'll be here soon.'

'It'll stop in a minute.'

'Look at my clothes!'

She shakes her head at me in despair. 'You better lie down.'

This is also the wrong thing to do, but it's not stopping, so everything's ruined anyway. Mum sits on the edge of the sofa. I lie back and watch shapes brighten and dissolve. I imagine I'm on a sinking ship. A shadow flaps its wings at me.

Mum says, 'Does that feel any better?'

'Much.'

I don't think she believes me, because she goes out to the

kitchen and comes back with the ice-cube tray. She squats next to the sofa and empties it onto her lap. Ice cubes skate off her jeans and onto the carpet. She picks one up, wipes the fluff off and hands it to me.

'Hold this on your nose.'

'Frozen peas would be better, Mum.'

She thinks about this for a second, then rushes off again, returning with a packet of sweetcorn.

'Will this do? There weren't any peas.'

It makes me laugh, which I guess is something.

'What?' she says. 'What's so funny?'

Her mascara is smeared, her hair flyaway. I reach for her arm and she helps me sit up. I feel ancient. I swing my legs onto the floor and pinch the top of my nose between two fingers like they showed me at the hospital. My pulse is pounding against my head.

'It's not stopping, is it? I'm going to call Dad.'

'He'll think you can't cope.'

'Let him.'

She dials his number quickly. She gets it wrong, re-dials.

'Come on, come on,' she says under her breath.

The room is very pale. All the ornaments on the mantelpiece bleached as bones.

'He's not answering. Why isn't he answering? How noisy can it be at a bowling alley?'

'It's his first night out for weeks, Mum. Leave him. We'll manage.'

Her face crashes. She hasn't dealt with a single transfusion or

216

lumbar puncture. She wasn't allowed near me for the bone-marrow transplant, but she could have been there for any number of diagnoses, and wasn't. Even her promises to visit more often have faded away with Christmas. It's her turn to taste some reality.

'You have to take me to hospital, Mum.'

She looks horrified. 'Dad's got the car.'

'Call a cab.'

'What about Cal?'

'He's asleep, isn't he?'

She nods forlornly, the logistics beyond her.

'Write him a note.'

'We can't leave him on his own!'

'He's eleven, Mum, practically a grown-up.'

She hesitates only briefly, then scrolls through her address book to dial a cab. I watch her face, but my focus won't really hold. All I get is an impression of fear and bewilderment. I close my eyes and think of a mother I saw in a film once. She lived on a mountain with a gun and lots of children. She was sure and certain. I stick this mother on top of mine, like plaster on a wound.

When I open my eyes again, she's clutching armfuls of towels and tugging at my coat. 'You probably shouldn't go to sleep,' she says. 'Come on, let's get you up. That was the door.'

I feel dazed and hot, as if everything might be a dream. She hauls me up and we shuffle out to the hallway together. I can hear whispering coming from the wall.

But it's not the cab, it's Adam, all dressed up for our date. I try and hide, try and stumble back into the lounge, but he sees me.

'Tess,' he says. 'Oh my God! What's happened?'

'Nosebleed,' Mum tells him. 'We thought you were the cab.'

'You're going to the hospital? I'll take you in my dad's car.'

He steps into the hallway and tries to put his arm around me as if we're all just going to walk to his car and get in. As if he's going to drive and I'm going to bleed all over the upholstery and none of it matters. I look like road kill. Doesn't he understand that he really shouldn't be seeing me like this?

I shove him off. 'Go home, Adam.'

'I'm taking you to the hospital,' he says again, as if perhaps I didn't hear him the first time, or maybe the blood has made me stupid.

Mum takes his arm and gently leads him back out of the door. 'We'll manage,' she says. 'It's all right. Anyway, look, the cab's here now.'

'I want to be with her.'

'I know,' she tells him. 'I'm sorry.'

He touches my hand as I walk past him up the path. 'Tess,' he says.

I don't answer. I don't even look at him, because his voice is so clear that if I look I might change my mind. To find love just as I go and have to give it up – it's such a bad joke. But I have to. For him and for me. Before it starts hurting even more than this.

Mum spreads towels across the back seat of the cab, makes sure we're belted up, then encourages the driver to do a very dramatic U-turn outside the gate.

'That's it,' Mum tells him. 'Put your foot down.' She sounds as if she's in a movie.

Adam watches from the gate. He waves. He gets smaller and smaller as we drive away.

Mum says, 'That was kind of him.'

I close my eyes. I feel as if I'm falling even though I'm sitting down.

Mum nudges me with her elbow. 'Stay awake.'

The moon bounces through the window. In the headlights – mist.

We were going dancing. I wanted to try alcohol again. I wanted to stand on tables and sing cheering songs. I wanted to climb over the fence in the park, steal a boat and circle the lake. I wanted to go back to Adam's house and creep up to his room and make love.

'Adam,' I say under my breath. But it gets covered in blood like everything else.

At the hospital, they find me a wheelchair and make me sit in it. I'm an emergency, they tell me as they rush me away from the reception area. We leave behind the ordinary victims of pub brawls, bad drugs and late-night domestics and we speed down the corridor to somewhere more important.

I find the layers of a hospital strangely reassuring. This is a duplicate world with its own rules and everyone has their place. In the emergency rooms will be the young men with fast cars and crap brakes. The motorcyclists who took a bend too sharply.

In the operating theatres are the people who mucked around

with air rifles, or who got followed home by a psychopath. Also, the victims of random accident – the child whose hair got caught in an escalator, the woman wearing an underwired bra in a lightning storm.

And in bed, deep inside the building, are all the headaches that won't go away. The failed kidneys, the rashes, the ragged-edged moles, the lumps on the breast, the coughs that have turned nasty. In the Marie Curie Ward on the fourth floor are the kids with cancer. Their bodies secretly and slowly being consumed.

And then there's the mortuary, where the dead lie in refrigerated drawers with name tags on their feet.

The room I end up in is bright and sterile. There's a bed, a sink, a doctor and a nurse.

'I think she's thirsty,' Mum says. 'She's lost so much blood. Shouldn't she have a drink?'

The doctor dismisses this with a wave of his hand. 'We need to pack her nose.'

'Pack it?'

The nurse ushers Mum to a chair and sits down next to her. 'The doctor will put strips of gauze in her nose to stop the blood,' she says. 'You're welcome to stay.'

I'm shivering. The nurse gets up to give me a blanket and pulls it up to my chin. I shiver again.

'Someone's dreaming about you,' Mum says. 'That's what that means.'

I always thought it meant that, in another life, someone was standing on my grave.

The doctor pinches my nose, peers in my mouth, feels my throat and the back of my neck.

'Mum?' he says.

She looks startled, sits upright in her chair. 'Me?'

'Any signs of thrombocytopenia before today?'

'Sorry?'

'Has she complained of a headache? Have you noticed any pin-prick bruising?'

'I didn't look.'

The doctor sighs, clocks in a moment that this is a whole new language for her, yet, strangely, persists.

'When was the last platelet transfusion?'

Mum looks increasingly bewildered. 'I'm not sure.'

'Has she used aspirin products recently?'

'I'm sorry. I don't know any of this.'

I decide to save her. She's not strong enough, and she might just walk out if it gets too difficult.

'December the twenty-first was the last platelet transfusion,' I say. My voice sounds raspy. Blood bubbles in my throat.

The doctor frowns at me. 'Don't talk. Mum, get yourself over here and take your daughter's hand.'

She obediently comes to sit on the edge of the bed.

'Squeeze your mum's hand once for yes,' the doctor tells me. 'Twice for no. Understand?'

'Yes.'

'Shush,' he says. 'Squeeze. Don't talk.'

We go through the same routine – the bruising, the headaches, the aspirin, but this time Mum knows the answers.

'Bonjela or Teejel?' the doctor asks.

Two squeezes. 'No,' Mum tells him. 'She hasn't used them.'

'Anti-inflammatories?'

'No,' Mum says. She looks me in the eyes. She speaks my language at last.

'Good,' the doctor says. 'I'm going to pack the front of your nose with gauze. If that doesn't do it, we'll pack the back, and if the bleeding still persists, we'll have to cauterize. Have you had your nose cauterized before?'

I squeeze Mum's hand so hard that she winces. 'Yes, she has.'

It hurts like hell. I could smell my own flesh burning for days.

'We'll need to check your platelets,' he goes on. 'I'd be surprised if you weren't below twenty.' He touches my knee through the blanket. 'I'm sorry. It's a rotten night for you.'

'Below twenty?' Mum echoes.

'She'll probably need a couple of units,' he explains. 'Don't worry, it shouldn't take more than an hour.'

As he packs sterile cotton into my nose, I try and concentrate on simple things – a chair, the twin silver birch trees in Adam's garden and the way their leaves shiver in sunlight.

But I can't hold onto it.

I feel as if I've eaten a sanitary towel; my mouth is dry and it's hard to breathe. I look at Mum, but all I see is that she's feeling squeamish and has turned her face away. How can I feel older than my own mother? I close my eyes so I don't have to see her fail.

'Uncomfortable?' the doctor asks. 'Mum, any chance of distracting her?'

I wish he hadn't said that. What's she going to do? Dance for us? Sing? Perhaps she'll do her famous disappearing act and walk out of the door.

The silence goes on a long time. Then, 'Do you remember the day we all tried oysters, and how your dad was sick in the bin at the end of the pier?'

I open my eyes. Whatever shadows are in the room disappear with the brightness of her words. Even the nurse smiles.

'They tasted exactly of the sea,' she says. 'Do you remember?'

I do. We bought four, one for each of us. Mum tipped her head right back and swallowed hers whole. I did the same. But Dad chewed his and it got stuck in his teeth. He ran down the pier clutching his stomach, and when he came back, he drank a whole can of lemonade without pausing for breath. Cal didn't like them either. 'Perhaps they're a female thing,' Mum said, and she bought us both another one.

She goes on to describe a seaside town and a hotel, a short walk to the beach and days when the sun shone bright and warm.

'You loved it there,' she says. 'You'd collect shells and pebbles for hours. Once you tied some rope to a lump of driftwood and spent an entire day dragging it up and down the beach pretending you had a dog.'

The nurse laughs at this and Mum smiles. 'You were a wonderfully imaginative little girl,' she tells me. 'Such an easy child.'

And if I could talk, I'd ask her why, then, did she leave me? And maybe she'd speak at last of the man she left Dad for. She might tell me of a love so big that I'd begin to understand.

But I can't talk. My throat feels small and feverish. So instead, I listen as Mum explores an old sun, faded days, past beauty. It's good. She's very inventive. Even the doctor looks as if he's enjoying himself. In her story, the sky shimmers, and day after day we see dolphins playing in the sea.

'Supplementary oxygen,' the doctor says. And he winks at me as if he's offering me dope. 'No need to cauterize. Well done.' He has a word with the nurse, then turns in the doorway to wave goodbye. 'Best customer tonight so far,' he tells me, then he gives Mum a little bow. 'And you weren't so bad either.'

'Well, what a night that was!' Mum says as we finally climb into a cab to take us home.

'I liked you being with me.'

She looks surprised, pleased even. 'I'm not sure how much use I was.'

Early-morning light spills from the sky onto the road. It's cold in the taxi, the air rarefied, like inside a church.

'Here,' Mum says, and she unbuttons her coat and wraps it round my shoulders.

'Step on it,' she tells the driver, and we both chuckle.

We drive back the way we came. She's very talkative, full of plans for spring and Easter. She wants to spend more time at our house, she says. She wants to invite some of her and Dad's old friends for dinner. She might want a party for my birthday in May.

Perhaps she means it this time.

'Do you know,' she says, 'every night when the market stalls are being packed away, I go out and collect vegetables and fruit off the ground. Sometimes they chuck away whole boxes of mangoes. Last week I got five sea bass just lying there in a plastic bag. If I begin to put things in Dad's freezer, we'll have plenty for parties and dinners and it won't cost your father a penny.'

She gets lost in party games and cocktails. She talks of bands and entertainers; she hires the local community hall and covers it in streamers and balloons. I nudge up next to her and put my head on her shoulder. I'm her daughter after all. I try and keep really still because I don't want it to change. It's lovely being lulled by her words and the warmth of her coat.

'Look,' she says. 'That's strange.'

It's a struggle to open my eyes. 'What is?'

'There on the bridge. That wasn't there before.'

We've stopped at the traffic lights outside the railway station. Even at this early hour it's busy, with taxis dropping off commuters determined to beat the rush. On the bridge, high above the road, letters have blossomed during the night. Several people are looking. There's a wobbly T, a jagged E, and four interlinked curves for the double S. At the end, bigger than the other letters, there's a mountainous A.

Mum says, 'That's a coincidence.'

But it's not.

My phone's in my pocket. My fingers furl and unfurl.

He would've done this last night. It would've been dark. He climbed the wall, straddled it, then leaned right over.

My heart hurts. I get out my phone and text: R U ALIVE?

The lights change through amber to green. The cab moves under the bridge and along the High Street.

It's half past six. Will he even be awake? What if he lost his balance and plummeted onto the road below?

'Oh my goodness,' Mum says. 'You're everywhere!'

The shops in the High Street still have their metal grilles down, blank-eyed and sleeping. My name is scrawled across them all. I'm outside Ajay's newsagent's. I'm on the expensive shutters of the health food store. I'm massive on Handie's furniture shop, King's Chicken Joint and the Barbecue Café. I thread the pavement outside the bank and all the way to Mothercare. I've possessed the road and am a glistening circle at the roundabout.

'It's a miracle!' Mum whispers.

'It's Adam.'

'From next door?' She sounds amazed, as if there's magic afoot.

My phone bleeps. AM ALIVE. U?

I laugh out loud. When I get back, I'm going to knock on his door and tell him I'm sorry. He's going to smile at me the way he did yesterday when he was carrying garden rubbish down the path and he saw me watching and said, 'Just can't keep away, can you?' It made me laugh, because actually it was true, but saying it out loud made it not so painful.

'Adam did this for you?' Mum shivers with excitement. She always did believe in romance.

226

I text him back. AM ALIVE 2. CMING HME NOW.

Zoey asked me once, 'What's the best moment of your life so far?' And I told her about the time I was practising handstands with my friend Lorraine. I was eight, the school fair was the next day, and Mum had promised to buy me a jewellery box. I lay on the grass holding Lorraine's hand, dizzy with happiness and absolutely certain that the world was good.

Zoey thought I was nuts. But really, it was the first time I'd ever known I was happy in such a conscious way.

Kissing Adam replaced it. Making love replaced that. And now he's done this for me. He's made me famous. He's put my name on the world. I've been in hospital all night, my head's stuffed with cotton. I'm clutching a paper bag full of antibiotics and painkillers, and my arm aches from two units of platelets delivered through my portacath. And yet, it's extraordinary how happy I feel.

Thirty

'I want Adam to move in.'

Dad turns from the sink, his hands dripping soapsuds onto the floor. He looks utterly stunned. 'Don't be ridiculous!'

'I mean it.'

'Where's he supposed to sleep?'

'In my bedroom.'

'There's no way I'm agreeing to that, Tess!' He turns back to the sink, clunks bowls and plates about. 'Is this on your list? Is having a live-in boyfriend on your list?'

'His name's Adam.'

He shakes his head. 'Forget it.'

'Then I'll move into his house.'

'You think his mother will want you there?'

'We'll bugger off to Scotland and live in a croft then. Would you prefer that?'

His mouth twitches with anger as he turns back to me. 'The answer's no, Tess.'

I hate the way he pulls authority, as if it's all sorted because he says so. I stomp upstairs to my room and slam the door. He thinks it's about sex. Can't he see it's deeper than that? And can't he see how difficult it is to ask for?

Three weeks ago, at the end of January, Adam took me out on the bike, faster than before and further – to a place on the borders of Kent where there's flat marshy land sloping down to a beach. There were four wind turbines out at sea, their ghostly blades spinning.

He skimmed stones at the waves and I sat on the shingle and told him how my list is sprawling away from me.

'There are so many things I want. Ten isn't enough any more.'

'Tell me,' he said.

It was easy at first. On and on I went. Spring. Daffodils and tulips. Swimming under a calm blue evening sky. A long train journey, a peacock, a kite. Another summer. But I couldn't tell him the thing I want the most.

That night he went home. Every night he goes home to keep his mother safe. He sleeps just metres away from me, through the wall, on the other side of the wardrobe.

The next day he turned up with tickets for the zoo. We went on the train. We saw wolves and antelopes. A peacock opened its tail for me, emerald and aquamarine. We had lunch in a café and Adam bought me a fruit platter with black grapes and vivid slices of mango.

A few days later he took me to a heated outdoor pool. After swimming, we sat on the edge, wrapped in towels, and dangled our feet in the water. We drank hot chocolate and laughed at the children hollering in the cold air.

One morning he delivered a bowl of crocuses to my room.

'Spring,' he said.

He took me to our hill on his bike. He'd bought a pocket kite from the newsagent's and we flew it together.

Day after day it was as if someone had taken my life apart and polished every bit of it really carefully before putting it all back together.

But we never shared a single night.

Then, on Valentine's day, I got anaemic only twelve days after a blood transfusion.

'What does it mean?' I asked the consultant.

'You've moved nearer the line,' he said.

It's getting harder to breathe. The shadows under my eyes have deepened. My lips look like plastic stretched over a gate.

Last night I woke up at two in the morning. My legs were hurting, a dull throbbing, like a toothache. I'd taken paracetamol before going to bed, but I needed codeine. On the way to the bathroom I passed Dad's open bedroom door and Mum was in there – her hair spilling across the pillow, his arm flung protectively across her. That's three times she's stayed over in the last two weeks.

I stood on the landing watching them sleep and I knew for a fact that I couldn't be alone in the dark any more.

Mum comes upstairs and sits on my bed. I'm standing at the window watching the dusk. The sky is full of something, the clouds low down and expectant.

'I hear you want Adam to move in,' she says.

I write my name in condensation on the window. My finger marks smeared across the glass make me feel young.

She says, 'Your dad might agree to the occasional night, Tess, but he's not going to let Adam live here.'

'Dad said he'd help me with my list.'

'He *is* helping. He's just bought us all tickets to go to Sicily, hasn't he?'

'Because he wants to spend a whole week with you!'

When I turn to look at her, she frowns at me as if I'm someone she's never seen before.

'Did he actually say that?'

'He's in love with you, it's obvious. Travel isn't even on my list any more.'

She looks bemused. 'I thought travel was number seven.'

'I swapped it for getting you and Dad back together.'

'Oh, Tessa!'

It's weird, because of all people, she should understand about love. I fold my arms at her. 'Tell me about him.'

'Who?'

'The man you left us for.'

She shakes her head. 'Why are you bringing this up now?'

'Because you said you didn't have a choice. Isn't that what you said?'

'I said I was unhappy.'

'Lots of people are unhappy, but they don't run away.'

'Please, Tess, I really don't want to talk about this.'

231

'We loved you.'

Plural. Past tense. But still it sounds too big for this little room.

She looks up at me, her face pale and angular. 'I'm sorry.'

'You must've loved him more than you'd ever loved anyone. He must've been wonderful, some kind of magical person.'

She doesn't say anything.

Simple. A love that big. I turn back to the window. 'Then you should understand how I feel about Adam.'

She gets up and comes over. She doesn't touch me, but stands very close. 'Does he feel the same way about you, Tess?'

'I don't know.'

I want to lean on her and pretend that everything's going to be OK. But I just smear my name off the window and look out at the night instead. It's strangely gloomy out there.

'I'll talk to Dad,' she says. 'He's seeing Cal to bed, but when he's finished, I'll take him out for a beer. Will you be all right by yourselves?'

'I'll ask Adam over. I'll make him supper.'

'All right.' She turns to go, then at the doorway turns back. 'You want some sweet and lovely things, Tessa, but be careful. Other people can't always give you what you want.'

I cut four giant slices of bread onto the chopping board and put them under the grill. I get tomatoes from the vegetable rack, and because Adam stands with his back against the sink watching me, I hold a tomato cupped in each hand at breast height and shimmy back to the counter with them.

He laughs. I slice both tomatoes and place them on the grill next to the toast. I get the grater from the cupboard, the cheese from the fridge, and grate a pile of cheese onto the chopping board while the toast cooks. I know there's a gap between the bottom of my T-shirt and the waistband of my trousers. I know there's a particular curve (the only curve I have left) where my spine meets my bum, and that when I lean on one hip, that curve pushes itself towards Adam.

After grating the cheese I lick each finger in turn, very deliberately, and it does just what I knew it would. He walks over and kisses the back of my neck.

'Want to know what I'm thinking?' he whispers.

'Tell me.' Although I already know.

'I want you.' He turns me round and kisses me on the mouth. 'A lot.'

He talks as if he's been grabbed by a force that he doesn't understand. I love it. I press myself against him.

I say, 'Want to know what I want?'

'Go on then.'

He smiles. He thinks he knows what I'm going to say. I don't want to stop him smiling. 'You.'

The truth. And not the truth.

I turn the gas off before we go upstairs. The toast has turned to charcoal. The smell of burning makes me sad.

In his arms I forget. But afterwards, as we lie quietly together, I remember.

'I have bad dreams,' I say.

He strokes my hip, the top of my thigh. His hand is warm and firm. 'Tell me.'

'I go somewhere in them.'

I walk bare-footed over fields to a place at the edge of this world. I climb stiles and trek through tall grass. Every night I go further. Last night I got to a wood – gloomy and not very big. On the other side was a river. Mist hovered above the surface. There were no fish, and as I waded out, mud oozed between my toes.

Adam brushes my cheek with one finger. Then he pulls me close and kisses me. On my cheek. On my chin. On my other cheek. Then on my mouth. Very gently.

'I'd come with you if I could.'

'It's very scary.'

He nods. 'I'm very brave.'

I know he is. How many people would be here with me in the first place?

'Adam, there's something I need to ask you.'

He waits. His head next to mine on the pillow, his eyes calm. It's difficult. I can't find the words. The books on the shelf above seem to sigh and shuffle.

He sits up and hands me a pen. 'Write it on the wall.'

I look at all the things I've written there over the months. Scrawls of desire. There's so much more I could add. A joint bank account, singing in the bath with him, listening to him snore for years and years.

'Go on,' he says. 'I have to go soon.'

And it's these words, with an edge of the outside world in

them, of things to do and places to be, that allows me to write.

I want you to move in with me. I want the nights. I write it quickly in really bad handwriting, so maybe he won't be able to read it. Then I hide under the duvet.

There's a second's pause.

'I can't, Tess.'

I struggle out from the duvet. I can't see his face, just a glimpse of light reflected in his eyes. Stars shining there perhaps. Or the moon.

'Because you don't want to?'

'I can't leave my mum by herself.'

I hate his mother, the lines on her forehead and round her eyes. I hate her wounded look. She lost her husband, but she didn't lose anything else.

'Can't you come back when she's asleep?'

'No.'

'Have you even asked her?'

He gets out of bed without touching me and puts on his clothes. I wish it was possible to smear cancer cells onto his arse. I could reach from here, and he'd be mine for ever. I'd lift the carpet and haul him under the floor to the foundations of the house. We'd make love in front of the worms. My fingers would reach under his skin.

'I'll haunt you,' I tell him. 'But from the inside. Every time you cough you'll think of me.'

'Stop messing with my head,' he says.

And then he leaves.

I grab my clothes and follow him. He gets his jacket from the banister. I hear him walk through the kitchen and open the back door.

He's still standing on the step when I catch up. Beyond him, out in the garden, great flakes of snow are swirling down. It must have started when we went upstairs. The path's covered, the grass too. The sky's full of it. The world seems silent and smaller.

'You wanted snow.' He puts out a hand to catch a flake and shows it to me. It's a proper one, like I used to cut out of doilies and stick on the windows at primary school. We watch it melt into his palm.

I get my coat. Adam finds my boots, scarf and hat, and helps me down the step. My breath is frost. It's snowing so much our footprints are wiped out as soon as we make them.

The snow on the lawn is deeper; it creaks as we stand on it. We cross the newness of it together. We tramp our names, trying to wear it out, to reach the grass beneath. But fresh snow covers every mark we make.

'Watch,' Adam says.

He lies flat on his back and flaps his arms and legs. He yells at how cold it is on his neck, his head. He jumps up again, stamps the snow off his trousers.

'For you,' he says. 'A snow angel.'

It's the first time he's looked at me since I wrote on the wall. His eyes are sad.

'Ever had snow ice cream?' I ask.

I send him indoors for a bowl, icing sugar, vanilla, a spoon. He follows my instructions, scoops handfuls of snow into the bowl, whisks all the ingredients together. It turns to mush, goes brown, tastes weird. It isn't how I remember it when I was a kid.

'Maybe it's yoghurt and orange juice.'

He rushes off. Comes back. We try again. It's worse, but this time he laughs.

'Beautiful mouth,' I tell him.

'You're shivering,' he says. 'You should go in.'

'Not without you.'

He looks at his watch.

I say, 'What do you call a snowman in the desert?'

'I need to go, Tess.'

'A puddle.'

'Seriously.'

'You can't leave now, there's a snowstorm. I'll never find my way back home.'

I undo my zip. I let my coat fall open so my shoulder's exposed. Earlier, Adam spent minutes kissing this particular bit of shoulder. He blinks at me. Snow falls onto his eyelashes.

He says, 'What do you want from me, Tess?'

'Night time.'

'What do you *really* want?'

I knew he'd understand.

'I want you to be with me in the dark. To hold me. To keep loving me. To help me when I get scared. To come right to the edge and see what's there.'

He looks really deeply at me. 'What if I get it wrong?'

'It's impossible to get wrong.'

'I might let you down.'

'You won't.'

'I might get freaked out.'

'It doesn't matter. I just want you to be there.'

He gazes at me across the winter garden. His eyes are very green. In them I see his future stretching before him. I don't know what he sees in mine. But he's brave. I always knew it about him. He takes my hand and leads me back inside.

Upstairs I feel heavier, like the bed glued itself to me and is sucking me down. Adam takes ages getting undressed, then stands there shivering in his boxer shorts.

'Shall I get in then?'

'Only if you want to.'

He rolls his eyes, as if there's no winning with me. It's so difficult to get what I want. I worry that people only give me things because they feel guilty. I want Adam to *want* to be here. How will I ever tell the difference?

'Shouldn't we tell your mum?' I ask as he climbs in beside me.

'I'll tell her tomorrow. She'll survive.'

'You're not doing this because you feel sorry for me, are you?'

He shakes his head. 'Stop it, Tess.'

We wrap ourselves together, but the shiver of snow is still with us; our hands and feet are ice. We cycle our legs to keep warm. He rubs me, strokes me. He scoops me into his arms again. I feel his prick grow. It makes me laugh. He laughs too, but nervously, as if I'm laughing at him.

'Do you want me?' I say.

He smiles. 'I always want you. But it's late, you should go to sleep.'

The snow makes the world outside brighter. Light filters through the window. I fall asleep watching the glimmer and sheen of it on his skin.

When I wake up, it's still night and he's asleep. His hair is dark on the pillow, his arm slung across me as if he can hold me here. He sighs, stops breathing, stirs, breathes again. He's in the middle bit of sleep – a part of this world, but also part of another. This is strangely comforting to me.

His being here doesn't stop my legs hurting though. I leave him the duvet, wrap myself in the blanket and stumble to the bathroom for codeine.

When I come out, Dad's on the landing in his dressing gown. I'd forgotten he even existed. He's not wearing slippers. His toes look very long and grey.

'You must be getting old,' I tell him. 'Old people get up in the night.'

He pulls his dressing gown tighter. 'I know Adam's in there with you.'

'And is Mum in there with you?'

This seems an important point, but he chooses to ignore it. 'You did this without my permission.'

I look down at the carpet and hope he gets this over with quickly. My legs feel full up, as if my bones are swelling. I shuffle my feet.

'I'm not out to spoil the fun, Tess, but it's my job to look after you and I don't want you hurt.'

'Bit late for that.'

I meant it as a joke, but he's not smiling. 'Adam's just a kid, Tessa. You can't rely on him for everything: he might let you down.'

'He won't.'

'And if he does?'

'Then I've still got you.'

It's weird hugging him in the dark on the landing. We hold each other tighter than I ever remember. Eventually he eases his grip and looks at me very seriously.

'I'll always be here for you, Tess. Whatever you do, whatever you still have left to do, whatever your stupid list makes you do. You need to know that.'

'There's hardly anything left.'

Number nine is Adam moving in. Deeper than sex. It's about facing death, but not alone. My bed, no longer frightening, but a place where Adam lies warm and waiting for me.

Dad kisses the top of my head. 'Off you go then.'

He goes off to the bathroom.

I go back to Adam.

Thirty-one

Spring is a powerful spell.

The blue. The clouds high up and puffy. The air warmer than it's been for weeks.

'The light was different this morning,' I tell Zoey. 'It woke me up.'

She shifts her weight in the deck chair. 'Lucky you. Leg cramp woke me up.'

We're sitting under the apple tree. Zoey's brought a blanket from the sofa and wrapped herself up in it, but I'm not cold at all. It's one of those mellow days in March that feel as if the earth is tipping forwards. Daisies sprinkle the lawn. Clusters of tulips sprout at the edges of the fence. The garden even smells different – moist and secretive.

'You all right?' Zoey says. 'You look a bit weird.'

'I'm concentrating.'

'On what?'

'Signs.'

She groans softly, picks up the holiday brochure from my lap and flicks through the pages. 'I'll just torture myself with this then. Tell me when you're done.'

I'll never be done.

That rip in the clouds where the light falls through.

That brazen bird flying in a straight line right across the sky.

There are signs everywhere. Keeping me safe.

Cal's got into it too now, although in a more practical way. He calls them 'keep-death-away spells'.

He's put garlic above all the doors and at the four corners of my bed. He's made KEEP OUT boards for the front and back gates.

Last night, when we were watching TV, he tied our legs together with a skipping rope. We looked as if we were entering a three-legged race.

He said, 'No one will take you if you're tied to me.'

'They might take you as well!'

He shrugged, as if that didn't matter to him. 'They won't get you in Sicily either; they won't know where you are.'

Tomorrow we fly. A whole week in the sun.

I tease Zoey with the brochure, run my finger over the volcanic beach with black sand, the sea edged by mountains, the cafés and piazzas. In some of the photos, Mount Etna squats massively in the background, remote and fiery.

'The volcano's active,' I tell her. 'It sparks at night, and when it rains, everything gets covered in ash.'

'It's not going to rain though, is it? It must be about thirty degrees.' She slaps the brochure shut. 'I can't believe your mum gave her ticket to Adam.'

'My dad can't believe it either.'

Zoey thinks about this for a moment. 'Wasn't getting them back together on your list?'

'Number seven.'

'That's terrible.' She flings the brochure on the grass. 'I feel sad now.'

'It's the hormones.'

'Sadder than you'd ever believe.'

'Yeah, it's the hormones.'

She gazes hopelessly at the sky, then almost immediately turns back to me with a smile on her face. 'Did I tell you I'm picking the keys up in three weeks?'

Talking about the flat always cheers her up. The council has agreed to give her a grant. She'll be able to swap vouchers for paint and wallpaper, she tells me. She gets quite animated describing the mural she plans for her bedroom, the tropical fish tiles she wants in the bathroom.

It's strange, but as she talks, her body begins to waver at the edges. I try and concentrate on her plans for the kitchen, but it's as if she's caught in a heat haze.

'Are you OK?' she says. 'You've got that weird look on your face again.'

I sit forward and massage my scalp. I focus on the pain behind my eyes and try and make it go away.

'Shall I get your dad?'

'No.'

'A glass of water?'

'No. Stay there. I'll be back in a minute.'

'Where are you going?'

I can't see Adam, but I can hear him. He's turning over the soil so his mum can plant flowers while we're away. I can hear the push of his boot on the spade, the wet resistance of the earth.

I go through the gap in the fence. There's the whisper of growing things – buds opening, delicate fronds of green pushing their way into the air.

He's got his jumper off, is only wearing a vest top and jeans. He had his hair cut yesterday and the arc of his neck as it joins his shoulder is shockingly beautiful. He grins when he sees me watching, puts the spade down and walks over.

'Hey, you!'

I lean in to him and wait to feel better. He's warm. His skin is salty and smells of baked sunlight.

'I love you.'

Silence. Startling. Did I mean to say that?

He smiles his tilted smile. 'I love you too, Tess.'

I put my hand over his mouth. 'Don't say it if you don't mean it.'

'I do mean it.' His breath makes my fingers humid. He kisses my palm.

I bury these things in my heart – the feel of him under my fingers, the taste of him on my mouth. I'll need them, like talismans, to survive an impossible journey.

He brushes my cheek with one finger, from my temple to my chin and then across my lips. 'You OK?'

I nod.

He looks down at me, gently puzzled. 'You seem quiet. Shall I come and find you when I'm done? We could go out on the bike if you like, say goodbye to the hill for a week.'

I nod again. Yes.

He kisses me goodbye. He tastes of butter.

I hold onto the fence as I go back through the gap. A bird is singing a complicated song and Dad's standing on the back step holding a pineapple. These are good signs. There's no need to be afraid.

I go back to my chair. Zoey's pretending to be asleep, but she opens one eye as I sit down. 'I wonder if you'd fancy him if you weren't sick.'

'I would.'

'He's not as good-looking as Jake.'

'He's a lot nicer.'

'I bet he gets on your nerves sometimes. I bet he talks utter crap, or wants to shag you when you don't feel like it.'

'He doesn't.'

She scowls at me. 'He's a bloke, isn't he?'

How can I explain it to her? The comfort of his arm around my shoulder at night? The way his breathing changes with the hours, so that I know when it's dawn? Every morning when he wakes up, he kisses me. His hand on my breast keeps my heart beating.

Dad comes up the path, still clutching his pineapple. 'You need to come in now. Philippa's here.'

But I don't want to be inside. I'm having trouble with walls. I want to stay under the apple tree, out in the spring air.

'Ask her to come out, Dad.'

He shrugs, turns back to the house.

'I need to have a blood test,' I tell Zoey.

She wrinkles her nose. 'All right. It's freezing out here anyway.'

Philippa squeezes her fingers into sterile gloves. 'Love still working its magic then?'

'It's our tenth anniversary tomorrow.'

'Ten weeks? Well, it's doing wonders for you. I'm going to start recommending all my patients fall in love.'

She holds my arm up to the sky and cleans round the portacath with swabs of gauze.

'You packed yet?'

'A couple of dresses. Bikini and sandals.'

'That all?'

'What else will I need?'

'Sun cream, sun hat and a sensible cardigan for a start! I don't want to be treating you for sunburn when you get back.'

I like her fussing over me. She's been my regular nurse for weeks now. I think I might be her favourite patient.

'How's Andy?'

She smiles wearily. 'He's had a cold all week. Although of course, he says it's flu. You know what men are like.'

I don't really, but I nod anyway. I wonder if her husband loves her, if he makes her feel gorgeous, if he lies entranced in her fat arms.

'Why don't you have any children, Philippa?'

She looks right at me as she draws blood into the syringe. 'I couldn't manage that kind of fear.'

She draws a second syringe of blood and transfers it to a bottle, flushes my port with saline and heparin, then packs her things away into her medical bag and stands up. For a moment I think she's going to reach down and hug me, but she doesn't.

'Have a lovely time,' she says. 'And don't forget to send me a postcard.'

I watch her waddle up the path. She turns on the step to wave.

Zoey comes back out. 'What's she looking for in your blood exactly?'

'Disease.'

She nods sagely as she sits back down. 'Your dad's making lunch by the way. He's going to bring it out in a minute.'

A leaf dances. A shadow travels the length of the lawn.

There are signs everywhere. Some you make. Some come to you.

Zoey grabs my hand and presses it to her belly.

'She's moving! Put your hand here – no, here. That's it. Feel it?'

It's a slow roll, as if her baby's spinning the laziest of somersaults. I don't want to take my hand away. I want the baby to do it again.

'You're the first person ever to feel that. You did feel it, didn't you?'

'I felt it.'

'Imagine her,' Zoey says. 'Really imagine her.'

I often do. I've drawn her on the wall above my bed. It's not a great drawing, but all the measurements are accurate – femur, abdomen, head circumference.

Number ten on my list. Lauren Tessa Walker.

'The structures of the spine are in place,' I tell Zoey. 'Thirty-three rings, one hundred and fifty joints and one thousand ligaments. The eyelids are open, did you know that? And the retinas are formed.'

Zoey blinks at me, as if she can't quite believe anyone would know this information. I decide not to tell her that her own heart is working twice as fast as usual, circulating six litres of blood every minute. I think it would freak her out.

Dad walks up the path. 'Here you go, girls.' He puts the tray down on the grass between us. Avocado and watercress salad. Pineapple and kiwi slices. A bowl of redcurrants.

Zoey says, 'No chance of a burger then?'

He frowns at her, realizes she's joking and grins. 'I'm going to get the lawnmower out.' He goes off to the shed.

Adam and his mum appear at the gap in the fence. 'Lovely day, isn't it?' Sally calls.

'It's spring,' Zoey says, her mouth sprouting watercress.

'Not until the clocks change.'

'Must be pollution then.'

Sally looks alarmed. 'A man on the radio said if we stop using cars we could buy the human race another thousand years on the planet.'

Adam laughs, jangles the car keys at her. 'Shall we walk to the garden centre then, Mum?'

'No, I want to buy bedding plants. We'd never be able to carry them.'

He shakes his head. 'We'll be back in an hour.'

We watch them walk down the path. At the gate he gives me a wink.

Zoey says, 'Now that would definitely annoy me.'

I ignore her. I eat a slice of kiwi. It tastes of somewhere else. The sky skitters with clouds, like spring lambs in a strange blue field. The sun comes and goes. Everything feels volatile.

Dad hauls the lawnmower from the shed. It's covered in old towels, as if it's been hibernating. He used to look after the garden religiously, used to plant and prune, tie things back with bits of string and keep some general order. It's a wilderness now though – the grass bedraggled, the roses nudging their way into the shed.

We laugh at him when the lawnmower won't start, but he doesn't seem to mind, just shrugs at us as if he didn't want to mow the lawn anyway. He goes back into the shed, comes out with some shears and starts cutting back brambles from the fence.

Zoey says, 'There's this pregnant teens group, did I tell you? They give you cake and tea and show you how to change nappies and stuff. I thought it'd be rubbish, but we had a great laugh.'

A plane crosses the sky, leaving a smoky trail. Another plane crosses the first one, making a kiss. Neither plane falls.

Zoey says, 'Are you listening? Because you don't look as if you are.'

I rub my eyes, try to focus. She says she's made friends with a girl . . . something about their due dates being the same . . . something else about a midwife. She sounds as if she's speaking to me down a tunnel.

I notice how a button strains in the middle of her shirt.

A butterfly lands on the path and spreads its wings. Sunbathing. It's very early in the year for butterflies.

'You sure you're listening?'

Cal comes through the gate. He dumps his bike on the lawn and runs round the garden twice.

'Holidays start here!' he yells. He climbs the apple tree to celebrate, jamming his knees between two branches and squatting there like an elf.

He gets a text, the blue light on his phone flashing amongst the new leaves. It reminds me of a dream I had a few nights ago. In the dream, a blue light shone from my throat every time I opened my mouth.

He sends a text back, quickly receives one in return. He laughs. Another text arrives, then another, like a flock of birds landing in the tree.

'Year Seven won!' he announces cheerfully. 'There was a water fight in the park against Year Ten and we won!'

Cal finding his way at secondary school. Cal with friends and a new mobile. Cal growing his hair because he wants to look like a skateboarder.

'What are you staring at?' He sticks his tongue out at me, jumps out of the tree and runs into the house.

The garden's sunk into shadow. The air feels damp. A sweet wrapper blows down the path.

Zoey shivers. 'I think I might go.' She holds me tight, as if one of us might fall. 'You're very hot. Are you supposed to be?'

Dad sees her out.

Adam comes through the gap in the fence. 'All done.' He pulls the deck chair closer to me and sits down. 'She bought half the garden centre. It cost a fortune, but she was really into it. She wants to start a herb garden.'

Keep-death-away spells. Hold your boyfriend's hand very tight.

'You all right?'

I rest my head on his shoulder. I feel as if I'm waiting for something.

There are sounds – the vague chink of dishes from the kitchen, the rustle of leaves, the roar of a faraway engine.

The sun has turned to liquid, melting coldly into the horizon.

'You feel very hot.' He presses his hand against my forehead, brushes my cheek, feels the back of my neck. 'Don't move.'

He leaves me, runs up the path towards the house.

The planet spins, the wind sifts the trees.

I'm not afraid.

Keep breathing, just keep doing it. It's easy – in and out.

Strange how the ground comes up to meet me, but it feels better to be low. I think about my name while I lie here. Tessa Scott. A good name of three syllables. Every seven years our bodies change, every cell. Every seven years we disappear.

'Christ! She's burning up!' Dad's face glimmers right above me.

'Call an ambulance!' His voice comes from far away. I want to smile. I want to thank him for being here, but for some reason I don't seem able to get the words together.

'Don't close your eyes, Tess. Can you hear me? Stay with us!'

When I nod, the sky whirls with sickening speed, like falling from a building.

Thirty-two

Death straps me to the hospital bed, claws its way onto my chest and sits there. I didn't know it would hurt this much. I didn't know that everything good that's ever happened in my life would be emptied out by it.

it's happening now and it's really, really true and however much they all promise to remember me it doesn't even matter if they do or not because I won't even know about it because I'll be gone

A dark hole opens up in the corner of the room and fills with mist, like material rippling through trees.

I hear myself moaning from a distance. I don't want to listen. I catch the weight of glances. Nurse to doctor, doctor to Dad. Their hushed voices. Panic spills from Dad's throat.

Not yet. Not yet.

I keep thinking about blossom. White blossom from a spinning blue sky. How small humans are, how vulnerable compared to rock, stars.

Cal comes. I remember him. I want to tell him not to be scared. I want him to talk in his normal voice and tell me something funny. But he stands next to Dad, quiet and small, and whispers, 'What's wrong with her?'

'She's got an infection.'

'Will she die?'

'They've given her antibiotics.'

'So she'll get better?'

Silence.

This isn't how it's supposed to be. Not sudden, like being hit by a car. Not this strange heat, this feeling of massive bruising deep inside. Leukaemia is a progressive disease. I'm supposed to get weaker and weaker until I don't care any more.

But I still care. When am I going to stop caring?

I try to think of simple things – boiled potatoes, milk. But scary things come into my mind instead – empty trees, plates of dust. The bleached angle of a jaw bone.

I want to tell Dad how frightened I am, but speaking is like climbing up from a vat of oil. My words come from somewhere dark and slippery.

'Don't let me fall.'

'I've got you.'

'I'm falling.'

'I'm here. I've got you.'

But his eyes are scared and his face is slack, like he's a hundred years old.

Thirty-three

I wake to flowers. Vases of tulips, carnations like a wedding, gypsophila frothing over the bedside cabinet.

I wake to Dad, still holding my hand.

All the things in the room are wonderful – the jug, that chair. The sky is very blue beyond the window.

'Are you thirsty?' Dad says. 'Do you want a drink?'

I want mango juice. Lots of it. He plumps a pillow under my head and holds the glass for me. His eyes lock into mine. I sip, swallow. He gives me time to breathe, tips the glass again. When I've had enough, he wipes my mouth with a tissue.

'Like a baby,' I tell him.

He nods. Silent tears fill his eyes.

I sleep. I wake up again. And this time I'm starving.

'Any chance of an ice cream?'

Dad puts his book down with a grin. 'Wait there.' He's not gone long, comes back with a Strawberry Mivvi. He wraps the stick in tissue so it doesn't drip and I manage to hold it myself. It's utterly delicious. My body's repairing itself. I didn't know it could still do that. I know I won't die with a Strawberry Mivvi in my hand.

'I think I might want another one after this.'

Dad tells me I can have fifty ice creams if that's what I want. He must've forgotten I'm not allowed sugar or dairy.

'I've got something else for you.' He fumbles in his jacket pocket and pulls out a fridge magnet. It's heart-shaped, painted red and badly covered in varnish. 'Cal made it. He sends you his love.'

'What about Mum?'

'She came to see you a couple of times. You were very vulnerable, Tessa. Visitors had to be kept to a minimum.'

'So Adam hasn't been?'

'Not yet.'

I lick the ice-cream stick, trying to get all the flavour from it. The wood rasps my tongue.

Dad says, 'Shall I get you another one?'

'No. I want you to go now.'

He looks confused. 'Go where?'

'I want you to go and meet Cal from school, take him to the park and play football. Buy him chips. Come back later and tell me all about it.'

Dad looks a bit surprised, but he laughs. 'You've woken up feisty, I see!'

'I want you to phone Adam. Tell him to visit me this afternoon.'

'Anything else?'

'Tell Mum I want presents – expensive juice, loads of magazines and new make-up. If she's going to be crap, she can at least buy me stuff.'

Dad looks gleeful as he grabs a bit of paper and writes down the brand of foundation and lipstick I want. He encourages me to think of other things I might like, so I order blueberry muffins, chocolate milk and a six-pack of Creme Eggs. It's nearly Easter after all.

He kisses me three times on the forehead and tells me he'll be back later.

After he's gone, a bird lands on the window ledge. It's not a spectacular bird, not a vulture or a phoenix, but an ordinary starling. A nurse comes in, fiddles about with the sheets, fills up my water jug. I point the bird out to her, joke that it's Death's look-out. She sucks her teeth at me and tells me not to tempt fate.

But the bird looks right at me and cocks its head.

'Not yet,' I tell it.

The doctor visits. 'So,' he says, 'we found the right antibiotic in the end.'

'Eventually.'

'Bit scary for a while though.'

'Was it?'

'I meant for you. That level of infection can be very disorientating.'

I read his name badge as he listens to my chest. Dr James Wilson. He's about my dad's age, with dark hair, receding at the crown. He's thinner than my dad. He looks tired. He checks my arms, legs and back for bleeding under the skin, then he sits down on the chair next to the bed and makes notes on my chart.

Doctors expect you to be polite and grateful. It makes their job easier. But I don't feel like being tactful today.

'How much longer do I have?'

He looks up, surprised. 'Shall we wait for your dad to be here before we have this discussion?'

'Why?'

'So that we can look at the medical options together.'

'It's me that's sick, not my dad.'

He puts his pen back in his pocket. The muscles round his jaw tighten. 'I don't want to be drawn into time scales with you, Tessa. They're not helpful at all.'

'They're helpful to me.'

It's not that I've decided to be brave. This isn't a new year's resolution. It's just that I have a drip in my arm and I've lost days of my life to a hospital bed. Suddenly, what's important seems very obvious.

'My best friend's having a baby in eight weeks and I need to know if I'm going to be there.'

He crosses his legs, then immediately uncrosses them. I feel a bit sorry for him. Doctors don't get much training in death.

He says, 'If I'm over-optimistic, you'll be disappointed. It's equally unhelpful to give you a pessimistic prediction.'

'I don't mind. You've got more of an idea than I have. Please, James.'

The nurses aren't allowed to use doctors' first names, and

normally I'd never dare. But something's shifted. This is my death and there are things I need to know.

'I won't sue you if you're wrong.'

He gives me a grim little smile. 'Although we managed to cure your infection and you're obviously feeling much better, your blood count didn't pick up as much as we'd hoped, so we ran some tests. When your father gets back, we can discuss the results together.'

'Have I got peripheral disease?'

'You and I don't know each other very well, Tessa. Wouldn't you rather wait for your father?'

'Just tell me.'

He sighs very deeply, as if he can't quite believe he's about to give in. 'Yes, we found disease in your peripheral blood. I'm very sorry.'

That's it then. I'm riddled with cancer, my immune system is shot and there's nothing more they can do for me. I had weekly blood tests to check for it. And now it's here.

I'd always thought that being told for definite would be like being punched in the stomach – painful, followed by a dull ache. But it doesn't feel dull at all. It's sharp. My heart's racing, adrenalin surges through me. I feel absolutely focused.

'Does my dad already know?'

He nods. 'We were going to tell you together.'

'What options do I have?'

'Your immune system is in collapse, Tessa. Your options are limited. We can keep going with blood and platelets if you want

259

to, but it's likely their benefit will be short-lived. If you became anaemic straight after a transfusion, we would have to stop.'

'What then?'

'Then we would do everything we could to make you comfortable and leave you in peace.'

'Daily transfusions aren't feasible?'

'No.'

'I'm not going to make eight weeks then, am I?'

Dr Wilson looks right at me. 'You'll be very lucky if you do.'

I know I look like a pile of bones covered in cling film. I see the shock of it in Adam's eyes.

'Not quite how you remembered me, eh?'

He leans down and kisses me on the cheek. 'You're gorgeous.'

But I think this is what he was always scared of – having to be interested when I'm ugly and useless.

He's brought tulips from the garden. I stuff them in the water jug while he looks at my get-well cards. We talk about nothing for a bit – how the plants he bought in the garden centre are coming along, how his mum is enjoying the weather now that she's outside more often. He looks out of the window, makes some joke about the view across the car park.

'Adam, I want you to be real.'

He frowns as if he doesn't understand.

'Don't pretend to care. I don't need you as an anaesthetic.'

'What's that supposed to mean?'

'I don't want anyone being fake.'

'I'm not being.'

'I don't blame you. You didn't know I'd get this sick. And it's only going to get worse.'

He thinks about this for a moment, then kicks off his shoes.

'What are you doing?'

'Being real.'

He pulls back the blanket and climbs into bed next to me. He scoops me up and wraps me in his arms.

'I love you,' he whispers angrily into my neck. 'It hurts more than anything ever has, but I do. So don't you dare tell me I don't. Don't you ever say it again!'

I lay the flat of my palm against his face and he pushes into it. It crosses my mind that he's lonely. 'I'm sorry.'

'You should be.'

He won't look at me. I think he's trying not to cry.

He stays all afternoon. We watch MTV, then he reads the paper my dad left behind and I have another sleep. I dream of him, even though he's right next to me. We walk together through snow, but we're hot and wearing swimming costumes. There are empty lanes and frosty trees and a road that curves and never ends.

When I wake up, I'm hungry again, so I send him off for another Strawberry Mivvi. I miss him as soon as he goes. It's like the whole hospital empties out. How can this be? I claw my hands together under the blanket until he climbs back into bed beside me.

He unwraps the ice cream and passes it over. I put it on the bed-side table.

'Touch me.'

He looks confused. 'Your ice cream will melt.'

'Please.'

'I'm right here. I am touching you.'

I move his hand to my breast. 'Like this.'

'No, Tess, I might hurt you.'

'You won't.'

'What about the nurse?'

'We'll chuck the bed-pan at her if she comes in.'

He very gently cups my breast through my pyjamas. 'Like this?'

He touches me as if I'm precious, as if he's stunned, as if my body amazes him, even now, when it's failing. When his skin touches mine, skin to skin, we both shiver.

'I want to make love.'

His hand stalls. 'When?'

'When I get back home. One more time before I die. I want you to promise.'

The look in his eyes frightens me. I've never seen it before. So deep and real, it's as if he's seen things in the world that others could only imagine.

'I promise.'

Thirty-four

They swap like porters. Dad comes every morning. Adam comes every afternoon. Dad comes back in the evening with Cal. Mum visits randomly, managing to sit through an entire blood transfusion on her second visit.

'Haemoglobin and platelets coming right up,' she said as they hooked me up.

I liked her knowing the words.

But ten days. I even missed Easter. That's too much time to lose.

Every night I lie in my single hospital bed and I want Adam, his legs entwined with mine, his warmth.

'I want to go home,' I tell the nurse.

'Not yet.'

'I'm better.'

'Not better enough.'

'What're you hoping for? A cure?'

The sun hoists itself up every morning and all the lights in the town wink off. Clouds rush the sky, frenzied traffic dips in and out of the car park, then the sun plummets back to the

263

horizon and another day is over. Time rush. Blood rush.

I pack my bag and get dressed. I sit on the bed trying to look perky. I'm waiting for James.

'I'm going home,' I tell him as he examines my chart.

He nods as if he was expecting this. 'Are you determined?'

'Very. I'm missing the weather.' I point at the window just in case he's been too busy to notice the mellow light and the blue-sky clouds.

'There's a certain rigour needed to maintain this blood count, Tessa.'

'Can't I be rigorous at home?'

He looks at me very seriously. 'There's a fine line between the quality of the life you have left and the medical intervention necessary to maintain it. You're the only one who can judge it. Are you telling me you've had enough?'

I keep thinking about the rooms in our house, the colours of the carpets and curtains, the exact positioning of furniture. There's a journey I really like making from my bedroom, down the stairs, through the kitchen and into the garden. I want to make that journey. I want to sit in my deck chair on the lawn.

'The last transfusion only lasted for three days.'

He nods sympathetically. 'I know. I'm sorry.'

'I had another one this morning. How long do you reckon that's going to last?'

He sighs. 'I don't know.'

I stroke the bed sheet with the flat of my hand. 'I just want to go home.'

'Why don't I talk to the community care team? If I can get them to guarantee daily visits, then perhaps we can reassess.' He clips my chart back onto the end of my bed. 'I'll phone them and come back when your dad gets here.'

After he leaves, I count to one hundred. A fly grazes the table. I reach out my finger for a touch of those flimsy wings. It senses me coming, sputters into life and zigzags up to the light fitting, where it circles out of reach.

I put on my coat, drape my scarf round my shoulders and pick up my bag. The nurse doesn't even notice as I walk past her desk and get into the lift.

When I reach the ground floor, I text Adam: REMEMBER YR PROMISE?

I want to die in my own way. It's my illness, my death, my choice.

This is what saying yes means.

It's the pleasure of walking, one foot in front of the other, following the yellow lines painted on the floor of the corridor all the way to reception. It's the pleasure of revolving doors – going round twice to celebrate the genius of the person who invented them. And the pleasure of the air. The sweet, cool, shocking outside world.

There's a kiosk at the gate. I buy a Dairy Milk and a packet of Chewits. The woman behind the counter looks at me strangely as I pay her. I think I might glow a bit from all my treatments, and some people are able to see it, like a neon wound that flares as I move.

I walk slowly to the taxi rank, savouring details – the CCTV camera on the lamppost swinging on its axis, the mobile phones chirruping all about me. The hospital seems to retreat as I whisper goodbye, the shade from the plane trees turning all the windows to darkness.

A girl swings past, high heels clicking; there's a fried-chicken smell about her as she licks her fingers clean. A man holding a wailing child shouts into his phone: 'No! I can't bloody carry pot-atoes as well!'

We make patterns, we share moments. Sometimes I think I'm the only one to see it.

I share my chocolate with the taxi driver as we join the lunchtime traffic. Today he's on a double shift, he tells me, and there are too many cars on the road for his liking. He waves at them in despair as we crawl through the town centre.

'Where's it all going to end?' he asks.

I offer him a Chewit to cheer him up. Then I text Adam again: U HVE PROMISES 2 KEEP.

The weather's changed, the sun hidden by cloud. I open the window. Cold April air shocks my lungs.

The driver drums his fingers impatiently on the steering wheel. 'It's complete gridlock!'

I like it – the stall and shove of traffic, the deep thrum of a bus engine, an urgent siren in the distance. I like creeping so slowly down the High Street that I have time to notice Easter eggs still unbought in the newsagent's window, the cigarette butts swept into a neat pile outside the Chicken Joint. I see children carrying the strangest things – a polar bear, an octopus. And under the wheels of a buggy outside Mothercare I see my name, faded now, but still weaving the pavement all the way to the bank.

I phone Adam's mobile. He doesn't pick up, so I leave another message: I WANT YOU.

Simple.

At the junction, an ambulance stands skewed, its doors open, the blue of its light flashing across the road. The light even flashes onto the clouds, low above us. A woman is lying in the road with a blanket over her.

'Would you look at that,' the taxi driver says.

Everyone's looking – people in other cars, office workers out for their lunchtime sandwich. The woman's head is covered, but her legs stick out. She's wearing tights; her shoes are at strange angles. Her blood, dark as rain, pools beside her.

The taxi driver flicks me a glance in his mirror. 'Makes you realize, doesn't it?'

Yes. It's so tangible. Being and not being.

I feel as if I have sap in my toes, running up my ankles and into my shins, as I knock on Adam's door.

Sally opens it a crack and peeps at me. I feel a surge of love for her.

'Is Adam in?'

'Aren't you supposed to be in hospital?'

'Not any more.'

She looks confused. 'He didn't say they were letting you out.'

'It's a surprise.'

'Another one?' She sighs, opens the door a bit further and looks at her watch. 'He won't be back until five.'

'Five?'

She frowns at me. 'Are you all right?'

No. Five's too late. I might be completely anaemic again by then.

'Where is he?'

'He's gone to Nottingham on the train. They've agreed to interview him.'

'For what?'

'University. He wants to start in September.'

The garden spins.

'You look as surprised as I was.'

I fell asleep in his arms in that hospital bed. 'Touch me,' I said, and he did. 'I love you,' he said. 'Don't you dare tell me I don't.' He made me a promise.

It starts to rain as I walk back down the path to the gate. A fine silver rain, like cobwebs falling.

Thirty-five

I rip my silk dress from its hanger in the wardrobe and cut a gaping mouth in it just below the waist. These scissors are sharp so it's easy, like sliding metal through water. My blue wrap-dress gets a diagonal slit across the chest. I lay them side by side on the bed like a couple of sick friends and stroke them.

It doesn't help.

The stupid jeans I bought with Cal never fitted anyway, so I hack the legs off at the knee. I split the pockets of all my jogging pants, gash holes in my sweatshirts and chuck the lot next to the dresses.

It takes ages to stab my boots. My arms ache and I'm wheezing. But I had a transfusion this morning and other people's blood runs hot through my veins, so I don't stop. I slit each boot along its length. Two startling wounds.

I want to be empty. I want to live somewhere uncluttered.

I open the window and throw the boots out. They land on the lawn.

The sky is solid cloud, grey and low. There's a thin rain falling.

The shed's wet. The grass is wet. The barbecue set is rusting on its wheels.

I haul the rest of my clothes out of the wardrobe. My lungs wheeze, but I'm not stopping. Buttons ping across the room as I slash my coats. I shred my jumpers. I lacerate every pair of trousers. I line my shoes up on the window ledge and cut off their tongues.

It's good. I feel alive.

I grab the dresses from the bed and push them out with the shoes. They tumble onto the patio together and lie there in the rain.

I check my phone. No messages. No missed calls.

I hate my room. Everything in it reminds me of something else. The little china bowl from St Ives. The brown ceramic jar Mum used to keep biscuits in. The sleeping dog with its silent slipper that belonged on Nanna's mantelpiece. My green glass apple. They all make it to the lawn except for the dog, which smashes against the fence.

Books fall open as I chuck them. Their pages flap like exotic birds, rip and flutter. CDs and DVDs like Frisbees over next door's fence. Adam can play them to his new friends at university when I'm dead.

Duvet, sheets, blankets, all out. Medicine bottles and boxes from my bedside table, syringe driver, Diprobase cream, aqueous cream. My jewellery box.

I slash my beanbag, decorate the floor with polystyrene balls and throw the empty sack out into the rain. The garden's looking very busy. Things will grow. Trouser trees. Book vines. I'll chuck myself out later and take root in that dark space by the shed.

Still no message from Adam. I throw my phone over his fence.

The TV is heavy as a car. It hurts my back. It makes my legs burn. I drag and heave it across the carpet. I can't breathe, have to stop. The room tilts. Breathe. Breathe. You can do this. Everything's got to go.

Onto the ledge with the TV.

And out.

It roars, explodes in a dramatic smash of glass and plastic.

That's it. Everything gone. Finished.

Dad crashes in. He stands for a moment, still and open-mouthed.

'You monster,' he whispers.

I have to cover my ears.

He comes over and takes me by both arms. His breath smells of stale tobacco. 'Do you want to leave me with nothing?'

'There was nobody here!'

'So you thought you'd wreck the place?'

'Where were you?'

'I was at the supermarket. Then I went to the hospital to visit you but you weren't there. We were all frantic.'

'I don't give a shit, Dad!'

'Well, I do! I absolutely give a shit! This will completely exhaust you.'

'It's my body. I can do what I like!'

'So you don't care about your body now?'

'No, I'm sick of it! I'm sick of doctors and needles and blood tests and transfusions. I'm sick of being stuck in a bed day after day while the rest of you get on with your lives. I hate it! I hate all of you! Adam's gone for a university interview, did you know that? He's going to be here for years doing whatever he likes and I'm going to be under the ground in a couple of weeks!'

Dad starts to cry. He sinks onto the bed and puts his head in his hands and just weeps. I don't know what to do. Why is he weaker than me? I sit next to him and touch his knee. 'I'm not going back to the hospital, Dad.'

He wipes his nose on his shirt sleeve and looks at me. He looks like Cal. 'You've really had enough?'

'I've really had enough.'

I put my arm round him and he leans his head on my shoulder. I stroke his hair. It's as if we're floating about on a boat. There's even a breeze from the open window. We sit for ages.

'You never know, maybe I won't die if I'm at home.'

'It'd be lovely if you didn't.'

'I'll do my A-levels instead. Then I'll go to university.'

He sighs, stretches himself out on the bed and closes his eyes. 'That's a good idea.'

'I'll get a job, and maybe one day I'll have children – Chester, Merlin and Daisy.'

Dad opens one eye briefly. 'God help them!'

'You'll be a grandad. We'll visit you loads. For years and years we'll visit, until you're ninety.'

'And then what? You'll stop coming?'

'No, then you'll die. Before me. The way it's supposed to be.'

He doesn't say anything. Where the dark filters through the window and shadow touches his arm, he seems to vanish.

'You won't live in this house any more, but somewhere smaller near the sea. I've got keys because I visit you so often, and one day I let myself in as usual, but the curtains aren't open and the post is on the mat. I go up to the bedroom to see where you are. I'm so relieved to see you lying peacefully in bed that I laugh out loud. But when I pull the curtains, I notice your lips are blue. I touch your cheek and it's cold. Your hand's cold as well. I say your name over and over, but you can't hear me and you don't open your eyes.'

Dad sits up. He's crying again. I hold him close and pat his back.

'Sorry. Am I freaking you out?'

'No, no.' He pulls away, sweeps a hand across his eyes. 'I better go and clear up outside before it gets dark. Will you be all right if I go and do that?'

'Sure.'

I watch him from the window. It's raining hard now and he's put his wellies on and an anorak. He gets a broom and the wheelbarrow from the shed. He puts on gardening gloves. He picks up the telly. He sweeps up the broken glass. He gets a cardboard box and piles all the books in it. He even picks up the pages that lie shivering against the fence.

Cal turns up in his school uniform with his rucksack and bike. He looks sane and healthy. Dad goes over and hugs him.

Cal dumps his bike and joins in the clearing up. He looks like a treasure hunter, holding each ring up to the sky. He finds the silver necklace I got for my last birthday, my amberlite bracelet. Then he

Thirty-six

'So, were you ever going to tell me?'

Adam regards me grimly from his perch on the edge of the chair. 'It was difficult.'

'That's a no then.'

He shrugs. 'I tried a couple of times. It just felt so unfair, like how come I get to have a life?'

I sit forwards in the bed. 'Don't you dare feel sorry for yourself because you get to stay behind!'

'I'm not.'

'Because, if you want to die too, then here's a plan. We go out on the bike. You take a hairpin bend really fast just as a juggernaut's coming the other way, and we'll die together – loads of blood, joint funeral, our bones entwined for eternity. How about that?'

He looks so horrified it makes me laugh. He grins back at me, relieved. It's like breaking through fog, as if the sun comes out in the room.

'Let's just forget about it, Adam. It was bad timing, that's all.'

'You threw everything out the window!'

'Not just because of you.'

He leans his head back against the chair and closes his eyes. 'No.'

Dad told him I'm finished with the hospital. Everyone knows. Philippa's coming in the morning to discuss options, although I don't think there'll be much to discuss. Today's transfusion is already wearing out.

'What was it like at university anyway?'

He shrugs. 'It was big, lots of buildings. I got a bit lost.'

But he glows with the future. I can see it in his eyes. He got on a train and he went to Nottingham. He'll go to so many places without me.

'Did you meet any girls?'

'No!'

'Isn't that why people go to university?'

He gets up from the chair and sits on the edge of the bed. He looks at me very seriously. 'I'm going because my life was crap until I met you. I'm going because I don't want to be here when you're not, still living with my mum and nothing being any different. I wouldn't even be thinking about going if it hadn't been for you.'

'I bet you forget me by the end of the first term.'

'I bet I won't.'

'It's practically the law.'

'Stop it! Do I have to do something outrageous to make you believe me?'

'Yes.'

He grins. 'What do you suggest?'

'Keep your promise.'

He reaches over to lift the duvet, but I stop him. 'Turn the light off first.'

'Why? I want to see you.'

'I'm a pile of bones. Please.'

He sighs, switches off the main light and sits back on the bed. I think I've scared him because he doesn't try to get in, but strokes me through the duvet – the length of my leg from thigh to ankle, the length of my other leg. His hands are sure. I feel like I'm an instrument being tuned up.

'I could spend hours on every bit of you,' he says. Then he laughs, as if it wasn't cool to say that. 'You really are gorgeous.'

Beneath his hands. Because his fingers give my body dimension.

'Is this OK, me stroking you like this?'

When I nod, he slides off the bed, kneels on the rug and holds my feet between both his hands, warming me through my socks.

He massages them for so long I nearly fall asleep, but I wake up when he pulls off my socks, lifts both feet to his mouth and kisses them. He swims his tongue around each toe. He scrapes his teeth along the soles. He licks the run of my heels.

I thought my body wouldn't feel heat again, not the kind of urgent heat I've felt with him before. I'm amazed as it comes surging back. He feels it too, I know. He pulls off his T-shirt and kicks off his boots. Our eyes lock as he unbuckles his jeans.

277

He's astonishingly beautiful – the way his hair is short now, shorter than mine, the arc of his back as he pulls off his jeans, his muscles firm from gardening.

'Get in,' I tell him.

The room is warm, the radiators piping hot, but still I shiver as he lifts the duvet and climbs in beside me. He's careful not to put weight on me. He leans up on one elbow to kiss me very gently on the mouth.

'Don't be afraid of me, Adam.'

'I'm not.'

But it's my tongue that finds his. It's me that moves his hand to my breast and encourages him to undo my buttons.

He makes a noise in the back of his throat, a deep groan, as his kisses move down. I cradle his head. I stroke his hair as he gently sucks, like a baby might, at my breast.

'I missed you so much,' I tell him.

His hand slides to my waist to my belly to the top of my thigh. His kisses follow his hand, work their way down until his head is between my legs and then he looks at me, asking permission with his eyes.

It spills me, the thought of him kissing me there.

His head is in shadow, his arms scooped under my legs. His breath is warm on my thigh. He very slowly begins.

If I could buck, I would. If I could howl at the moon, then I would. To feel this, when I'd thought it was over, when my body's closing down and I thought I'd have no pleasure from it again.

I am blessed.

'Come here. Come up here.'

Concern flickers in his eyes. 'Are you OK?'

'How did you know how to do that?'

'Was it all right?'

'It was amazing!'

He grins, ridiculously pleased at himself. 'I saw it in a film once.'

'What about you though? You're left out now.'

He shrugs. 'It's all right, you're tired. We don't have to do anything else.'

'You could touch yourself.'

'In front of you?'

'I could watch.'

He blushes. 'Seriously?'

'Why not? I need more memories.'

He smiles shyly. 'You really want me to?'

'I really do.'

He kneels up. I might have no energy left, but I can give him my gaze.

He looks at my breasts as he touches himself. I have never shared anything so intimate, never seen such a look of bewildered love as his mouth opens and his eyes widen.

'Tess, I love you! I really bloody love you!'

Thirty-seven

'Tell me how it will be.'

Philippa nods as if she was expecting this question. She has a strange look on her face – professional, distant. She's begun to retreat, I think. What else can she do? Her job is to administer to the dying, but if she gets too close, she might fall into the abyss.

'You won't want to eat much from now on. You'll probably want to sleep a lot. You might not want to talk, but you may feel energized enough for good ten-minute chats between sleeps. You may even want to go downstairs or outside if it's warm enough, if your dad is able to carry you. But mostly you'll sleep. In a few days you'll begin to drift in and out of consciousness, and at this stage you may not be able to respond, but you'll know people are with you and you'll be able to hear them talk to you. Eventually you'll just drift away, Tess.'

'Will it hurt?'

'I think your pain will always be manageable.'

'In the hospital it wasn't. Not at first.'

'No,' she admits. 'At first they had trouble getting the drugs right. But I've got you morphine sulphate here, which is slow release. I've also got Oramorph, so we can top up if necessary. You shouldn't feel any pain.'

'You think I'll be scared?'

'I think there's no right or wrong way to be.' She sees from my face that I think this is rubbish. 'I think you've had the worst luck in the world, Tessa, and if I was in your shoes, I'd be scared. But I also believe that however you handle these last days will be exactly how it should be done.'

'I hate it when you say *days*.'

She frowns. 'I know. I'm sorry.'

She talks to me about pain relief, shows me packets and bottles. She talks softly, her words washing over me, her instructions lost. I feel as if everything is zeroing in, a strange hallucination that all my life has been about this moment. I was born and grew up in order to receive this news and be handed this medicine by this woman.

'Do you have any questions, Tessa?'

I try to think of all the things I should ask. But I just feel blank and uncomfortable, as if she's come to see me off at the station and we're both hoping the train hurries up so we can avoid all the ridiculous small talk.

It's time.

Out there is a bright April morning. The world will roll on without me. I have no choice. I'm full of cancer. Riddled with it. And there's nothing to be done.

Philippa says, 'I'm going downstairs now to talk to your dad. I'll try and see you again soon.'

'You don't have to.'

'I know, but I will.'

Fat, kind Philippa, helping all the people between London and the south coast to die. She reaches down and hugs me. She's warm and sweaty and smells of lavender.

After she's gone I have a dream where I walk into the lounge and everyone's sitting there. Dad's making a sound I've never heard before.

'Why are you crying?' I ask. 'What's happened?'

Mum and Cal are next to each other on the sofa. Cal's dressed in a suit and tie, like a mini snooker player.

And then it hits me – I'm dead.

'I'm here, right here!' I yell, but they don't hear me.

I saw a film once about the dead – how they never really go away, but live silently amongst us. I want to tell them this. I try to knock a pencil off the table but my hand moves right through it. And through the sofa. I walk through the wall and back again. I dabble my fingers in Dad's head and he shifts in his chair, perhaps wondering at the thrill of the cold.

Then I wake up.

Dad's sitting on a chair beside the bed. He reaches for my hand. 'How are you feeling?'

I think about this, scan my body for signs. 'I'm not in pain.'

'That's good.'

'I'm a bit tired.'

He nods. 'Are you hungry?'

I want to be. For him. I want to ask for rice and prawns and treacle pudding, but I'd be lying.

'Is there anything I can get you, anything you want?'

Meet the baby. Finish school. Grow up. Travel the world.

'A cup of tea?'

Dad looks pleased. 'Anything else? A biscuit?'

'A pen and paper.'

He helps me sit up. He plumps pillows behind me, turns on the bedside light and passes me a notepad and pen from the shelf. Then he goes downstairs to put the kettle on.

Number eleven. A cup of tea.

Number twelve . . .

Instructions for Dad

I don't want to go into a fridge at an undertaker's. I want you to keep me at home until the funeral. Please can someone sit with me in case I get lonely? I promise not to scare you.

I want to be buried in my butterfly dress, my lilac bra and knicker set and my black zip boots (all still in the suitcase that I packed for Sicily). I also want to wear the bracelet Adam gave me.

Don't put make-up on me. It looks stupid on dead people.

I do NOT want to be cremated. Cremations pollute the atmosphere with dioxins, hydrochloric acid, hydrofluoric acid, sulphur dioxide and carbon dioxide. They also have those spooky curtains in crematoriums.

I want a bio-degradable willow coffin and a woodland burial. The people at the Natural Death Centre helped me pick a site not far from where we live, and they'll help you with all the arrangements.

I want a native tree planted on or near my grave. I'd like an oak, but I don't mind a sweet chestnut or even a willow. I want a wooden plaque with my name on. I want wild plants and flowers growing on my grave.

I want the service to be simple. Tell Zoey to bring Lauren (if she's born by then). Invite Philippa and her husband Andy (if he wants to come), also James from the hospital (though he might be busy).

I don't want anyone who doesn't know me saying anything about me. The Natural Death Centre people will stay with you, but should also stay out of it. I want the people I love to get up and speak about me, and even if you cry it'll be OK. I want you to say honest things. Say I was a monster if you like, say how I made you all run around after me. If you can think of anything good, say that too! Write it down first, because apparently people often forget what they mean to say at funerals.

Don't under any circumstances read that poem by Auden. It's been done to death (ha, ha) and it's too sad. Get someone to read Sonnet 12 by Shakespeare.

Music – 'Blackbird' by the Beatles. 'Plainsong' by the Cure. 'Live Like You Were Dying' by Tim McGraw. 'All the Trees of the

Field Will Clap Their Hands' by Sufjan Stevens. *There may not be time for all of them, but make sure you play the last one. Zoey helped me choose them and she's got them all on her iPod (it's got speakers if you need to borrow it).*

Afterwards, go to a pub for lunch. I've got £260 in my savings account and I really want you to use it for that. Really, I mean it – lunch is on me. Make sure you have pudding – sticky toffee, chocolate fudge cake, ice-cream sundae, something really bad for you. Get drunk too if you like (but don't scare Cal). Spend all the money.

And after that, when days have gone by, keep an eye out for me. I might write on the steam in the mirror when you're having a bath, or play with the leaves on the apple tree when you're out in the garden. I might slip into a dream.

Visit my grave when you can, but don't kick yourself if you can't, or if you move house and it's suddenly too far away. It looks pretty there in the summer (check out the website). You could bring a picnic and sit with me. I'd like that.

OK. That's it.

I love you.

Tessa xxx

Thirty-eight

'I'm going to be the only kid at school with a dead sister.'

'It'll be cool. You'll get out of homework for ages, and all the girls will fancy you.'

Cal thinks about this. 'Will I still be a brother?'

'Of course.'

'But you won't know about it.'

'I bloody will.'

'Are you going to haunt me?'

'You want me to?'

He smiles nervously. 'I might be scared.'

'I won't then.'

He can't keep still, is pacing the carpet between my bed and the wardrobe. Something has shifted between us since the hospital. Our jokes aren't as easy.

'Throw the telly out the window if you want, Cal. It made me feel better.'

'I don't want to.'

'Show me a magic trick then.'

He runs off to get his stuff, comes back wearing his special jacket, the black one with the hidden pockets.

'Watch very carefully.'

He ties two silk handkerchiefs together at one corner and pushes them into his fist. He opens his hand finger by finger. It's empty.

'How did you do that?'

He shakes his head, taps his nose with his wand. 'Magicians never give their secrets away.'

'Do it again.'

Instead, he shuffles and spreads a pack of cards. 'Choose one, look at it, don't tell me what it is.'

I choose the queen of spades, and then replace her in the pack. Cal spreads the cards again, face-up this time. But she's gone.

'You're good, Cal!'

He slumps down on the bed. 'Not good enough. I wish I could do something bigger, something scary.'

'You can saw me in half if you like.'

He grins, but almost immediately starts to cry, silently at first, and then great gulping sobs. As far as I know this is only the second time he's ever cried, so maybe he needs to. We both act as if he can't help it, like it's a nosebleed that has nothing to do with how he might be feeling. I pull him close and hold him. He sobs into my shoulder, his tears melt through my pyjamas. I want to lick them. His real, real tears.

'I love you, Cal.'

It's easy. Even though it makes him cry ten times harder, I'm really glad I dared.

Number thirteen, to hold my brother as dusk settles on the window ledge.

Adam climbs into bed. He pulls the duvet right up under his chin, as if he's cold or as if he's afraid that the ceiling might fall on his head.

He says, 'Tomorrow your dad's going to buy a camp bed and put it on the floor down there for me.'

'Aren't you going to sleep with me any more?'

'You might not want it, Tess. You might not want to be held.'

'What if I do?'

'Well, then I'll hold you.'

But he's terrified. I see it in his eyes.

'It's all right, I let you off.'

'Shush.'

'No, really. I free you.'

'I don't want to be free.' He leans across and kisses me. 'Wake me up if you need me.'

He falls asleep quickly. I lie awake and listen to lights being switched off all over the town. Whispered goodnights. The drowsy creak of bedsprings.

I find Adam's hand and hold it tight.

I'm glad that night porters and nurses and long-distance lorry drivers exist. It comforts me to know that in other countries with different time zones, women are washing clothes in rivers and children are filing to school. Somewhere in the world right now, a boy is listening to the merry chink of a goat's bell as he walks up a mountain. I'm very glad about that.

Thirty-nine

Zoey's sewing. I didn't know she could. A lemon-coloured baby suit is draped across her knees. She threads the needle, one eye shut, pulls the thread through and rolls a knot between licked fingers. Who taught her that? For minutes I watch her, and she sews as if this is how it's always been. Her blonde hair is piled high, her neck at a tender angle. She bites her bottom lip in concentration.

'Live,' I tell her. 'You will live, won't you?'

She looks up suddenly, sucks bright blood from her finger. 'Shit!' she says. 'I didn't know you were awake.'

It makes me chuckle. 'You're blooming.'

'I'm fat!' She heaves herself upright in the chair and thrusts her belly at me to prove it. 'I'm as big as a bear.'

I'd love to be that baby deep inside her. To be small and healthy.

Instructions for Zoey
Don't tell your daughter the planet is rotting. Show her lovely

things. Be a giant for her, even though your parents couldn't do it for you. Don't ever get involved with any boy who doesn't love you.

'When the baby's born, do you think you'll miss the life you had before?'

Zoey looks at me very solemnly. 'You should get dressed. It's not good for you to sit around in your pyjamas all day.'

I lean back on the pillows and look at the corners of the room. When I was a kid, I always wanted to live on the ceiling – it looked so clean and uncluttered, like the top of a cake. Now it just reminds me of bed sheets.

'I feel like I've let you down. I won't be able to babysit or anything.'

Zoey says, 'It's really nice outside. Shall I ask Adam or your dad to carry you out?'

Birds joust on the lawn. Ragged clouds fringe a blue sky. This sun lounger is warm, as if it's been absorbing sunlight for hours.

Zoey's reading a magazine. Adam's stroking my feet through my socks.

'Listen to this,' Zoey says. 'This won the funniest joke of the year competition.'

Number fourteen, a joke.

'*A man goes to the doctor's and says, "I've got a strawberry stuck up my bottom." "Oh," says the doctor, "I've got some cream for that."'*

I laugh a lot. I'm a laughing skeleton. To hear us – Adam, Zoey and me – is like being offered a window to climb through. Anything could happen next.

Zoey shoves her baby into my arms. 'Her name's Lauren.'

She's fat and sticky and drooling milk. She smells good. She waves her arms at me, snatching at air. Her little fingers with their half-moon nails pluck at my nose.

'Hello, Lauren.'

I tell her how big and clever she is. I say all the silly things I imagine babies like to hear. And she looks back at me with fathomless eyes and gives a great big yawn. I can see right inside her little pink mouth.

'She likes you,' Zoey says. 'She knows who you are.'

I put Lauren Tessa Walker at my shoulder and swim my hand in circles over her back. I listen to her heart. She sounds careful, determined. She is ferociously warm.

Under the apple tree, shadows dance. Sunlight sifts through the branches. A lawnmower drones far away. Zoey's still reading her magazine, slaps it down when she sees I'm awake.

'You've been asleep for ages,' she tells me.

'I dreamed Lauren was born.'

'Was she gorgeous?'

'Of course.'

Adam looks up and smiles at me. 'Hey,' he says.

Dad walks down the path filming us with his video camera.

'Stop it,' I tell him. 'It's morbid.'

He takes the camera back into the house, comes out with the recycling box and puts it by the gate. He dead-heads flowers.

'Come and sit with us, Dad.'

But he can't keep still. He goes back inside, returns with a bowl of grapes, an assortment of chocolate, glasses of juice.

'Anyone want a sandwich?'

Zoey shakes her head. 'I'm all right with these Maltesers thanks.'

I like the way her mouth puckers as she sucks them.

Keep-death-away spells.

Ask your best friend to read out the juicy bits from her magazine – the fashion, the gossip. Encourage her to sit close enough for you to touch her tummy, the amazing expanse of it. And when she has to go home, take a deep breath and tell her you love her. Because it's true. And when she leans over and whispers it back, hold onto her tight, because these are not words you would normally share.

293

Make your brother sit with you when he gets back from school and go through every detail of his day, every lesson, every conversation, even what he had for dinner, until he's so bored he begs to be allowed to run off and play football with his friends in the park.

Watch your mum kick off her shoes and massage her feet because her new job in the bookshop means she has to stand up all day and be polite to strangers. Laugh when she gives your dad a book because she gets a discount and can afford to be generous.

Watch your dad kiss her cheek. Notice them smile. Know that whatever happens, they are your parents.

Listen to your neighbour pruning her roses as shadows lengthen across the lawn. She's humming some old song and you're under a blanket with your boyfriend. Tell him you're proud of him, because he made that garden grow and encouraged his mother to care about it.

Study the moon. It's close and has a pink flare around it. Your boyfriend tells you it's an optical illusion, that it only seems big because of its angle to the earth.

Measure yourself against it.

And, at night, when you're carried back upstairs and another day is over, refuse to let your boyfriend sleep in the camp bed. Tell him you want to be held and don't be afraid that he might not want to, because if he says he will, then he loves you and that's all that matters. Wrap your legs with his. Listen to him sleep, his gentle breathing.

And when you hear a sound, like the flapping of a kite getting closer, like the sails of a windmill slowly turning, say, 'Not yet, not yet.'

Keep breathing. Just keep doing it. It's easy. In and out.

Forty

The light begins to come back. The absolute dark fades at the edges. My mouth's dry. The grit of last night's medication lines my throat.

'Hey,' Adam says.

He's got a hard-on, apologizes for it with a shy smile, then opens the curtains and stands at the window looking out. Beyond him, the dull pink clouds of morning.

'You're going to be here for years without me,' I tell him.

He says, 'Shall I make us some breakfast?'

Like a butler, he brings me things. A lemon ice lolly. A hot-water bottle. Slices of orange cut onto a plate. Another blanket. He puts cinnamon sticks to boil on the oven downstairs, because I want to smell Christmas.

How did this happen so quickly? How did it really come true?

please get into bed and climb on top of me with your warmth and wrap me with your arms and make it stop

'Mum's putting up a trellis,' he says. 'First it was a herb garden, then roses, now she wants honeysuckle. I might go out and give her a hand when your dad comes to sit with you. Would that be OK?'

'Sure.'

'You don't fancy sitting outside again today?'

'No.'

I can't be bothered to move. The sun grinds into my brain and everything aches.

this mad psycho tells everyone to get into a field and says I'm going to pick one of you just one of you out of all of you to die and everyone's looking around thinking it's so unlikely to be me because there's thousands of us so statistically it's completely unlikely and the psycho walks up and down looking at everyone and when he gets near me he hesitates and he smiles and then he points right at me and says you're the one and the shock that it's me and yet of course it's me why wouldn't it be I knew all along

Cal crashes in. 'Can I go out?'

Dad sighs. 'Where?'

'Just out.'

'You need to be a bit more specific.'

'I'll let you know when I get there.'

'Not good enough.'

'Everyone else is allowed randomly out.'

'I'm not interested in everyone else.'

Wonderful rage as Cal stomps to the door. The bits of garden in his hair, the filth of his fingernails. His body able to yank the door open and slam it behind him.

'You're all such bloody bastards!' he yells as he races down the stairs.

Instructions for Cal
Don't die young. Don't get meningitis, or Aids or anything else
ever. Be healthy. Don't fight in any war, or join a cult, or get reli-
gion, or lose your heart to someone who doesn't deserve it.
Don't think you have to be good because you're the only one
left. Be as bad as you like.

I reach for Dad's hand. His fingers look raw, as if they've been
through a grater.

'What have you done?'

He shrugs. 'I don't know. I didn't even notice.'

Further instructions for Dad – Let Cal be enough for you.

I love you. I love you. I send this message through my fingers
and into his, up his arm and into his heart. Hear me. I love you.
And I'm sorry to leave you.

I wake up hours later. How did that happen?

Cal's here again, sitting next to me on the bed propped up with pillows. 'Sorry I shouted.'

'Did Dad tell you to say that?'

He nods. The curtains are open and somehow the darkness is back.

'Are you scared?' Cal says this very softly, as if it's something he's thinking, but didn't mean to say.

'I'm scared of falling asleep.'

'That you won't wake up?'

'Yes.'

His eyes shine. 'But you know it won't be tonight, don't you? I mean, you'll be able to tell, won't you?'

'It won't be tonight.'

He rests his head on my shoulder. 'I really, really hate this,' he says.

Forty-one

The bell they gave me is loud in the dark, but I don't care. Adam comes in, bleary-eyed, in his boxers and T-shirt.

'You left me.'

'I just this second went down to make a cup of tea.'

I don't believe him. And I don't care about his cup of tea. He can drink tepid water from my jug if he's desperate.

'Hold my hand. Don't let go.'

Every time I close my eyes, I fall. Endlessly falling.

Forty-two

All qualities are the same – the light through the curtains, the faraway hum of traffic, the boiler rush of water. It could be groundhog day, except that my body is more tired, my skin more transparent. I am less than yesterday.

And

Adam is in the camp bed.

I try to sit up, but can't quite muster the energy. 'Why did you sleep down there?'

He touches my hand. 'You were in pain in the night.'

He opens the curtains just like he did yesterday. He stands at the window looking out. Beyond him, the sky is pale and watery.

we made love twenty-seven times and we shared a bed for sixty-two nights and that's a lot of love

'Breakfast?' he says.

I don't want to be dead.
    I haven't been loved this way for long enough.

Forty-three

My mum was in labour for fourteen hours with me. It was the hottest May on record. So hot I didn't wear any clothes for the first two weeks of my life.

'I used to lay you on my tummy and we'd sleep for hours,' she says. 'It was too hot to do anything but sleep.'

Like charades, this going over of memories.

'I used to take you on the bus to meet Dad in his lunch break and you'd sit on my lap and stare at people. You had such an intense look about you. Everyone used to comment on it.'

The light is very bright. A great slab of it falls through the window and lands on the bed. I can rest my hand in sunshine without even moving.

'Do you remember when we went to Cromer and you lost your charm bracelet on the beach?'

She's brought photos, holds them up one by one.

A green and white afternoon threading daisies.

The chalk light of winter at the city farm.

Yellow leaves, muddy boots and a proud black bucket.

'What did you catch, do you remember?'

Philippa said my hearing would be the last thing to go, but she didn't say I'd see colours when people talk.

Whole sentences arc across the room like rainbows.

I get confused. I'm at the bedside and Mum's dying instead of me. I pull back the sheets to look at her and she's naked, a wrinkled old woman with grey pubic hair.

I weep for a dog, hit by a car and buried. We never had a dog. This is not my memory.

I'm Mum on a pony trotting across town to visit Dad. He lives on a council estate, and me and the pony get into the lift and go up to the eighth floor. The pony's hooves clatter metallically. It makes me laugh.

I'm twelve. I get home from school and Mum's on the doorstep. She has her coat on and a suitcase at her feet. She gives me an envelope. 'Give this to your dad when he gets home.'

She kisses me goodbye. I watch her until she reaches the horizon, and at the top of the hill, like a puff of smoke, she disappears.

Forty-four

The light is heart-breaking.

Dad sips tea by the bed. I want to tell him that he's missing GMTV, but I'm not sure that he is. Not sure of the time.

He's got a snack as well. Cream crackers with piccalilli sauce and old mature cheddar. I'd like to want that. To be interested in taste – the crumb and dry crackerness of things.

He puts down the plate when he sees me looking and picks up my hand. 'Beautiful girl,' he says.

I tell him thanks.

But my lips don't move and he doesn't seem to hear me.

Then I say, I was just thinking about that netball post you made me when I got into the school team. Do you remember how you got the measurements wrong and made it too high? I practised so hard with it that I always overshot at school and they chucked me out of the team again.

But he doesn't seem to hear that either.

So then I go for it.

Dad, you played rounders with me, even though you hated it and wished I'd take up cricket. You learned how to keep a stamp collection because I wanted to know. For hours you sat in hospitals and never, not once, complained. You brushed my hair like a mother should. You gave up work for me, friends for me, four years of your life for me. You never moaned. Hardly ever. You let me have Adam. You let me have my list. I was outrageous. Wanting, wanting so much. And you never said, 'That's enough. Stop now.'

I've been wanting to say that for a while

Cal peers down at me. 'Hello,' he says. 'How are you?'

I blink at him.

He sits in the chair and studies me. 'Can't you actually talk any more?'

I try and tell him that yes, of course I can. Is he stupid, or what?

He sighs, gets up and goes over to the window. He says, 'Do you think I'm too young to have a girlfriend?'

I tell him yes.

'Because loads of my friends have got one. They don't actually go out. Not really. They just text each other.' He shakes his head in disbelief. 'I'm never going to understand love.'

But I think he already does. Better than most people.

Zoey says, 'Hey, Cal.'

He says, 'Hey.'

She says, 'I've come to say goodbye. I mean, I know I did already, but I thought I'd say it again.'

'Why?' he says. 'Where are you going?'

I like the weight of Mum's hand in mine.

She says, 'If I could swap places with you, I would, you know.'
   Then she says, 'I just wish I could save you from this.'
   Maybe she thinks I can't hear her.

She says, 'I could write a story for one of those true story magazines, about how hard it was to leave you. I don't want you
thinking it was easy.'

when I was twelve I looked Scotland up on a map and saw that
beyond the Firth were the Islands of Orkney and I knew they'd
have boats that would take her even further away than that

Instructions for Mum
*Don't give up on Cal. Don't you ever slide away from him,
move back to Scotland or think that any man is more important. I'll haunt you if you do. I'll move your furniture around,
throw things at you and scare you stupid. Be kind to Dad.
Serious. I'm watching you.*

She gives me a sip of iced water. She gently places a cold flannel on my forehead.

Then she says, 'I love you.'
Like three drops of blood falling onto snow.

Forty-five

Adam gets into his camp bed. It creaks. Then it stops.

I remember him sucking my breast. It wasn't long ago. We were in this room, both in my bed, and I held him in the crook of my arm and he nestled against me and I felt like his mother.

He promised he'd come to the edge. I made him promise. But I didn't know he'd lie next to me at night like a good boy scout. I didn't know it would hurt to be touched, that he'd be too scared to hold my hand.

He should be out in the night with some girl with lovely curves and breath like oranges.

Instructions for Adam
Look after no one except yourself. Go to university and make lots of friends and get drunk. Forget your door keys. Laugh. Eat pot-noodles for breakfast. Miss lectures. Be irresponsible.

Adam says, 'Goodnight, Tessa.'
Goodnight, Adam.

'I phoned the nurse. She says we should top up the morphine with Oramorph.'

'Won't anyone come out?'

'We can manage.'

'She was calling for her mum again when you were on the phone.'

I keep thinking of fires of smoke rising of the crazed jangle of bells and the surprised faces of a crowd as if something has been snatched from them

'I'll sit with her if you like, Adam. Go down and watch TV, or catch up on some sleep.'
'I said I wouldn't leave her.'

It's like turning off the lights one by one.

rain drizzles gently onto sand and bare legs as Dad puts the finishing touches to the castle and even though it's raining me and Cal collect sea water in a bucket for the moat and later when the sun comes out we put flags on each tower so they flutter and we get ice cream from the hut at the top of the dunes and later still Dad sits with us as the tide comes in and together we try and push all that water back out so the people in the castle don't drown

'Go on, Adam. None of us will be any good to her if we're exhausted.'
  'No, I'm not leaving.'

when I was four I almost fell down the shaft of a tin mine and when I was five the car rolled over on the motorway and when I was seven we went on holiday and the gas ring blew out in the caravan and nobody noticed

I've been dying all my life

'She's more peaceful now.'
 'Hmm.'

I hear only the fraction of things. Words fall down crevices, get lost for hours, then fly back up and land on my chest.

'I'm grateful to you.'
 'For what?'
 'For not backing off. Most lads would've run a mile by now.'
 'I love her.'

Forty-six

'Hey,' Adam says, 'you're awake.'

He leans over and moistens my mouth with a sponge. He dabs my lips dry with a flannel and smears them with Vaseline.

'Your hands are cold. I'll hold them for a bit and warm them up, shall I?'

I stink. I smell myself farting. I hear the ugly tick of my body consuming itself. I'm sinking, sinking into the bed.

Fifteen, to get out of bed and go downstairs and it's all a joke.

Two hundred and nine, to marry Adam.

Thirty, to go to parents' evening and our child's a genius. All three of our children in fact – Chester, Merlin and Daisy.

Fifty-one, two, three. To open my eyes. Bastard open them.

I can't. I'm falling.

Forty-four, to not be falling. I don't want to fall. I'm afraid.

Forty-five, to not be falling.

Think of something. I won't die if I'm thinking of Adam's hot breath between my legs.

But I can't hold onto anything.

Like a tree losing its leaves.

I forget even the thing I was thinking.

'Why is she making that noise?'

'It's her lungs. Fluid can't drain away because she's not moving around.'

'It sounds horrible.'

'It sounds worse than it is.'

Is that Cal? I hear the tug of a ring pull, the fizz of a Coke can.

Adam says, 'What's your dad up to?'

'On the phone. He's telling Mum to come over.'

'Good.'

What happens, Cal, to dead bodies?

Dust, glitter, rain.

'You think she can hear us?'

'Definitely.'

''Cos I've been telling her stuff.'

'What kind of stuff?'

'I'm not telling you!'

the big bang was the origin of the solar system and only then was the earth formed and only then could life appear and after all the rain and fire had gone fish came then insects amphibians dinosaurs mammals birds primates hominids and finally humans

'Are you sure she should be making that noise?'

'I think it's OK.'

'It's different from just now.'

'Shush, I can't hear.'

'That's worse. That sounds like she can't even breathe.'

'Shit!'

'Is she dying?'

'Get your dad, Cal. Run!'

a little bird moves a mountain of sand one grain at a time it picks up one grain every million years and when the mountain has been moved the bird puts it all back again and that's how long eternity is and that's a very long time to be dead for

Maybe I'll come back as somebody else.

I'll be the wild-haired girl Adam meets in his first week at university. 'Hi, are you on the horticultural course as well?'

'I'm here, Tess. I'm right here, holding your hand. Adam's here too, he's sitting on the other side of the bed. And Cal. Mum's on her way, she'll just be a minute. We all love you, Tessa. We're all right here with you.'

'I hate that noise. It sounds like it's hurting her.'

'It's not, Cal. She's unconscious. She's not in pain.'

'Adam said she could hear us. How can she hear us if she's unconscious?'

'It's like sleeping, except she knows we're here. Sit with me, Cal, it's all right. Come and sit on my lap. She's peaceful, don't worry.'

'She doesn't sound peaceful. She sounds like a broken boiler.'

I turn inwards, their voices the sound of water murmuring.

Moments gather.

Aeroplanes crash into buildings. Bodies sail through the air. Tube trains and buses explode. Radiation seeps from the pavements. The sun turns to the tiniest black spot. The human race dies out and cockroaches rule the world.

Anything could happen next.

Angel Delight on a beach.

A fork whisking against a bowl.

Seagulls. Waves.

'It's all right, Tessa, you can go. We love you. You can go now.'

'Why are you saying that?'

'She might need permission to die, Cal.'

'I don't want her to. She doesn't have my permission.'

Let's say yes then.

Yes to everything for just one more day.

'Maybe you should say goodbye, Cal.'

   'No.'

'It might be important.'

'It might make her die.'

'Nothing you say can make her die. She wants to know you love her.'

One more moment. One more. I can manage one more.

   A sweet wrapper whips up the path in the wind.

'Go on, Cal.'

   'I feel stupid.'

'None of us are listening. Get close and whisper.'

My name encircles a roundabout.

   Cuttlefish washed up on a beach.

   A dead bird on the lawn.

   Millions of maggots stunned by sunlight.

'Bye, Tess. Haunt me if you like. I don't mind.'

A duck goes into a chemist's to buy some lipstick.
   A mouse dunked in water and held down with a spoon.
   Three tiny air bubbles escaping, one after the other.

Six snowmen made of cotton wool.
   Six serviettes folded into origami lilies.
   Seven stones, all different colours, bound with a silver chain.

There's sun in my teacup.
   Zoey stares out of the window and I drive out of town. The sky
gets darker and darker.

Let them go.

Adam blows smoke at the town below. Says, 'Anything could be happening down there, but up here you just wouldn't know it.'

Adam strokes my head, my face, he kisses my tears.
  We are blessed.

Let them all go.

The sound of a bird flying low across the garden. Then nothing. Nothing. A cloud passes. Nothing again. Light falls through the window, falls onto me, into me.

Moments.

All gathering towards this one.